LYING
FOR A
LIVING

In Memory of David G. Hayes
(August 29, 1951 – December 31, 2014)
Bro Davey—Always the First Man IN

1

IF JESSE FEW WERE EVER GRANTED A SUPERHERO power, he'd make damn sure it gave him the ability to defeat the evils of suburban gridlock. Until then, all he could do was curse.

"Screw this traffic light to the headboard," Jesse muttered, gunning his pearl-white Cadillac Escalade past a line of docile commuters, down the side of the road, through a path of mud, grass, and potholes, red clay and rocks rooster-tailing in the air. Rolling through two stop signs, unconcerned about the Dwyer Police, he power-slid into his mother's narrow driveway, barely missing her mailbox.

The front door to Momma's house was wide open.

He took a deep breath and hopped out. Adrenaline flooded his arms; his hands quivered. He tried forcing himself to stand still, but the current flowing through his body made him quake even more. He was supposed to be recuperating from his traditional Thursday night drinking binge and working on tomorrow's hangover, enjoying a rare Friday afternoon off and nursing a cocktail with all the other sales rep slackers—not playing amateur detective. A bead of sweat trickled down his spine.

"Shit fire," he said. "Shit, shit, shit. Where's my gun?"

Leaning back into the car, he opened the center console, frantically searching past his iPod, cell phone chargers, and breath mints, finding his 9mm buried at the bottom. He pulled the black pistol out of its holster; the chamber was open and the magazine empty.

"Bullets." The instructor at the range had told him that in a gunfight an unloaded weapon was as useless as a rubber knife. But Jesse was a business guy, not the town marshal, and he felt safer keeping his pistol unloaded. He dug back into the center console looking for a cartridge, scrambling like a bungling deputy. He found one but almost jammed it in backwards. Flipping the cartridge around, he chambered the round, another rush filling him as he became aware that he held a live weapon.

Jesse had been in Chicago on a business trip, and he'd received Momma's voicemail—along with a dozen others—as soon as he landed back home in Atlanta almost two hours ago, skipping over it to get to the messages from work.

"Jesse...Jesse...is that you? There's a strange man in my yard. He's trampling on my rose bushes...peering in my windows ..." Next was the plastic rattle of the receiver as Momma either dropped or attempted to hang up the phone. He tried calling her back umpteen dozen times and got umpteen dozen busy signals. Momma was eighty-one, widowed three times, and lived alone right off Lewallen Courthouse Square. This was the first time she'd ever called about someone in her backyard, and Jesse, forty-nine, was her only relative living close enough to respond to her call.

Pointing his pistol at the ground like he had been taught in the self-defense course, he walked slowly down the driveway. He reached the backyard and scanned the area. The flowerbeds were covered in dandelions, and the honeysuckle was overtaking the back fence. His tremors had diminished, but perspiration was dripping into his eyes.

Jesse eyed the back door. He couldn't hear any commotion coming from inside; it was all quiet. He contemplated calling 911—didn't the hard-nosed cop always radio for backup?—but he'd left his cell phone in the car. He peeked around the side of the house. At the far end of the driveway were his car and his phone. A flush of heat inched up his neck. Silence had never been so baffling.

Opening the back door, Jesse crept past the laundry room into the kitchen and was caught by the blare of Howard Cosell.

"Down goes Frazier! Down goes Frazier! Down goes Frazier!"

The nasal bellowing jerked Jesse's head back as he walked into the den, pistol still at his side. He entered the den as Momma was taking a sip from her afternoon cocktail. She looked up from her chair.

"Jesse?" Momma shouted above Cosell. Like Jesse, his mother was an avid sports fan, and there were a dozen digital cable channels of classic sports reruns, allowing her ample occasion to reminisce about the good old days of the '70s and the '80s.

"Yes, ma'am," he replied, his eyes ricocheting around the room. He tucked the pistol into the back of his waistband, praying he wouldn't shoot himself in the ass.

"I didn't hear you come in the front door, sweetie."

"Well, I didn't really. I got your voicemail."

"Voicemail? What?"

"Your message, Momma, about some man in your backyard, but I couldn't get you on the phone."

He saw the phone on the table next to her, laying on its side off the hook.

"Don't be silly," Momma said.

He walked to the back of the house and checked Momma's bedroom, her cedar closet, and her bathroom, flipping back the shower curtain. He opened the linen closet and jumped back as a comforter landed on his head; the tip of the pistol dug into his butt. Wadding up the comforter, he pushed it back onto the top shelf. Halfheartedly, he scanned the spare bedrooms and decided against looking in the closets, but a pang sent him back to check—no escaped prisoners or greasy perverts hiding anywhere.

He shut the front door. Everything was in order.

Leaning over the kitchen sink, Jesse splashed cool water on his face; the excitement churned in his gurgling stomach. He planned to stop for some takeout on his way home and eat dinner in front of an old Western movie, preferably John Wayne. Ted Turner, the media mogul, had launched SuperStation WTCG when Jesse was nine or ten, allowing him to devote his weekday afternoons immersed in black-and-white cowboy movies like *The Wyoming Outlaw* and *The Night Riders*, learning how to talk, how to walk, and how to drink whiskey. He pulled the 9mm out of his waistband and ejected the round, setting his pistol on the counter and sticking the bullet in his shirt pocket. The self-defense course had paid off: no intruder in the house and his ass was safe.

Momma was gnawing on the orange slice from her cocktail as Jesse came back into the den. After he put the phone back on the hook and turned the TV down, he kissed Momma on the forehead, and she patted his back. He plopped down in the twin Queen Anne chair next to her, the well-worn, brown leather cushioning his descent.

Ever since grade school, people had told Jesse how much he resembled his mother. They both had lanky frames and shared the family face—long and narrow with high cheekbones and sharp, angular noses. Their hazel eyes could appear green or blue, depending on their clothes or their mood. Jesse kept his thick, light-brown hair in a crew cut, minimizing the gray. For years, Momma hid her own gray hair with regular trips to the beauty parlor, but looking at her now, he presumed it'd been months since her last trip. Her shoulder-length hair was in a loose bun, poking out in all directions, a trilogy of tarnished gold, honey brown, and stark white from the tips to the roots.

"You care for a cool drink?" she asked, a slur in her drawl. Despite the smothering August humidity, Momma had a red cardigan sweater over her blue flowered housedress, coupled with a pair of pink slippers. She fished the cherry out of her glass and washed it down with the last of her drink. "I've got a beer in the fridge."

"No, thank you," Jesse replied, recognizing the thickening of her tongue. He hesitated before taking his cue. "Let me fix one for you," he said, taking Momma's glass.

"Would you? Thank you, Man-o," she said, calling him by the pet name she'd given him as a baby, which she'd somehow derived from Sammy Davis Jr.'s 1960s TV ad slogan, "Man-o, Manischewitz! What a wine!"

Before he made the drink, he took his pistol to his car, swapping it for his cell phone. He checked for missed calls before tucking it in his shirt pocket next to the bullet.

Jesse returned to the kitchen and saw all the ingredients laid out on the counter: Old Forester Kentucky bourbon, sweet and sour mix, an orange, a jar of cherries, a jigger, and an ice bucket.

At thirteen, Jesse had learned from William "Mr. Billy" Few, Jr.—Gennifer Few's third husband and Jesse's adopted father— the science of making cocktails, not just drinks. He remembered his basic instructions: "Use the right stuff, in the right way, and you get it right every time." Jesse added fresh ice to the old-fashioned glass engraved with a WFJ monogram, then two jiggers of bourbon, followed by a jigger of sweet and sour mix. He stirred the mixture with an iced tea spoon, topping it off with a wilted orange slice and a bloated maraschino cherry.

Jesse went back to the den and handed Momma the cocktail.

She took a sip and smiled. "Puuuurfect, Man-o," she said.

"Just like y'all taught me," Jesse said, slumping back in his chair with a shy smile.

They sat in silence, watching Foreman and Frazier fight.

"Remember when you boys were young and Mr. Billy took me to see Muhammad Ali?" Momma asked.

"Versus Quarry at the old Municipal Auditorium," Jesse said. His parents had hired a sitter to stay with Ricky, his older brother, and Jesse while they got a suite at the Hyatt Regency, the trendiest Atlanta hotel at the time, with its glass elevators and blue flying-saucer top.

"Ursula Andress—you know, the Swedish movie star—was real popular. I wore that tiger-print minidress and some white knee boots. I may have even dyed my hair sort of dishwater blonde. Mr. Billy loved that James Bond movie she did. There's a picture or something of us...somewhere."

"I seem to recall seeing one," Jesse said, fidgeting. After all these years, he guessed now was not the time to confess that Ricky had found Mr. Billy's homemade 8mm movies of Gennifer doing a striptease in that dress. His brother had tried to make

Jesse watch their mother's silent movie—her straddling a chair, unfettered breasts flickering on the dining room wall—but Jesse had run away, locking himself in his room, finding solace in a stack of records. Not even Sonny & Cher could erase the image of his mother unzipping her dress, wriggling first one shoulder, then two, from its top, eyeing the camera lustfully. "Didn't Ali end that bout early?" he asked.

"As I recollect, our rounds of champagne lasted longer than the fight. We were up at that revolving rooftop restaurant thingy... what was it called?"

"The Polaris, I believe," Jesse said, crossing his legs and wiggling his foot, taking refuge in avoidance and denial. According to his ex-wife's therapist, those were his preferred communication tools. "You want some pretzels or nuts?"

"Our suite...it had such mirrors...wall-length mirrors." Momma raised her cocktail and paused, holding it before her lips. "Mirrors galore," she said, as if she were reciting an incantation into the bottom of the glass, turning the liquid into a potion that would allow her to go back in time and seductively twist in front of the looking glass. "Mirrors galore."

"Foreman gets some huge shots in this next round," Jesse said, interrupting her spell. He bore down on the commercial and away from the specter of Momma's hand sliding over her body. He knew Momma never liked "Smokin' Joe" Frazier; he was a Philly fighter, and for her, nothing good ever came from Philadelphia, so watching Foreman pummel Frazier would put her in a festive mood.

"How's Denise and the babies?" she asked, setting her glass down.

"They're good," Jesse said.

"Aren't they coming to dinner tonight?"

Jesse and Denise Hill Few had ended their twenty-year marriage two years ago, and before he could tell her there was no dinner planned, his phone erupted with a blaring siren like a French police car, his personalized ringtone for his boss, Jean-Paul Gandois, North American president of Papier Mondiale—PM—the French conglomerate's Atlanta-based paper division.

"Excuse me a second, Momma. I gotta take this call," Jesse said, jumping up. He hit the green answer button as soon as he was on the front stoop.

"Hello, this is Jesse Few...Jean-Paul, *bonsoir.*"

Jesse had been expecting this phone call all afternoon. He'd been in Chicago the past three days on a mission for Jean-Paul, collecting money and laying off the sales staff.

"No, no, you're not bothering me at all," he said, pacing across the front lawn. Jesse was vice president of paper sales and marketing, a corporate troubadour, exchanging a weekly routine of airport security lines, stripped-down, four-door sedans, and spongy pillows for the rewards of first-class upgrades, six-figure annual bonuses, and stock options.

"Ralph and everyone signed the termination paperwork. Nope, there were no issues," Jesse told Jean-Paul, leaving out the six-hour drinking binge with Ralph Rigget, the sales manager he had known for fifteen years, and his attempted drunken hookup with the young woman he'd flirted with on the plane, who'd somehow reminded him of his ex-wife. Jesse was still unable to remember how the night ended.

He and Jean-Paul spent another several minutes rehashing the details of the layoffs and the collections, and then concluded with chitchat. Jean-Paul and his wife were driving down to Destin,

Florida, for what Jean-Paul described as "a weekend at the sea."

"You do the same. You and Jolie enjoy the sea," Jesse said, trying to sign off. The perpetual people-pleasing brown-noser in him would never allow him to tell Jean-Paul that Americans went to the beach, and the Gulf of Mexico wasn't the sea. "I'll speak to you Monday. *Au revoir.*"

Jesse glanced at his watch. The call had taken fifteen minutes, and he supposed Momma had either fallen asleep or was waiting for a whiskey sour. He wanted to say a quick good-bye and head home for a rib-eye sandwich and *The Searchers.*

As he walked back into the house, he saw Momma's red cardigan and pink slippers scattered across the foyer floor. He turned and looked in the dining room, and then into the living room, drawn to an aberration in the large, golden-framed mirror.

"No, sweet Jesus," he said, his eyes locking with his mother's reflection, interrupting her slow, sensual dance. The only thing missing was a chair for her to straddle. Momma paused and then winked, her fingers circling the tip of her naked breast, massaging her erect nipple.

2

JESSE TURNED AND DARTED OUT THE FRONT DOOR, jumped into his Escalade, and backed out of the driveway, mowing over Momma's mailbox in his rush to escape.

In all his years entertaining clients, from the Vegas Strip to Bourbon Street, he had seen a cascade of girls slide down poles and grind on middle-age laps, but nothing could have prepared him for Momma's gyrating figure. The image of her strawberry-red areola ran on a haunting loop. The Oedipal overload hypnotized him as he drove toward the interstate, away from his rib-eye sandwich and his sofa on the other side of the county.

The honk of a car brought him around as he realized the traffic light was green. He had forgotten about his take-out dinner; he needed booze to cleanse his brain, but he didn't want to see his regular drinking pals, who might read the shock in his face.

Spying a restaurant near Ansley Place with a bright banner advertising "Cool Summer Cocktails," he turned into the parking lot of the Brick Oven. It looked suitable for a drink, so he headed inside.

~~~

"Welcome to the Brick Oven. I'm Sabrina," said the bartender, placing a napkin in front of Jesse. "Would you like to try this month's cool summer cocktail?"

She handed Jesse a laminated menu with a photo of a perfectly frosted cocktail glass filled with an orange-colored drink and topped with peaches and grapefruit slices. Mr. Billy would have been jealous.

"What's this?" Jesse asked.

"It's our peach grapefruit margarita."

"Really?"

"They're delish, and they'll get you."

"I'll bet," Jesse said. "Have you got a long neck Budweiser and Jim Beam?"

"I'm pretty sure we do." She turned to sort through the bottles behind her, pulling out a dusty, half-full bottle. "Here we go."

"Great. I'll have one of each," Jesse said, placing the drink menu back on the bar.

Jesse downed the shot of whiskey, washing it back with plenty of beer. He wanted a numbing hum—fast. Not a cool summer cocktail, thought Jesse, but brown liquor and cold beer were the perfect sidekicks; they wouldn't ask why he didn't call 911 on the way to Momma's house, or how he could be so irresponsible as to abandon her, leaving her naked and shimmying in her living room.

Jesse had never been to the Brick Oven; it resembled an Italian villa with a brown-tile roof, mustard walls trimmed in brick, and faux stone archways. Three or four years ago, when the developers had free-flowing cash, they built Ansley Place, the new heart of Dwyer, inundating Lewallen with a surge of big-box retailers and corporate chain eateries. You could smell the smoke lingering in the air from the stacks of fallen trees, burning day and night. Several miles away from I-85 and the trendy lifestyle center, the marble sentinel on the Confederate War Memorial remained at his post, serving as a lookout over Lewallen Courthouse Square, Dwyer's forgotten hub, the once-vibrant city center, sacrificed for the greater tax base.

The TV in the corner was showing a news show. Jesse would've preferred the Braves game, but he was thankful it wasn't boxing, even though he hated listening to the talking dickheads blathering about the increasing unemployment rate. They could rattle off the latest jobless numbers, but Jesse could provide them names and faces to match.

Jesse caught the busy bartender's eye and motioned for more whiskey and beer, needing his two faithful pals to lubricate the cogs in his head and lead him in a barstool brainstorming session. Momma's bizarre behavior jammed up his mind like suddenly slamming a moving car from drive into park. Other than Daniel "Haymaker" Hay, Jesse's longtime friend, transient housemate, and unemployed investment partner, and his other golf buddies, there was no place he could go for answers—not a priest, not his married girlfriend, and, especially, not his asshole brother in Florida. He supposed he could visit Momma's sister, Aunt Lizzy, but he wasn't sure how to describe his mother's striptease.

Jesse pulled out his phone and checked his email. He scrolled down the fifteen new messages he had received since he had last looked while sitting in traffic. He looked at the usual follow-up emails regarding yesterday's layoffs in Chicago, no surprises for those who still had jobs. Jesse had woken up with a hangover this morning, but he knew he'd get better with time. Ralph Rigget's hangover probably felt worse and would last longer. Jesse imagined Ralph donning his unflappable corporate mask and telling his wife and kids that he'd lost his job, the entire time feeling as if a stranger—or worse, a trusted friend—had randomly crashed his car through Ralph's living room wall.

Jesse's balance was off-kilter, yet his mind was expanding. Like a pair of reliable buddies, the beer and the bourbon were pouring out new ideas: *If you gouge out your eyes, you might stop thinking about Momma's milky-white backside.*

Draining his shot, Jesse listened as the bourbon tossed out another suggestion: *Hey, Slick, isn't your ex-wife the perfect, and maybe only, person to help you with Momma? Before you let her get away, she spent more time with your mother than you did, and you know how much it upset Momma when you told her about the divorce. You just need her to drop by a couple times a week. Besides, it might just give you the second chance you've been dreaming of.*

He'd met Denise at a Halloween party—Jesse was Joe Strummer of The Clash, and she was Debbie Harry of Blondie. Within six months, they were married, and Denise wanted to start a family immediately. She charted her basal body temperature and did mucus exams like she was competing in the eighth-grade science fair, but Jesse wasn't sure if he was her partner in the project or part of the experiment. Jesse Eugene Few, Jr.—JJ—was born on their second anniversary, and Amie Barbara Few was born eighteen months later. It was then that Jesse began to travel. When he came off the road, he wanted to bury his problems of sales quotas and upset customers, not replace them with ear tubes and pimply diaper rash. They'd arranged a Friday to Monday marriage, and Jesse developed a penchant for conquering cocktail waitresses and receptionists. They split amicably.

Later—too much later—he felt like a lost puppy, and he fantasized about courting Denise again, winning her over with the perfect Christmas gift or surprising her by showing up at the kids' school award ceremonies. That's when the dreams started, choking him with an aching remorse, no matter whom he slept with or where he slept.

He'd be lingering over the Sunday paper, and Denise would call out for his help in carrying a box down to the basement. He'd lug the overstuffed load down the steep flight of stairs, and she would stand at the top, smiling. Halfway down, he'd recognize it wasn't real, and she'd shut off the lights and close the basement door, trapping him alone.

Jesse turned the bottom up on his beer, soothing his throat but not extinguishing the invading guilt. His booze buddy's proposal to turn his ex-wife into a caretaking partner was sound, but Jesse seriously doubted Denise would be willing to commit to helping him. She was probably super busy, and asking her for help would make him appear weak, especially if she were going to turn him down.

The bartender glanced his way. He smiled, nodded, and signaled for another round. She quickly set another Budweiser and Jim Beam in front of him, and he took half a shot and two more gulps of chaser.

He wasn't drunk enough to forget Ralph's doomed face or Momma's wink, but he couldn't remember what had happened with the cute girl from the plane. Serendipity had put her next to Jesse on the flight to Chicago, but he'd bungled his good fortune.

With the last of the bourbon disappearing, the booze began filling in the lapses in his memory like the shit-faced best man who grabs the microphone at the wedding reception, awkwardly slurring out tales of the groom's sleazy past.

Earlier that morning, Jesse had studied her business card one more time before tossing it in the trash can: Beth Montgomery, Account Executive. In her early thirties, she was part of the new generation of ambitious female business travelers whom Jesse encountered at the rental car counter or the hotel gym. With one phone call, the aspiring Beth had appeared at the hotel bar, right after Ralph stumbled away, as if Jesse materialized her with his breezy promises of connections. After a few chocolate martinis, she'd kissed him once, squeezing his thigh. Leading her to his room, he'd envisioned an elevator ride of furious groping. But when the bell chimed and the brass doors opened, he'd said something that turned her to stone.

Jesse emptied his beer.

The girl had dainty ears like petite, pink seashells that were near replicas of his ex-wife's. Jesse recalled stroking her slender cheeks and tucking her straight blonde hair behind her ear, whispering, "Babe, forgive me if I'm too drunk to remember your name. Is it okay if I just call you Denise?"

Sighing on the verge of a groan, Jesse blocked out the girl's hardened glare.

After asking the bartender for the check, figuring he was still fine to drive, he reconsidered how his mother had forgotten her panicky phone call about the stranger in her backyard. He folded his arms and leaned back in his barstool, squinting at his comrades—an empty beer bottle and an upturned shot glass. Like a pair of wingmen turned cockblockers at closing time, they issued their final challenge: *So, we were thinking, on Sunday night, when you take the kids to dinner, that'd be the ideal time to convince Denise to help you with Momma. Who knows where it could lead? After all, don't you have higher aspirations than being half-drunk, sitting alone in a fake Italian villa?*

A LONG, RAINY WEEKEND AFFORDED JESSE PLENTY OF time to recover from his drinking spree and to formulate a plan for talking with Denise about Momma. His dinners with JJ and Amie were a remnant of the divorce that had formed into an irregular ritual, and he decided to arrive early to pick them up and wait inside for them to get ready. On Sunday evening, he stood in his old house and launched the conversation with a sales opener he'd used countless times.

"How's your mom and them?" Jesse asked his ex-wife, glancing around his former den and kitchen. They'd moved into the four-bedroom pink stucco house on the golf course at Quail Woods right after Amie was born. Jesse had given Denise the house, debt-free, and in the past six months, she had repainted all the rooms, hung all new pictures, and replaced all their classic-style furnishings with brighter and cozier sofas and chairs, rooting out any vestige of their twenty-year life together. "Ms. Mary and your daddy doing okay?"

"They're good, or at least they're both as good as Mother will ever let herself or my daddy be. I swear, every day, she's growing and he's shrinking," Denise said, her voice trailing off. She was unloading the dishwasher while kale steamed on the stove, giving off a misty funk, a chemical warfare to Jesse's steak-and-potatoes appetite. She'd always been more health conscious, and it had paid off for her. Only two years shy of fifty, her good looks had not diminished, the edges only gently shaped by time. Jesse still thought of kissing her every time he saw her thin up-turned nose that led to her full, pink lips. She wore her dirty-blonde hair twisted in a bun.

"You doing okay?" Jesse asked, preparing to move into the Momma subject.

"Funny you should ask," she said, turning away from Jesse and stepping on a stool to put a serving platter on the top shelf—a job she never would have asked Jesse to do, even if they'd still been married.

Jesse admired his ex-wife's round bottom, which was nicely displayed in her tight jeans.

Coming down off the stool, she turned back around to face him. She pinched the bridge of her nose and squeezed her eyes shut. "I apologize for this. I know I should've told you this earlier, but I assumed you were traveling or in meetings, so I didn't want to interrupt you with an email, a text, or, Lord forbid, a late-night phone call. It's not like you could've done anything about it from wherever you were."

"What is it? Don't worry about any of that. What is it?"

"Thursday night, JJ got arrested for a DUI." Denise stepped back, wilting against the refrigerator. "The police found a bottle of tequila and gin in his car, plus some pills. Evidently, he somehow managed to get a bottle of OxyContin prescribed to you. So they also charged him with illegal drug possession and intent to distribute or whatever."

"Christ almighty." Jesse's neck stiffened, and his thoughts about discussing Momma spun away like a hydroplaning car leaving the road. "You gotta be kidding me."

"I wish, but it gets worse because Melanie, JJ's girlfriend, the preacher's daughter, was with him. She's only seventeen, so they turned her over to her parents. You talk about awkward?" Denise said with a weak laugh. "You should've seen when I ran into her father, the Southern Baptist preacher, as he's leading his precious, plastered, underage daughter out of the police station. My apology not accepted. He even said something like bad company ruining good morals and the devil throwing sinful people in prison."

"What the hey?"

"I don't really know what he meant. I just wanted to get JJ and go home."

"How long was JJ in jail?"

"After his arraignment and me putting up the house as bond, I got him out Friday night, so I'd say almost a full day."

"I ain't believing this," Jesse said, images of flashing blue lights, emerald gin bottles, and peach-colored painkillers sailing through his mind until he landed on the figure of his skinny little boy in an orange jumpsuit huddled in the corner of a holding cell. JJ had never even been to the principal's office— much less county jail—so far as Jesse knew, but of course, he didn't ask; even before conception, the children were Denise's department. JJ had recently started attending community college so he could transfer to the University of Georgia after he got his associate degree. Melanie had come to dinner with them once or twice, and she seemed like a quiet girl, but apparently, underneath lurked the wild streak of a preacher's daughter. "How's he feeling? Is he doing all right?"

"Physically, I guess he's all normal, sleeping a lot, eating pretty much like usual," Denise said, stepping toward Jesse, closing the dishwasher. "Emotionally, who knows? This is a stretch of your comfort zone, but given the circumstances, you might want to consider talking to JJ tonight about some of this stuff. He may open up to you, a guy. His father."

"Tonight?" Jesse folded his arms across his chest.

Denise gave Jesse the same "don't be a dumbass" frown that she had been giving him ever since they met. "Yes, the sooner the better. You might start with illegal drinking, stealing drugs, going to jail, finishing college, or—heaven help us all—girls. You're a specialist in that field of study," she said, her knitted brow transforming the "don't be a dumbass" frown into a scowl.

"Sure, we could talk. I mean, we talk all the time," Jesse said, not wanting to acknowledge that most of the time, JJ and he talked about Bulldog football, Batman movies, Shelby GT Mustangs, and the latest addition to Jesse's gun collection. "But he probably just wants to relax tonight."

"Well, he stopped talking to me after you bought that gigantic TV for his bedroom. He only comes out to wolf down a meal and go see Melanie."

"He's got a lot on his mind," Jesse said, using his standard excuse throughout the years for distracted stares, extra golf games, and late-night drunks.

"That's fine. Maybe he'll talk to Jack," Denise said, crossing the room to pour herself a glass of wine. "He took JJ and Amie hiking somewhere this afternoon, see if being in the great outdoors would open him up. That's why they're running late."

When Jesse heard Jack's name and noticed the second wineglass on the counter, the tension hardened in his neck and traveled to his jawline. Jackoff the Painter Geek was what Jesse called him, but he was actually Jack Lafferty, Denise's boyfriend. They'd met on the festival circuit where she displayed and sold her photographs. He was young, tall, and had long, blonde hair down to his shoulders. He was an artist, a folk artist, meaning to Jesse that he produced stuff that looked like third-grade artwork and sold it to people wanting a picture of rural Southern Americana to hang in their guest room. The only painters Jesse knew painted either cars or houses, and most of those guys were always drunk from the fumes. He tried blocking his mind from any further thoughts of the redneck Rembrandt banging Denise.

"Did he now?" Jesse's heart wobbled.

"Jack just wants to help—be a friend—and as much as you and our son might think otherwise, JJ doesn't need to keep it all bottled up inside," Denise said, her voice steady and deep. "Anyway, we have an appointment this week, Wednesday, I think, with a lawyer."

"I suppose that's a good plan. What attorney?"

"I was told Blaire McMahon was good, but we'll need to give him some money—a retainer or whatever, around five grand."

"Jesus-jumping-jones, do you have five thousand bucks?" Jesse was paying her generous alimony and child support.

"Not and pay all our bills. I'm sorry, but I figured that you could possibly help." Denise looked down at the stovetop, checking on her steaming kale and sautéing chicken. "But if you can't, Jack promised to help. He had a good summer—he sold a lot of pieces."

"Really?" Jesse said with his chest bowed out. "When do you need a check?"

"Are you sure you have the money?"

"I got it covered. I sold some velvet finger paintings of Waylon

Jennings, Patsy Cline, and Jimi Hendrix at the gas station. When do you need the check?"

"Jesse, please, I don't need the jealous ex-husband game now," Denise said, standing on the opposite end of the kitchen island, clutching the wineglass to her breasts. "Those drugs, your pills, however he got them. They put people in prison for that sort of thing. And you should've seen the look on Melanie's father's face. It scared me almost."

The heat from the stove flushed Jesse's face. He wanted to grab hold of Denise and pull her close, offering solace that he knew wasn't his to provide anymore. A heavy craving filled his lungs. Despite the divorce and being a half-ass father, he still dreamed of one day being a hero to her and his family, and now he had his chance to ride in on the white horse for once. "When do you want the check?"

"I really kind of need it now."

"Okay, fine. How much?"

"Are you sure it's not a problem?"

"Denise, please."

"Four grand would be great."

"All right. I think I've got my checkbook in the car," Jesse said, hoping he only grimaced inside. Negotiating wouldn't be too gallant. He was always at the wrong end of an 80/20 split. He walked out, wondering if it were ever going to be possible to resurrect the Momma discussion and praying he had enough in his stock margin account to cover the check he was getting ready to write. "And I'll talk to JJ after dinner tonight."

4

MUSIC HAD ALWAYS BEEN ONE OF JESSE'S CONNECTIONS to his children. They'd named Amie after the song that was playing when he and Denise had their first kiss, and his memory told him that Al Green's "Tired of Being Alone" was playing the night JJ was conceived. When the kids were little, Jesse played music in the car to keep them content. If he felt really good, he'd sing along to "The Wheels on the Bus" or "The Bare Necessities," forgetting about his worries and his strife, hoping to make the kids laugh and Denise smile. Between the two children, they shared Jesse's varied taste in music: JJ liked Southern rock and country, and Amie more classic rock, heavy metal, and even punk.

On the way back from dinner, they listened to the Beatles' "Fixing a Hole," a deep track from *Sgt. Pepper's Lonely Heart Club Band*. JJ passively rode shotgun and Amie sat in the back-seat, carrying the conversation as she had all night.

"Fixing a hole where the rain comes in and stop my mind from wandering?" Amie said. She was waif-thin, wore large-gauge earrings, and that afternoon, she'd dyed her brown hair a cast-iron black. In the past two years, Jesse hadn't seen her in anything but jeans and a T-shirt, usually promoting a rock band that he didn't know. A senior in high school, she'd already decided she was going to study music therapy in college. "What in the world were these guys on?"

"Well, precious, I guess it was part of the magical mystery tour," Jesse said cautiously, not wanting to touch on the subject of the Fab Four's indulgence in psychedelics, or his own drug past and present. "I'm not sure, but I think they'd just got back from India or somewhere and were doing a lot of…meditation with a guru dude."

"Is that what the hippy geezers called it back then? Meditating?" JJ asked, lobbing his smart-ass grenade into the conversation before retreating back into his seat.

"Funny, whatever," she said with the skeptical tone of the teenage nonbeliever. "A friend of mine has this album. You know, like the old-fashioned vinyl?"

"I know vinyl very well, thanks. But, pray tell, what kind of friend?" Jesse asked, never missing the chance to tease his little girl about her newest romance.

"A friendly friend…for now. Enough about me," she said, switching to a nasal staccato speech. "What about your friend? Kimberly? When is her great unveiling?"

"Touché, precious." In a tipsy moment at a Sunday night dinner a few months back, Jesse had confessed to Amie the existence of Kimberly Roche, his married girlfriend, withholding her marital status. The accidental admission served as a counter-attack to all his kids' stories about the budding legend of Jackoff the Painter Geek.

"She can't not like me because she hasn't even met me."

"Oh, I'd like for you to meet her someday," Jesse said, startling himself with his own answer, hoping Kimberly's name was said aloud back in his old kitchen. Jealousy was a group sport. He knew envy didn't die on the elementary school playground. "And I'm sure you'll be best buds."

"Promises, promises. I still taste my burger. Have you got a breath mint in your saddlebag?" Amie asked, leaning into the front seat and opening the center console. "What the double deuce? Uh, Dad, there's a pistol in here. And it's kinda sorta in my way."

"Yeah, sorry. Let me help you. It's unloaded. The mints are down toward the bottom." Jesse steered the car with his knees—an expert skill of only the truly professional salesman—while he rummaged through the console, pulling out a box of Tic-Tacs and handing them to Amie.

"Thanks. That's still weird how you can like drive your car that way. But, anyway," she continued with a dash of Denise in her voice, "what's up with a gun even being in here in the first place?"

"I travel a lot, so I've got it here for, you know, personal protection, just in case." As he answered his daughter's question, the dilemma of who could help with Momma miraculously righted itself on the road. "What're you doing for extra spending money? Are you still babysitting for the neighborhood?"

"A little, every now and then, but ..." Amie briefly paused. "Mom and Jack are busy getting ready for the fall festival season, and I may have to get a regular job since this business with the police and your son that we're not talking about."

JJ sat upright in the passenger seat, whirled around to look at his younger sister, and quickly turned back around to the face the front.

Jesse playfully punched his son's upper arm. JJ rubbed his arm like the soft blow actually hurt and slouched deeper in his seat.

"Amie, you'd be perfect to sit with Grand."

"Sit? Why does Grand need a sitter?" Amie asked. "What's wrong?"

"Nothing really. I'm traveling a ton, and Momma could use a friendly face to drop by every day. Right now, she just needs someone to check in on her. I'm even going to ask Haymaker to stop in on her every now and then."

"Mr. Hay? That's totally off-the-chart crazy."

"He's got the time and the price is right."

"Yes, but he's—"

"I know. It's definitely a case of the inmate driving the short prison bus, but what else am I gonna do?"

"I can't even picture that," she said with her soft girlish giggle. "Can't you like hire a nurse-type lady?"

"I suppose, but Momma doesn't do well with strangers being in her house."

"Dad, people don't get any stranger than Mr. Hay."

"True, but I don't have other family around to help." Jesse pulled into the driveway of his old house.

"You've got me, and I'd be glad to help," Amie said, giving her dad a quick peck on the cheek. "But you'll have to help with transportation. I understand there's a certain black Mustang available now."

JJ spun around toward his sister again. His mouth was agape, but no words came out.

"I'll see what I can do," Jesse said, putting his hand on JJ's shoulder. "Your brother and I are going to talk about that right now."

JJ slumped deeper into the passenger seat.

"Hate that I'm going to miss that," Amie said, opening her car door. "Call me if you want me to help with Grand, but give me plenty of warning. I keep my social calendar very busy. Love you, Daddy."

"Will do, precious. Love you, too," Jesse said, wishing he had somebody to brag to about his flourishing daughter.

Amie ran inside, leaving Jesse and JJ alone in the car, idling in the driveway.

Jesse thought that father-and-son talks were always in black and white. The dad should be wearing a cardigan sweater, and he would sit his mischievous little boy down in his wood-paneled study, solving all their problems by the end of the thirty-minute episode. But Jesse didn't own a cardigan, and the front seat of his Cadillac would have to serve as the family study. Furthermore, television fathers never fortified themselves with a couple of double Jack and Cokes before their inspirational chats.

"Your mom and me are worried about you." Jesse wasn't totally sure about the objective of their heart-to-heart, but he dove forward using the same open-ended questions that could make even the most closed-mouth purchasing agent open up. "Everything going okay?"

"I know, I know. I'm fine. She told me that I needed to—had to—talk to Mr. Jack or you, somebody." JJ kept his eyes trained on the front door that Amie had just shut behind her, as if any second he would run from the passenger seat, before his escape route was totally cut off.

"Believe me, I know it's not always easy being good all the

time," Jesse said, changing to a quieter, softer tone. "But criminal charges, traffic tickets, court dates, and meeting with lawyers? You want to tell me what happened?"

Jesse studied his skinny young son's skimpy goatee and sandy-brown mop of hair and could see him caught in the middle ground between being a boy and becoming his own man, yet already overwhelmed by the daily struggles of adult life. This was more than a bloody knee or a trip to the principal's office.

"I was just stupid unlucky, I guess. But everything happens for a reason," JJ said with clear certainty, tapping his fist on his thigh.

"Yeah, I guess you're right." Jesse was slightly amazed at his son's philosophical attitude toward his trouble. "But you've gotten yourself in a helluva mess. You're talking a major pain in the ass, even if everything goes right. You know that, don't you?"

"Sure, and I'm sorry—really, really sorry—that I got me...us... in this fiasco, but I can deal with this on my own." JJ unclenched his fist and began to flip the air-conditioning vent open and closed. "Mom has the festivals coming up, and you've got enough problems with work and Grand. I'll pay whoever back for the lawyer—Mom, or Mr. Jack, or you."

"Don't worry about that for now," Jesse said, ready to let his son know that it was him, his father, not a broke-dick painter from Lower Alabama, paying the majority of his legal fees, but hesitant to add any competitive stress to the situation, especially until he knew his check cleared the bank. "Let me ask you this—how can I help you? What's the biggest problem you've got now?"

There was a clumsy silence.

"You really want to know?" JJ stopped playing with the vent.

"Of course. I wouldn't have asked if I didn't."

"Melanie."

"Melanie, okay," Jesse said, not completely shocked that problems with a blue-eyed blonde would rank higher than going to jail. The preacher's daughter wasn't your typical seventeen-year-old. "What's going on there?"

"It's her dad, Pastor Sonny."

"Pastor Sonny?"

"Sonny is his first name. He used to be in some bad-ass motorcycle gang."

"I assume that was before he got the job at First Baptist?"

"Yeah, a long time ago, like when he was my age. But Melanie says he's got a couple of creepy guys who used to be in the gang with him working for him at the church. They're like security dudes or something."

"That's weird. Why does a church need security?"

"I don't know; that's just what Melanie told me. But here's the thing," JJ said, turning and looking at his father directly. "He won't let me see her anymore. He says I'm a dangerous influence and something like I'm leading her down the path of destruction."

"Path of destruction? That's pretty heavy." Jesse figured that picking up the pastor's daughter at the police station had embarrassed him before his flock. "Pastor Sonny is just upset with Melanie about the other night is all."

"Upset? He's wigging out."

"It'll blow over. Give it some time." Jesse knew that he was lying to his son and that JJ and Melanie were finished as a couple.

"He keeps sending me text messages and posting these things on Facebook about me."

"What?" Jesse could see the pastor being angry about Melanie, but he couldn't understand him harassing JJ. "What kind of things?"

"Weird stuff about the Bible, verses, I think—flames being thrown into a pit, weeping and gnashing of teeth. He said I was going to hell if I didn't repent or whatever."

"He put this on your Facebook deal? Have you talked to Melanie?"

"I tried to call her tonight before dinner, but he answered the phone and told me to stop calling or he'd put me in jail."

"He doesn't know you like I do." Jesse put his arm on JJ's shoulder, giving it a squeeze. "You're a good boy, and I think Melanie's dad is just scared is all. But if he really knew you, he wouldn't say things like that."

"Can you talk to him for me?"

"I could, but I'm not sure it would do any good." Jesse preferred to risk kiting a check for a lawyer rather than talk to an angry preacher about daughters and damnation. "Just give her some space for now."

"I don't want to give her space," JJ said, pulling back, his voice rising. "She needs my help. You don't understand."

"Wow, what don't I understand?"

"Everything. Melanie and me. Do you know why I took those pills?"

"I will if you tell me." A chill passed along the back of Jesse's neck. He leaned back against the car door. He'd forgotten the Oxy. Last winter, he'd had his left knee scoped, and the doctor had given him a prescription for twenty 40-milligram tablets. Jesse learned that they were an excellent remedy for his pain, and they also turned a lonely January evening into a night of dreamless sleep. He'd easily gotten a refill, and then another through a pain-management doctor.

But before he could make use of the third refill, one of his old fraternity brothers overdosed after a night of binge-drinking and Oxy kickers. At the funeral, Jesse heard rumors about his departed friend's bankrupt home-building business. He put the pills in the medicine cabinet and never touched them again.

"It's just that Melanie has this—I don't know how to say it—this thing going on, and I was hoping they'd make it go away."

"So she has this thing going on," Jesse said, considering the problems that Melanie might have that would require pain pills. "Has she got some sort of injury or something? Back pain? A girl thing?"

"Gosh, no. It's not physical so much—I mean, it's like really weird to explain."

"If you want me to help, you need to give me something to go on. Give it a try."

"She can see and hear things that other people can't," JJ mumbled.

"Do what? Say that again."

"She's able to tell about people who have died, to communicate sort of," JJ said, slowing down a bit.

"You mean she's some kind of psychic?"

"Mom and Mr. Jack say that she's more like a medium."

"Oh, I see. And how do they know this?" Jesse gripped the steering wheel.

"I guess 'cause they watched her do it one time."

"Do what now?" Jesse asked, his head swiveling back and forth. "When?"

"Mr. Jack was staying over at the house, and Melanie told him things about his brother that only he would know. She had visions and everything."

"His brother? Couldn't she have seen his brother on Facebook or Googled him?"

"Not really. He's been dead for like twenty years or something," JJ said. "She even knew about his car crash. Mom and Mr. Jack were convinced. It was pretty amazing."

"They were? I'm sure that being a half-ass Norman Rockwell qualifies you to judge paranormal abilities like that," Jesse said, now his voice rising. He fought off the idea of Jackoff leading a séance around his kitchen table, right before he had all-night tantric sex with Denise.

"Mom says that Melanie has some sort of gift."

"I suppose anything is possible," Jesse said, easing his choke hold on the steering wheel. "But what's this gift got to do with you taking OxyContin from my bathroom cabinet? You don't mess with booze and those pills together. You can't do it."

JJ started mashing the door lock button up and down. Jesse listened as the rhythm of the metallic clicking grew louder and louder, realizing his biggest problem wouldn't be curing JJ's blue balls or convincing him he wasn't destined for the fiery pit of hell. Just then Jesse's phone chimed and vibrated with a new text message. Only one person sent Jesse text messages—Kimberly.

"If I tell you, Dad," JJ said, taking his hand off the switch, the abrupt silence startling Jesse, "will you promise to talk to Pastor Sonny for me?"

In twenty years, JJ had never really asked Jesse for anything more than a new video game, but now he had worked Jesse into a corner and then hit him with a sharp-angled question to close the deal.

"Okay, sure."

"You promise?"

"Yeah, yeah, I promise."

"Remember, you promised," JJ said, now looking out the front of the Cadillac. "I was hoping the pills would help calm her down or something, 'cause sometimes when she senses the dead people's feelings—it freaks her out. It's like she can't handle them 'cause she hasn't learned how to control it and it stresses her out, making her go a little off the walls."

"All right. I guess I can see how if that were really happening, you would be a bit anxious, but popping my pain pills and shooting tequila ain't the answer. Ever."

"I'm sorry, but that's why you need to talk to Pastor Sonny so I can see Melanie again," JJ said, pleading. "I'm the only one who she can actually tell what's going on. Without me, she's going crazy. That's why you have to convince him to change his mind. You're the super-sales guy, and he'll listen to you way more than if Mom and Mr. Jack tried to tell him."

"Okay, yeah, I will," Jesse said, JJ's last sentence making him willing to go see an ex-biker turned preacher about his pill-popping, soothsayer daughter. Just like when he'd found Momma's front door open, a rush of energy flowed through his arms. He needed to be the guy wearing the white hat, offering his son relief that he didn't have. There was no one who could approach Denise for him, tell her about his nightmares, and convince her the bad puppy was now housebroken. "I gotta see some folks in south Florida first to pay the bills, but you've got my word, as soon as I get back."

"Thanks, Dad. You know, you kinda surprised me." JJ leaned over and gave his dad a man-hug. "I love you."

"Love you, too. Sleep good." Jesse watched his son walk into the house and smiled, thinking he kind of surprised himself, too. His phone chirped a reminder about the unread text from Kimberly. Picking it up, he opened the message.

"I'm shopping for pleasure!?! Little B boy and chubby hubby are asleep...I'm drinking white z all by myself ☹"

Jesse flipped his phone over and over in his hands. In the saga of his late-night carousing, there usually came a moment when he had the choice to call in the hounds and get back on the porch or throw more kerosene on the fire and let the dogs run wild. He remembered a famous quote about valor and discretion, but then he imagined Kimberly's ass arching up to greet his thrust and wondered if a valiant knight would deny a tipsy damsel's request for a late-night hookup.

5

A YEAR AGO, PM HAD HOSTED A SEMINAR FOR GRAPHIC
design firms in Atlanta at the High Museum of Art. At the time,
they had the naive notion that the market was only in a slight
downturn, and they could sell their way out of the problem.
In Jesse's presentation, he had mentioned he lived in Dwyer.
Kimberly, a print buyer for Metro Graphic Designs (MGD), had
enjoyed his speech and thought he was cute; she made a point of
introducing herself, telling Jesse she lived in Dwyer, too. They
learned that they lived about five miles apart and even shopped
at the same grocery store. Flirting openly while they enjoyed
French wine and crudités, Jesse took the opportunity to set up a
lunch date. He was dating a series of divorced real estate agents
at the time, regularly hosting late-night hot tub parties, but he
didn't connect with any of them the way he had with his ex-wife;
Jesse couldn't explain what was missing. But Kimberly was a
stunner, born the same year he started tenth grade, and Jesse was
flattered by her attention.

He noticed her wedding ring, but he rationalized the morality
away, figuring there was little chance of anything happening.

It didn't hurt to contemplate the notion of upgrading if he ever happened to marry again. Besides, she had relationships inside the graphic design world that he ordinarily couldn't reach.

Kimberly and Nick, her husband, celebrated their seventh anniversary on Valentine's Day 2007, the same month Nick lost his job with a failing sub-prime mortgage lender. In the two and a half years since then, he hadn't found another position, and she hadn't given up her weakness for Saks Fifth Avenue, monthly spa appointments, and luxury car leases. Kimberly loved her four-year-old son, Brandon, but she didn't want to be a minivan carpooler married to an accidental househusband.

Jesse and Kimberly had their lunch meeting two weeks later on a Friday afternoon at the Sushi House in Buckhead. It was a two-hour lunch, fueled by a bottle or two of cold *sake* and plenty of time spent talking about the latest deals and gossiping about people in the design world. Their attraction was confirmed and continued to grow, beginning a daily correspondence of texts, each one developing a bolder, more enticing tone. They decided to meet again for lunch.

Jesse picked the Phipps Tavern across the street from the Buckhead Ritz-Carlton, where he had already checked into a room. They started with a couple of glasses of wine and never ordered lunch; in less than thirty minutes, they were across the street at the Ritz.

~~~

Staring out at his ex-house now, filled with his ex-wife and her current boyfriend, Jesse pondered his next best move. Haymaker was entertaining a recent divorcee from his support group, so Jesse couldn't sneak Kimberly into his house. He offered Kimberly his alternative.

How about a getaway? Hotel sex!

AYS? Where??

Holiday Inn Express at Ansley Place

It's not the Ritz!?

Like old times...turns me on

CU in 30...text me the room #

After he checked into the hotel, he texted Kimberly the number:

317

K

He brewed a pot of coffee and dug into his goody bag, pulling out a mini-bottle of Bailey's Irish Cream he had stashed. Adding the Bailey's to his coffee, he popped a Viagra—his blue diamond party pill—with a sip of coffee while he watched sports news, struggling not to doze off.

Jesse snapped awake to a loud knock on the door, taking a second to right himself to the stark-white surroundings at the Holiday Inn Express.

"That took forever," Kimberly said as Jesse let her in. "I thought you gave me the wrong room number."

"Nope, you're in the right spot and looking mighty damn good."

A teacup of a woman, slightly over five feet, Kimberly was wearing a sapphire corset tank top, a white denim miniskirt, and nothing underneath. She matched her straight platinum blonde hair with an all-over, year-round tan. Her brown eyes beamed above her slender cheeks and thin lips, which shone an impetuous pink.

"I'm supposed to be on a late-night run to Kroger," she said. "What if someone sees my car?"

"Soooo did it rain much at your house?" Jesse said.

"Are you drunk? You feel okay?"

"Come feel." He pulled her in close and pinned her up against the wall with a kiss, a familiar move they both enjoyed. He lifted off her top and paused, gazing at her tanned breasts, gently clutching them. Flicking his tongue across her rosy nipples, he took in the orange blossom fragrance of her perfume. "Thank you, sweet Jesus."

Later, they lie in bed, their bodies intertwined with the twisted sheets while Kimberly chattered and Jesse fought to keep his eyes open.

"How's next quarter's bonus looking?" she said.

"Nonexistent."

"Don't say that. You sound like Nick. He's working my last nerve with his whiny voice. I swear, he's not even trying to find a job." Kimberly twirled Jesse's chest hair around her finger.

"Speaking of bonus, how's that deal looking with that Chinese car company? That thing was loaded down with print work. I mean tons."

"This is kinky," she said, giving him a playful slap. "But it's not looking good for the home girls. I think those bitches at Iron Designs start each presentation on their knees."

"That must be interesting in an all-women meeting." Jesse made a note to have his sales rep follow up with the Iron Designs people. There was no point in everyone losing business.

"Ha, I bet you'd love to watch me in some girl-on-girl. You do have delusions of grandeur," she said with a breathy tease. "But who knows what the future holds."

Jesse rested on the idea of Kimberly and the sexy account executive at Iron Designs sprawled out on a conference room table, their creamy thighs and tongues locked together; just as quickly, the idea of Kimberly as an ally in the business world—a husband-wife sales team—entered his head. "Shit, just getting a paycheck is like making a bonus these days. I don't dare complain about the unreachable goal I've got. I'm not too keen on upsetting the status quo by riling up the French."

"True enough. I keep my head down and look busy every time Mark walks through the office."

"How is Darth Design doing these days?"

"His face seems frozen in a permanent pout, but he keeps yakking about some energy boom and opening an office in Houston." Kimberly rolled over, away from Jesse, and propped herself up on the pillows. "All I know is I'm the only bitch taking care of me and Brandon. So I gotta keep working on turning Marky-Mark's frown upside down."

"I am Kimba, the white lion. Hear me roar," Jesse said, imitating a deep, booming voice. He knew that Texas wasn't suffering like the rest of the country, and he'd welcome the potential for new contacts if Kimberly's company expanded. Anything to get him closer to his bonus and avoid more firings.

"You'll help me, won't you, baby?" she said, returning to nuzzle up against Jesse's neck.

"You wanna go again?" He lifted up the sheet and peeked at his limp dick, hoping she'd move her hand down to get him hard again. It would just take the touch of her long fingernails, the image of her writhing in unison on a black lacquered conference table, and his blue diamond party pill would do the rest, allowing him to compete with any younger man Kimberly might meet.

"Not this time, big boy. You're gonna have to handle that all by yourself. I gotta go in case Brandon wakes up."

"So soon?" Jesse asked, watching her leave the bed for the bathroom. He fought to stay awake, listening to the shower run, curious what it would be like to pay her water bill.

"Call me," she said, bending down to kiss him after she was dressed again, nibbling his lip.

"Roger that," he said, his eyelids fluttering.

"I'm going to that conference in New Orleans." Kimberly gave his nipple a hard twist. "I want you to meet me there."

"Owww!"

"We've got to do some talking."

In a twilight sleep, Jesse heard the loud slam of the door and then passed out, blissfully spent and temporarily oblivious to any dreams of Denise.

ON SATURDAY MORNING, JESSE STOOD ON THE FIRST TEE with "The Brothers"—Haymaker, Alton "Schaff" Schaffer, and Paul "Bubba" Babineaux—watching their pre-game rituals while they waited for the foursome in the fairway. Weather and life permitting, Saturday at the golf course had been Jesse's weekend custom since they all moved into Quail Woods in the mid-1990s. The smell of freshly mowed fairways and Bubba honking with his grass allergies, the *pssschh* sound of Schaff opening his first breakfast beer, and the aromatic bite of Haymaker puffing on his bootleg Cuban cigar all created a sense of sanctuary for Jesse. They'd been through tortuous bosses, lousy business ventures, and two divorces—one regrettable but agreeable and one inevitable and still nasty.

The cast-off pastureland converted to a golf course was as much home as his old house, except here, on the flat terrain running along a swampy bottom, he still felt welcome. On Saturday mornings, he still held the bonds of kinship; it was the solitude of Sunday mornings without Denise he hadn't yet learned to manage.

"I believe Mr. Hay and I are up," said Bubba, preparing to hit first. "Since the last time we played—one rain-out ago, I suppose—you gentlemen won."

"Sounds right," said Schaff. "Despite my crappy short game, I think we stomped a mudhole in you poor boys. Right, partner?"

"Oh, hell yes," Jesse said, giving his partner the first of many fist bumps.

Bubba Babineaux was short and wiry and was a regular runner who competed in marathons. He was a certified public accountant with his own firm, and he played a conservative game, always measuring the risk and reward of each shot.

"Hold on there, partner, before you bust 'em strong and long," Haymaker said. "We need to codify the stakes. It's time to get—"

"Okay, okay," said Schaff. "My back is really stiff, but what do you losers have in mind?"

"How about we up it this week? Nifty fifty a side and a honey-baked hundred overall?"

"Wait a second, not so fast," said Bubba.

"Have no fear, Underdog is here," said Haymaker, stepping up to hit after Bubba put his tee shot in perfect position. "Remember, there ain't no candy-asses in the hall of fame."

Haymaker was the least athletic of their foursome, with a soft, pear-shaped figure and a squishy potbelly, but he played the most golf and could produce a good round. He was a firm believer in using not only practice to lower his handicap, but also equipment, constantly trading sets of irons or woods. He smashed his tee shot past Bubba's, landing close to the hazard.

"What do you think, Jester?" said Schaff, getting ready to play next.

"I say screw it," Jesse said. "Let's double down."

"Back to you, big boy," said Haymaker before Bubba could object. "A honey a side and two honeys overall."

"Holy moly. I don't like the sound of this one," said Bubba with his usual pessimistic whine.

Schaff, who was already drenched in sweat, took a few practice swings before he hit. He was a large, barrel-chested man with a thick, black beard; he looked comical addressing the tiny white ball. He was a power hitter who could crush a golf ball, but he was the highest handicapper in the group; his tee shot sliced deep in the woods.

"Mulligan," said Schaff, reloading quickly and then hooking a towering tee shot deep into the driving range on the other side of the fairway. "That ain't gonna work."

"No worries," Jesse said as he did some fast windmill stretches. "Like James Brown said, I feel good, I knew that I would."

Jesse had won the Quail Woods Club Championship three years in a row. Three months before the annual club tournament, he would begin a practice regimen to tune up his game, including weightlifting, stretching exercises, and even a few classes of yoga. However, the strength of his game was his pre-shot routine that was impervious to the weather, his blood-alcohol level, or competitive pressures. Starting back low and slow with his club head, he let his well-rehearsed swing thought take over. Unleashed with a metallic *clank*, his tee shot sailed past Bubba's, with a clearer second shot than Haymaker's.

Jesse birdied the first hole and took honors away from Bubba and Haymaker. They waited to play the second hole, a par three.

"I noticed you didn't come home the other night. I was actually goin' to introduce you to my new divorcee friend," said Haymaker. "Shouldn't you have at least called?"

"I kind of had a strange night," said Jesse after he placed his tee shot on the green.

"Sounds like Mrs. Married with Child," said Haymaker. "Was it creepy strange or 'Super Freak' strange?"

"No, more like she said, 'We got to talk,' freaking-me-out."

They gathered on the green for their putts, and Jesse squatted by his ball, lining up his downhill putt to win the hole.

"I'd speculate that she's planning her exit strategy from husband number one to husband number two," Bubba said. "Let's make sure we get a prenuptial this go-around."

"Quiet, goofballs. Let my man putt," Schaff said.

"Not a problem," Jesse said, watching his putt drop into the center of the cup for birdie. "I think Kimba sorta clicks with me. It might be fun to have eye-candy strapped to my arm for some of those corporate dinners."

His friends looked at each other with bent grins as they walked off the green.

The match evened up over the next few holes as Bubba and Haymaker went on a barrage of birdies. They were tied on the front going into the ninth hole.

"Any of you gray-hairs got any aspirin?" Schaff asked. "My back is tightening up."

"You should try my landlord and very occasional roommate," said Haymaker, pointing to Jesse. "He's got all sorts of pills."

"Speaking of, Haymaker," said Jesse. "Did you see JJ around the house lately?"

"Yup—I think he and the preacher's daughter were over to the pool last week," Haymaker said, swatting at the grass with his driver. "They showed up right around cocktail time, and I was fixin' me a batch of margaritas, you know, and—how old is she?"

"Not old enough. Why?"

"Damn it. That girl said they were both twenty-one."

"You gave a seventeen-year-old girl margaritas?"

"We just had a couple of pitchers."

"Who's up on the tee box?" asked Bubba.

"That'd be you and Chester the Molester," said Schaff.

"Fine, but Bertram and his banker bunch are behind us, so we better hurry before they ask to play through. I'm not allowing your so-called banker buddies to slow up my afternoon." Bubba knocked a solid tee shot straight down the middle. Haymaker put one ten yards beyond Bubba's, and Schaff sprayed his ball deep into the rough.

Walking back to his cart, Jesse turned to Haymaker again. "Anything else happen at your impromptu pool party that I need to know about?"

"It wasn't no party," Haymaker said. "But JJ was sorta havin' problems with his stomach. Gas issues, I guess. I told him to go look in your medicine cabinet, that you had somethin' to help."

Jesse shook his head as their carts pulled away to the fairway; he had a clear vision of prescription bottles with his name on them sealed in plastic bags and labeled as Exhibit A in the prosecutor's case against his son.

At the turn, they made a short stop at the snack bar.

"Courtesy of my partner's dead-eye puttin', we won the front side's Benjamin, so we're buyin'," Haymaker said. "What'll you have, Jester? Mornin' beer or straight to clear liquids?"

"I'd love to be joining y'all," Jesse said, holding his hand up. "But I'll just be ordering my traditional hot dog at the turn, pure protein. I got a little sit-down meeting this afternoon."

"What sort of meeting?" Bubba asked. "You don't have meetings on Saturday."

"A Pastor Sonny sort of meeting."

"Yeah, I heard everything from the ever-nosy wife," Schaff said. His wife, Claire, had known Denise since their days together at Dwyer High School. Because of the women's friendship, Schaff often knew more about what was going on with the Few family than Jesse did.

"So I assume you guys heard the worst about JJ?" Jesse asked.

All three of his friends nodded and glumly gnarled their faces.

"It really sucks for JJ, and the pastor isn't allowing him to see Melanie anymore. I promised, so you'll see me going to church—on a Saturday afternoon. Watch out for thunderbolts." Jesse took a bite of his grilled hot dog, savoring the salty taste of the meat and the mustard and friends who didn't press him for details about juggling retainer payments, psychic girlfriends, or pissed-off preachers threatening damnation.

"Claire told me we had to change dentists because our old guy was a deacon, or choir leader dude, at Dwyer Baptist, but after he confronted the pastor about bopping one of his hygienists, he got booted from the church. His practice dried up and he had to move back to Folkston. Apparently, if you cock-block Pastor Sonny, all he needs to do is whisper and you're banished to purgatory in the Okefenokee Swamp."

"You know, he's well-connected, too," Bubba said, pontificating in his official CPA voice. "That braggart shyster Jenkins does their books, but on an off-the-cuff tally, I'd surmise there's five thousand attendees at his Sunday services, which means he's shepherding a fairly substantial revenue stream. There's even a rumor that he's forming a lobbying firm and a faith-based investment fund. I'd hazard the assumption that every candidate for every office has to kiss his ring to get his block of votes."

"Wow, not too shabby for an ex-biker. I may have to kiss something else to change his mind, but like I said, I promised."

"I'd tread lightly. He's used his newspaper column and a local cable talk show to shut down the sex toy head shop, the hippie bookstore, and that odd little bar out on the bypass that had the cross-dressing night."

"JJ told me he's even got like a security team or something," Jesse said, suppressing a belch. His savory snack tradition was fighting back. "How's that for weird?"

"That's as weird as a one-eyed wallflower. Keep an eye on your watch, your wallet, and your whitewalls." Haymaker crushed his empty beer can. "And let me know if you want me to do some unofficial background checkin'. That pastor is only as god-fearin' as the lies he's hidin'. I can dig up secrets the Holy Ghost don't know nothin' about."

"Let's go." Jesse rolled up his half-eaten hot dog in the wax paper wrapper, mashed it into a ball, and slam-dunked it into the trash can. He'd lost his taste for sodium nitrate bombs. "We gotta get our money back. We don't want to stare at the plaid-pants gang on the back nine."

They were all on the seventeenth green with Jesse looking at a long birdie putt to take the hole and even the match. Jesse rolled the ball toward the hole; it caught the right edge of the cup and lapped around the lip before dropping to the bottom of the cup.

"Yesss, babeeee," Jesse said, pumping his fist. "It's time to press on the last hole."

"Double it?" Haymaker looked at Bubba.

"Sure," Bubba said, fortified by a six-pack.

"Bet taken then," Haymaker said, pointing at Jesse. "Another hundred on this last hole, and two hundred more for the overall."

They made their way to the last hole where Jesse waited for the logjam in the fairway to clear.

"So in other wacky events since we gathered for our last meeting on the green, I didn't get a chance to tell y'all about me pulling out the nine, did I?" Jesse said. "I was ready to go all Mel Gibson or old-school Eastwood."

"I don't like the lead-in to this news flash," Bubba said. "What happened?"

"Momma called claiming there was a stranger in the backyard."

"A stranger? What type of stranger?"

"A disappearing one, I guess, 'cause when I got there, I couldn't find anything. She didn't even remember calling me," Jesse said, pinching his mind shut to Momma's burlesque show.

"Sounds like old-timer's disease to—" Haymaker said.

"You mean Alzheimer's?" Bubba rolled his eyes. "But it could be her thyroid or sleep apnea."

"I suppose," Jesse said, right before he blasted his best drive of the day, a pitching wedge away from the hole.

Schaff duck-hooked his shot way off to the left, crashing into a house. Bubba was short but safely in the middle, and Haymaker was off the edge of the fairway in the low-cut rough, but he had a clear shot to the green.

They pulled their carts together in the fairway as they waited for the green to clear.

"So what's your plan, big-money man?" Schaff asked.

"Knock it tight with my wedge and win the money."

"I meant the plan for your mom. 'Cause I hate to say it, but you could become your mother's babysitter. You ready for all that?"

"I had a client who had to hire a nurse for his mother and then put his mom-in-law in an assisted-living place," Bubba said after he put his second shot in the middle of the green. "Sets them all back well over two hundred thousand dollars a year."

"Like the Duke said, 'A man's gotta do what a man's gotta do.' I plan to live by that code, but I got no real plan, brother." Jesse got out of the cart and took a few practice swings. Mr. Billy had taught him how to make cocktails and entertain guests and told him every man should carry a pocketknife and handkerchief, so Jesse knew he was expected to care for Momma—no matter what. "Shit, I turn the TV station every time some old-fart cowboy actor tries to pitch long-term care insurance. I imagine it's tough picking up hot chicks in the adult diapers section of Kroger. Which reminds me, Haymaker, would you mind driving by my Momma's house every now and then? A neighborhood watch sort of deal."

"I'd consider it an honor to help with Mrs. Gennifer," Haymaker said, after he backed a nine iron up to within a few feet of the hole. "And I won't even dare ask you to deduct it from the rent I ain't payin', but you know, just because you didn't see nobody and she didn't remember, don't mean that no one hadn't been there."

"So what's your inference?" Bubba replied.

"I don't speak Latin, Mr. Big Words, but I'm just sayin' that some Nasonville white-trash meth-head could have slipped in her house and taken the family jewels without Jester's momma knowing. And I'd want my mammy to be prepared, you know? Get her one of those pink .38 specials with some full-metal rounds."

"Get serious," Bubba said with a grumpy grunt.

"I'm as serious as I get," Haymaker said as Jesse prepared to start his backswing. "I'd say we load her up and take Momma to the gun show."

The instinctive, orchestrated swing that Jesse had fine-tuned for years fled his mind and was replaced with the image of Momma shopping for a revolver like a modern-day Ma Barker while salacious gun dealers ogled her breasts. His smooth tempo was transformed into a fast whipping motion that sent his shot–and the bet–sailing over the green into the pond behind it.

IF IT WEREN'T FOR THE ENORMOUS IVORY CROSS ON TOP
of the dome, the circular, white-block building would have resembled a basketball arena more than the First Baptist Church of
Dwyer. The front of the sanctuary was three stories of gleaming
plate glass, and the blacktop parking lot was nearly as large as
the desert the Israelites had to cross to reach the Promised Land.
It had only taken an exchange of two short emails for Jesse
to set up an appointment with Melanie's father. He hadn't had
a one-on-one meeting in a church since his mother-in-law had
forced pre-marriage counseling on him more than twenty years
ago.

He thought the task of changing Pastor Sonny's mind was
improbable, like making a sales call on the customer who never,
ever bought anything from you. But he at least wanted to be able
to tell JJ he tried, and hopefully, by a miracle, he would live up
to his son's expectations.

When he entered the glossy lobby, Jesse almost expected to
be frisked by pony-tailed hoodlums with skull earrings and
walkie-talkies, but instead, a clean-shaven, cheery associate

minister escorted Jesse to the pastor's library where he could wait for his meeting.

Family photos were wedged throughout his overstuffed library: the mountain vista, the lake house, the pontoon boat, the snorkeling trip, the sweaty graduation, and the horrified candid shot from the hidden camera on Space Mountain. Jesse could mark Melanie's blossoming from a girl to a young woman who had obviously gotten her face and figure from her mother. Jesse thought the pastor's wife would look shapely in a choir robe, but she showed more of a thin, gloomy bend to her lips than an actual smile. There was a picture of a group of bikers in their leathers, posing with a small girl in a wheelchair. Pastor Sonny was a stocky man with a high, thick brow, which ran like a ridge across his forehead. His full head of hair was predominantly white, and he wore it spiked with hair gel.

The bookshelves were crammed with community awards, decrees, and honorary plaques. There were also pictures of Pastor Sonny alongside law enforcement officers, congressmen, senators, governors, both Bush Senior and Junior, and even Dick Cheney. The largest photo—and most recent—was of the pastor posing at a conference table next to a large man in a beige Western suit coat and bolo tie. A brown Stetson hat was on the table next to a stack of papers and two pens. Like all the pictures in the pastor's swollen shrine, Pastor Sonny was beaming, but the daunting gray-headed cowboy next to him had the tight-lipped glare of a man you wouldn't want to risk upsetting.

There was a wall-long display titled "Connecting to First Dwyer," illustrating in a lively cyan blue the church's extensive ministries, along with portraits of the staff responsible for each program. Jesse examined the exhibit of blithe faces with their crystal complexions, hearty and ready. Becky Carter, the youth and social media minister, caught Jesse's attention. He looked at the picture of the green-eyed brunette with the generous grin for several seconds before it clicked; he'd picked her up at T's one night.

Becky had been out with a girlfriend, drinking Long Island iced teas and celebrating the finalization of her divorce. Haymaker and he had bought them several drinks, and Jesse ended up spending the night at her place, reintroducing a bucking Becky to the uninhibited rewards of single life. The next morning, Jesse left before sunrise without saying a word. For the next couple of weeks, he'd avoided taking calls from unknown numbers or going back to T's.

He peeked at his watch. Pastor Sonny had kept him waiting for twenty minutes so far. The church was peaceful, and for the first time since he'd been waiting, Jesse heard muffled voices coming from the pastor's inner sanctum. The rumbles were joined by a brief series of thumps against the wall, and then it was quiet again. After a few more minutes, out came Pastor Sonny—alone.

"Mr. Few? Sorry to keep you waiting. Come on in," the pastor said, extending his hand to greet Jesse. "Pastor Sonny Suggs; I'm pleased to meet you. You can call me Sonny."

"Yeah, no, not a problem." Jesse sprang up and gave the pastor a firm handshake before following him into his private office. "And you can call me Jesse."

Pastor Sonny's office was much dimmer than the outer office. A desk lamp on the far side of the room gave off much of the light, shining on a pair of reading glasses laid across the pages of an open Bible. Jesse caught a hint of hand sanitizer in the air beneath the aroma of the scented pine candle burning on the pastor's desk. There were two guest chairs in front of the executive-size desk, and nearer the door was a seating area with a coffee table and two sofas, one backing up to the wall that adjoined the outer office.

Scanning the room, Jesse didn't see anyone else in the pastor's office. He assumed the pastor had been having an animated phone conversation or a direct talk with the Lord, until he noticed a partially concealed side door to the left of the desk, painted to blend in with the wall.

"Let's take a seat here on the sofas. They're a bit easier on the back," the pastor said, pointing to the seating area.

"That'll be good." Jesse sat down first while the pastor sat across from him. Sonny was dressed in a blue suit, white dress shirt, and red striped tie. Jesse noticed his lapel pin, an American flag overlaid with a pair of praying hands and a diamond accent. The pictures didn't do justice to his size or his silver-blue eyes, which still glowed in the subtle light.

"So we've got a few things to talk about, don't we?" Sonny said, his voice a rough boom. "Do you mind if I say a short prayer first?"

"Please. That'd be great." Despite the slight buzz of nerves, Jesse intended to follow a John Wayne strategy: "Talk low, talk slow, and don't say much."

Sonny closed his eyes and bowed his head, reaching his palms across the table. Jesse grabbed them, remembering that the Baptists were known for hugging and hand-holding. After his short prayer, Sonny asked a series of questions about Jesse's work at PM and hobbies. Sonny was a golfer, too, but not of Jesse's caliber. Jesse worked in a few questions about motorcycles, allowing the pastor to brag about the photo Jesse had seen.

"I'm in the Thundering Thumpers, a motorcycle club—a bit tongue in cheek, but it looks good on the back of our leather vests," Pastor Sonny said, using the same warmth he would for a welcomed visitor or an old-time deacon. "We do a lot of charity rides; it's a great way to spread the Gospel. You should do a ride with us sometime."

"I'd love to," Jesse said, not meaning it, but considering the pastor more of a regular guy than a killjoy. Now that they had talked about work, golf, and motorcycles, Jesse wondered if he should move on to guns, college football, and chicks.

"I've been riding for over thirty years, but not always with a higher purpose," Sonny said, now rolling up his sleeves. "I started as a bad seed on rocky ground, stealing cars, robbing people, selling drugs. We called ourselves Satan's Wolves—we were truly serving the devil."

"Really?" Jesse glanced at Sonny's forearms for tattoos, but none were showing.

"Yes, sir. We thought we had a bond as brothers, wearing our colors. But like all those who follow Satan, it led to destruction. We were coming back from Miami, me and a biker brother, smuggling a load of cocaine in our choppers, and the DEA was waiting for us. My so-called biker brother had flipped. He testified against me, and I went to the penitentiary.

"I got five-to-twenty, and it was a living hell of every degradation imaginable. It didn't matter—blacks or whites, inmates or guards—all you are is a piece of flesh. I'm not afraid to tell you, I was broken. But at my lowest moment, I found a Gideon Bible that had been tossed out on the rec yard. I began to read it and repeat the conversion prayer. My life changed. I was transferred to another prison. I got out on an early release. When I came back home, the only place I could get a job was as a janitor at First Baptist Dwyer."

"You've been here ever since?"

"Sure have. Reverend Rick, God rest his soul, helped me get my high school diploma; then he got me through junior college, and finally, seminary. I've done everything in this church there is to do. I was at the very first meeting when we had the vision for this new community of faith that you're in right now."

Jesse had now heard the condensed version of Sonny's testimonial, but he still needed to discuss his son's problems, and he wasn't sure how to bring it up, especially after a story about prison rape and jailhouse conversion.

"How many children do you have?" Jesse asked.

"My wife and I have two girls, more like grown women now. My oldest, Ellen, just graduated from Agnes Scott and is living in Decatur. And you know Melanie, of course."

"Yes, I do. Every time I've been around her, she's been a treat," Jesse said. "I can't tell you how sorry I am about the episode with the police. I take full blame; it's entirely my fault. I hope it hasn't caused your family too much grief."

"We're dealing with it like any other burden—we lay it down at the foot of the cross," the pastor said, tugging on his collar. "Melanie has always been a worrier, a nervous Nellie, we call them. We learned recently that she suffers from an anxiety disorder, and sadly, she's reached the age where she chooses to self-medicate and act out inappropriately in order to compensate for the stress."

"I'm sorry, but I had no idea," Jesse said, taking in the pastor's version of Melanie's behavior.

"It's a struggle not to allow these anxieties to rule her. Now, like all good papa bears, I'm protecting my cubs. It's my duty to them and the Lord. And I would suppose that JJ told you about the exchange that we've had."

"He has, and honestly, it's been a bit troubling. His mother and I tried to raise him right," Jesse said firmly, trying to decide if there were any upsides to growling back like a black bear in the wild. Sonny was a professional proselytizer who could make convicts cry and persuade sinners to give up cigarettes, beer, and R-rated movies for Sunday school and ice cream socials. Short of bludgeoning the pastor with the coffee table, Jesse didn't have much hope.

"I'm sure you have, and it should be troubling. I recognize the path your son is on. My calling as a pastor requires throwing out a lifeline, which comes in many different forms. JJ thinks I've been harsh, but Melanie needs time with her family. I trust you see that?"

"I do, I really do. It's just that Melanie means so much to JJ, and he's had a hard time not being part of her life."

"Has he got a court date set? Do you know who the judge is or the prosecutor?"

"I'm not sure about the date or that other stuff, but we've hired Blaire McMahon."

"Blaire is pretty capable."

"That's good to know," Jesse said, expecting him to be more than capable for five grand.

"Now it's all about the docket. There isn't really a giant blind lady holding scales; it's more like an assembly line of justice," the pastor said, shifting to the center of the sofa and lying back, his hands behind his head. "First, the police officer on the street has total power—discretionary law on the spot. Then the district attorney can steer your son's case whichever route he decides.

And lastly, it's the judge. He's got the final power over how to split your baby, forgive the expression. I've done a lot of prison ministry, and I've got a practical view of our criminal court system. I've seen it be influenced, one way or the other, time and again. It's the best system in the world, but any court can be swayed. Just ask Barabbas."

"I appreciate your advice. Would you maybe reconsider and at least let JJ talk to or text Melanie?" It was a desperate plea, but Jesse had to ask for the sale.

"I'd like to help, if I can." The pastor now leaned across the coffee table and put a hand on one thigh. "I know voters in Lewallen want stronger punishments for underage drinking-and-driving charges. They're even less tolerant of drug charges, prescription or otherwise. If he were my son, I'd want him concentrating on school, work, and, of course, church. I recommend that JJ and Melanie have a cooling-off period until after his court date. Then these young folks can decide if they want to start talking or seeing each other again."

"Honestly, I understand your point of view, and as tough as it'll be on JJ, I agree. Thank you for your time," Jesse said, considering the pastor's commitment a lame diplomatic victory. JJ wouldn't be pleased, and he remembered Haymaker's warning to "keep an eye on your watch, your wallet, and your whitewalls." It'd be interesting to see what his friend could discover about Sonny's "unofficial background." As he stood up to leave, he prepared himself for a possible Southern Baptist man-hug.

AFTER HIS SATURDAY AFTERNOON TRIP TO FIRST BAPTIST,
Jesse decided to take Momma to church. It was something that
he usually only did on Christmas Eve and Easter Sunday, but he
figured an hour mouthing a few hymns and tossing a fifty-dollar
bill in the offering plate could win him a divine blessing or two.
Besides, it got him out of the house and his own way on Sunday
morning. He confirmed the plans with her after his meeting with
the pastor and arrived early to take her to the eleven o'clock
service at Dwyer United Methodist. Jesse picked up the Sunday
paper on Momma's driveway.

Eugene Finch had built the Craftsman-style bungalow in
the late 1930s after Jesse's Aunt Lizzy was born. The red
brick house—with its white trim, shutters, and plain white
aluminum awnings—resembled Eugene and Barbara Finch.
Like his grandparents, it had an austere exterior with an affec-
tionate interior. Not unlike its current inhabitant, the house was
exhibiting signs of age with rotting and sagging roof fascia,
drooping front steps, and cracking in the brick veneer caused
by a settling foundation.

"Momma?" Jesse said, knocking on the front door before opening it. Getting no response, he stepped into the foyer. He walked into the kitchen, wishing he'd find Momma drinking a cup of coffee and reading a devotion from *The Upper Room*, but it was empty. He felt a crunch under his feet and looked down to see yellow corn puffs scattered across the floor.

"Momma...it's Jesse," he called out. "You about ready? We don't wanna have to sit in the front row."

Entering the dark den, he noticed a static screen on the TV and Momma curled up on the sofa in her housedress and slippers. He paused and listened for her breathing, relieved to see her chest rising up and down. He gave her shoulder a soft nudge, but there was no movement. Her empty cocktail glass with a half-eaten orange wedge and cherry stem floating in the bottom was sitting on the coffee table. He shook her a bit harder.

"Momma," he said, but still no reaction.

He sat down in the chair across the room and watched her sleep. On top of the TV console was a faded color photo taken from the captain's formal night on her honeymoon cruise with Mr. Billy. Momma—her sapphire-blue evening gown flattering her shapely figure and long legs—had stared straight into the camera with a glamorous smile and ruby red lips, her face framed by wavy, deep-brunette hair. His dad, equally dapper in his blue-and-green Black Watch tartan vest under his tuxedo dinner jacket, was captured in profile, his admiring eyes fixed on the lady he called "My Madame Queen."

His mother had never been divorced; all her husbands had just died on her. Rex Sherman, the Korean War hero from Philadelphia and Ricky's father, had been killed in an improbable Jeep accident at Fort McPherson right after Ricky was born in 1953. Preston Garrett, her second husband and Jesse's birth father, died while on a sales trip when his car slid off an icy rural highway, leaving Jesse temporarily fatherless at eighteen months. Billy Few and Gennifer had been married for thirty-six years before prostate cancer took away his manhood and then his life.

Grabbing the TV remote and muting the static, Jesse flipped the channels to see if he could find anything interesting on on Sunday morning; something like Eastwood's *Pale Rider* where Clint plays the preacher would be appropriate. Maybe he could put on his white collar, saddle up, and rescue his aging mother, his ex-wife, and his only son from any evil hounding them: roughneck outlaws, snake-oil artists, vengeful ex-bikers, and backyard strangers. But there was nothing but snow on all channels. Giving up, he turned the TV off and tossed the remote aside.

Next to him on the small end table was a stack of mail, with a neon-orange door flyer sticking out from the middle of the pile. Jesse pulled it out of the pile and read the cut-off notice from Dwyer Cable Company, dated Friday. That would explain the stranger in the backyard, but the timing wasn't right.

He sorted through the rest of the pile, finding her latest investment statement and her most recent bank statement. Creeping into the breakfast nook to open them up, he felt a mix of adventure and remorse, like a child exploring his parents' closet while they're gone.

She still had money in her investment account, but considerably less than Jesse expected. Based on what he knew Mr. Billy had left to Momma, nearly three-quarters of what his dad had left her had vanished. Jesse reviewed her list of stocks. Apparently, his mother favored investing in places she liked to eat and shop—O'Charley's and Macy's—businesses that scared consumers avoided first when the economy tanked. Her regional bank and airline stocks were trading for a fraction of her initial investment, and most frightening of all, her biggest single investment was in General Motors, which was now worthless. Momma wasn't on the verge of eating canned dog food to survive, but she hadn't ever asked Jesse for help or done anything to protect herself. A flush of indignation filled him, and he went back into the den with the firm resolve of a father to wake his slothful teenager.

"Time to wake up, Momma," he said in a loud voice, giving her a firm, steady shake.

Momma's eyes blinked open and she slowly rolled from her side to her back. She stared at the ceiling while Jesse sat back down.

"Am I dreaming?" Momma asked.

"Good morning. No, you're not dreaming. How'd you sleep? Why aren't you in your bedroom?" Jesse's displeasure was replaced with pity at the sound of her creaky morning voice.

"Can you fix my television?" Momma rubbed her eyes and stretched. "I was watching one of my stories after lunch. It wasn't yesterday, but anyway, I fell asleep, and when I woke up, it wasn't working. You don't suppose it's under warranty? You know, Mr. Billy was always real good about those things."

"I'll take a look at it, but it may be a problem with the cable bill."

"Oh me, oh my-o, Man-o," she said, patting her Medusa-style morning hairdo and shuffling to the bathroom. "I need to wash up and take my medicines."

"I'll find your pills for you."

Jesse went to the laundry room to get the broom and dustpan and found Momma's sheets in a heap on top of the washer. He detected the odor of stale urine and quickly returned to the unkempt kitchen.

After he put the broom away, he tried to decipher the array of pill bottles spread out on the kitchen counter, none with child-safe tops on them. There was a white oblong pill, a peach-colored square, a scored white barrel, and a light-yellow dot. He knew Momma had arthritis and either high blood pressure or high cholesterol, maybe both. One of the prescriptions was an opiate-type drug that was clearly labeled to avoid alcohol. There were three more prescriptions—for constipation, nausea, and heartburn—to offset the side effects of the other four drugs. Jesse pictured Momma as a bubbling cauldron of fire and trouble, stirred blindly by her doctors.

Momma padded into the kitchen, having changed her house-dress and tamed half of her hair.

"You look very sharp, Man-o," Momma said, noticing Jesse's church outfit of cream-colored linen slacks, a pink sports shirt, and a sky-blue blazer. "Are you going somewhere special?"

"No, ma'am. Just coming to see you." Jesse decided to skip church; the struggle wasn't worth the reward of bad singing, a muddled sermon, and smothering his guilt.

"That's sweet." Momma turned a circle in the center of the kitchen. "Now where're my medicines?"

"On the counter here. Let me get you a glass of water." He reached into the cabinet, happy to find a clean glass to fill at the sink. "Here you go."

"Thank you."

One by one, she poured a pill into her hand, popped it into her mouth, and swallowed each with a sip of water. Jesse was certain the old, bloated Elvis would have jones-upped at her swift user ritual.

"You need to eat something? You want me to carry you up to the club?"

"No, I'm a little tired. Besides, we've got plenty to eat right here at the house."

"Okay, I'll fix us something to eat. You go on in the den and read the Sunday paper."

"All righty then, but you holler when you need my help," she said, taking the paper into the other room.

Jesse opened the refrigerator door, thinking he would make a late breakfast of scrambled eggs and bacon, but her fridge was a wasteland. There was a jug of orange juice, a three-quarters-empty two-liter bottle of Coca-Cola with no cap, and two bottles of sweet and sour mix. The crisper was failing miserably at keeping a half-head of putrid brown lettuce fresh, which gave Jesse a slight gag. The door held her maraschino cherries but was otherwise jammed with an assortment of feckless condiments and salad dressings with nothing to accent or complement. He wondered what Momma had been eating, until he opened the freezer and came upon a bounty of frozen entrees.

Jesse surveyed the red, green, and orange boxes wedged into the racks. It was a single-serving cryonic cafeteria filled with pork cutlets, lasagna, spaghetti and meatballs, chicken Alfredo, Salisbury steak, fish sticks, turkey pot pies, and even enchiladas. He pulled out a beef pot roast for Momma and a fried chicken dinner for himself.

They sat quietly, enjoying their lunch.

"Is there anything I can do to help you today?" Jesse asked, breaking their silence.

"I'm good...other than that foolish TV set. I'll look for the warranty papers later."

"Don't worry over that. I'll get it fixed tomorrow, but I'll show you how to watch a movie if you want. Can I help you with your bed?" He took a long drink of water, hiding his face with his glass, embarrassed to be treading near the subject of her soiled linens.

"No, thank you," she said nonchalantly, wiping a bit of mashed potatoes from her chin. "I like the sofa much better."

"What do you mean? You like the sofa better? That can't be comfortable."

"It's comfy enough. I got the TV, when the silly thing works. The den is just right for me. Your daddy took many a nap on that sofa."

"Naps, yes, but not a full night's rest when you've got three bedrooms. I'll put a TV back there if you want."

"I don't want to be back there at night. You don't know how it feels," Momma murmured and looked down to pick a piece of pot roast off the table. "All alone with him out there, both of us just waiting."

"What are you talking about? Who, Momma?" Setting his knife and fork on his plate, Jesse leaned across the table, his earlier sense of frustration coming back.

"I'm not just some crazy old woman. I know it's hard for you to believe that he's out there," Momma said, easing herself up from the table. "He hasn't ever gone away. He wants me." She pointed a finger at her heart. "He's pressing for my soul on the other side." She took her plate into the kitchen and began rinsing it off in the sink.

Jesse looked down at his half-eaten fried chicken dinner and could practically hear John Wayne whisper in his ear, *"All battles are fought by scared men who'd rather be somewhere else."*

AFTER A FRUSTRATING TUTORIAL ON HOW TO USE THE
DVD player, Jesse left Momma asleep in her chair while an
episode of *The Honeymooners* played. He gathered up her checkbook, statements, and bills in a plastic grocery bag, planning to
take them by Bubba's office. Once Bubba reviewed Momma's
information, he'd give Jesse a summary of her financial condition.

On Monday morning, he stopped by his office in Midtown
for a brief meeting before a week-long trip to Philadelphia and
New Jersey. He asked Heather, his executive assistant, to call
the cable company and pay Momma's bill with his credit card,
declining Haymaker's offer of a free hookup from one of his
many conniving connections.

Late Wednesday afternoon, he called Heather to check in.

"I called the cable company and paid the bill with your card,"
she said.

"I thank you and my mother thanks you." Jesse asked. "Any
messages?"

"Elizabeth White left a message asking you to call her,"
Heather reported.

"My aunt?" Jesse said, scratching his head.

"Yes, sir, but she never told me she was your aunt. I'm sorry. Actually, she called once on Monday, twice on Tuesday, and three times today. This afternoon, she made me promise to call her back myself and tell her whether or not you were going to return her call."

"Okay, I'll call her," Jesse said. "I'm sorry you had to deal with her. She can be rather tenacious. What number did she leave?"

Elizabeth White, or Aunt Lizzy, was five years younger than Momma and was also a widow, but only once. She and her late husband, Archibald "Archie" White, had moved to north Florida fifty years ago, successfully investing in various business ventures and real estate projects. Aunt Lizzy never had any children, and she'd embraced Ricky and Jesse as her own when they were growing up, often inviting them to spend their summers at her beach house near Jacksonville.

Jesse paused before making the call, staring from his hotel room window at the statue of William Penn atop Philadelphia City Hall. He'd read the story of the famous Quaker who led the colonial settlement of the area, and he knew it would require Penn's diplomacy to call his aunt. It would be easier negotiating a peace treaty with the Delaware Indians. He'd learned that forty years ago.

Jesse couldn't recall if it was the mythical Summer of Love or not, but earlier in the week, they had watched Neil Armstrong walk on the moon. Uncle Archie had been away on a business trip. Jesse was ten, eleven at the most, and spent his summer enduring Ricky's barrage of Indian sunburns, red bellies, and his favorite little brother torture: "stop hitting yourself." The bridge club ladies were coming to the house, and Aunt Lizzy ordered the two boys down to the beach, warning them not to get separated or come back before dinnertime with sandy feet to plop down in front of the television.

On the beach, Ricky swiftly dumped Jesse to hunt for girls, so Jesse went in the ocean, contently playing alone in the shallow water. He was wading out to pee and dump sand from his suit when the riptide snatched him off the edge of the sandbar and into deeper water. Jesse could still remember fighting to feel bottom and the surf breaking directly on top of him, smacking him back down into the darkness. Bicycling his legs in a panic, he fought to the top. A wave peeled off near him, and he mustered the strength to take a couple of strokes, allowing it to carry him to shore.

Trying not to bawl, he raced up the dunes toward his aunt's house, not noticing the sandspurs. Certainly, she'd punish his older half-brother for leaving Jesse alone to practically drown. The sliding glass door was locked and the curtains were drawn. He ran around to the garage side door. His pursuit of justice was slowed only by the red MGB convertible parked in the garage where his uncle's Mercedes-Benz should have been. He limped toward the living room where she had intended to set up the card table. The card table was vacant, except for two empty wineglasses; the 5th Dimension's "Aquarius" was playing on the console stereo. Jesse heard a loud bump come from the back of the house, and he walked down the hall toward his aunt and uncle's bedroom. Hearing a faint cry, he peeked into their room. Jesse heard groans coming from the bathroom.

Guessing Aunt Lizzy may have fallen and busted her head in the shower, he inched the door open, detecting a strange voice with an English accent. His aunt screamed out while the red MGB stranger let out a growl that echoed off the bathroom tile. The steam filtered away, and Jesse saw Aunt Lizzy's breasts pressed against the glass shower door, peering out at him like a pair of angry clown eyes.

Jesse shut the door, ran back down to the beach, and sobbed uncontrollably for the last time in his life. He never told anyone about how he almost drowned or what he saw in the shower. Dialing his aunt's phone number, he realized he still looked at every red MGB with suspicion. After three rings, she answered.

"Hello."

"Aunt Lizzy? It's Jesse Few, your nephew."

"Of course, Jesse-akins. It's so nice to hear from you," his aunt said, her peachy accent undiminished despite her age. Mr. Billy always said the only thing Lizzy learned at Agnes Scott College was how to serve a cow patty casserole and make you ask for a second helping. "That young secretary gal that answers your phone is quite the gatekeeper. She was a little surly, but you can't talk to everyone who just calls up. I know how busy important people are."

"I apologize. She didn't know that you were my aunt. How are you?"

"I'm just fine. Who would've thought that a quadruple bypass could be such a blessing? I took my annual treadmill test two weeks ago and did wonderful."

"That's great. How's your new place? How's El Pueblo?"

"I absolutely love it. I golf three or four times a week right in the backyard, play bridge and backgammon. The biggest problem I've got is Yankee joggers on the golf course; but here's why I called," Aunt Lizzy said, a portion of the sugar leaving her voice. "How's your momma doing?"

"I had lunch with her on Sunday. She was doing fine...a little tired," he said, starting to doodle on the hotel notepad and trying to decide what cocktail to have before dinner.

"You know she calls me?"

"That's good." Jesse hadn't thought to look at her phone bill.

"She calls me every day, two or three times some days. It was four times yesterday. She needs help."

"How do you mean?" Jesse asked, setting down the pen.

"I mean that she can't take care of herself anymore. She tells me she's scared that someone—a man—is coming to get her."

"She told you about that?" A throbbing pain burst above Jesse's eyes. "About the stranger in her backyard?"

"You need to get her in a nursing home and get her some attention," his aunt said, now replacing genteel with plain-spoken, ensuring that her message penetrated the long-distance line.

"I wasn't sure what to make of it, but a nursing home? I've been checking in on her more. My daughter is going to help out and I've got a ..." Jesse thought of how to describe Haymaker's role. "A special service, a local company that just started. They're scheduled to drive by her house and check in, you know, just in case."

"It would be better for her and so much more convenient for you—not having to worry while you're off conquering the world—if she was in some type of nice care facility."

"I hear what you're saying, but I just ha—"

"Something needs to be done for my sister. There are things for her to do: trips, crafts, music. She isn't safe to drive. She's seeing things...men trying to get her. They have people and places to help her."

"I'm not sure she needs that just yet. Momma still gets around, and she likes the old house. I think she'd have a harder time adjusting to someplace new." Jesse considered faking bad cell service, hanging up, and cutting off his cell phone. It worked when irate customers called, and even Denise's therapist couldn't blame Jesse for dropped calls.

"There are ways for me to do it from down here, but don't you think it's better if you do it?"

"You've got a point, but I'm not sure where we'd look. I don't want her too far away," Jesse said, interested in the ways his aunt could get it done from Florida, but not really wanting to find out. "I suppose it won't hurt to see what's available around here. Maybe we'll see if we can go to Asbury Woods next week."

"That's smart," she said, resuming her saccharine tone. "That's a good idea. Do let me know how it goes, won't you? I've got a group of ladies coming over this evening and some deviled ham canapés to get out of the fridge. Bye-bye, now."

The early evening sun gleamed off the bronze statue atop City Hall, and Jesse was uncertain if it was William Penn or the tribal chief who traded his land and his heritage for a string of beads and some fur pelts. Perhaps a double Jameson or two would help him figure it out.

10

RESOLVED ON BEING PREPARED IF AUNT LIZZY CALLED
again, Jesse persuaded Momma to visit Asbury Woods with an
offer of fried pickles and spare ribs from Huck's BBQ. Of course,
it helped that he didn't mention their tour until they pulled into
the parking lot. It had taken him a couple of weeks to arrange for
a free Friday, and he'd made an appointment for mid-morning.

"Hey, Momma," Jesse said, pulling his Cadillac into the visitor's spot by the entrance. "I need you to do me a favor."

"What kind of favor?" She looked around. "Why are we here?"

"Denise wanted me to come by and tour Asbury Woods for
her. She's thinking it may be time for Mr. and Mrs. Hill to get a
little more help." Jesse wasn't worried that Momma would see
through his ruse; he just wanted to get her in the front door and
take it from there.

"I'm sure they're younger than I am. Aren't they younger?"
Momma adjusted her giant, dark sunglasses to the bright
sunshine. "I thought we were going to Huck's."

"We are," he said as they walked toward the main entrance.
"But I told Denise we'd meet this fellow and take a walk around

for her. I wanted your opinion, since this is where Granny Finch stayed and all."

Asbury Woods, operated by the United Methodists, was a few miles from downtown Dwyer. The design was functional to the point of dull, blending classic red brick and contemporary beige stucco trim, appealing to their Bible-believing tenants, as if the building committee had received divine revelation from a newly discovered epistle: Saint Paul's Letter to Colossian Architects. It made the old folks less cantankerous if they believed they were living in a church.

Greeting them at the reception desk was a tall man, large enough to fill a doorframe, with a pompadour of white hair. He was dressed in a gray pinstriped suit, maroon dress shirt, and matching paisley tie.

"Good morning," the man said in a deep voice with an upbeat tone. "I'm Reverend Lasher, but you can call me George. I'm director of sales here at Asbury Woods. Welcome, Mr. Few." He extended his hand and gave Jesse a firm shake, looking him straight in the eye.

"Not a problem," Jesse said, puzzled over the title of reverend and sales director. "This is my mother, Gennifer Few."

"How nice to meet you, Ms. Few." His large hands swallowed Momma's as he cupped them both. "We're so honored to have you for a visit. Let's get started, shall we?"

Jesse expected to smell bleach masking the underlying odors and hear the screeching sound of old ladies tied down to their beds, but instead, he was surprised by the aroma of freshly baked bread and the rhythmic beat of salsa music as they ventured down the carpeted hallway.

"On the left here is the dining area. We offer three full meals a day with a wide variety of choices, including a bistro, soups, salads, and my personal favorite, the ice cream bar. Do you like an old-fashioned ice cream sundae, Ms. Few?"

"Yes, she does," Jesse said before Momma could ask about old-fashioned cocktails.

"Across the way here is the activities center." Their guide pointed to his right. "In here, our residents can shoot billiards, hold card tournaments, and play board games. It sounds like they have a dance class going now."

The three of them peered through the plate glass door at the group of seniors paired up for the rumba, the muted beat of the music vibrating through the door.

"The activities center is really the heart and soul of our little community. It's a great place to meet new friends. Are you a dancer, Gennifer?"

Momma and Jesse both acted like they didn't hear the question. As they followed the Reverend Lasher down the hall, Jesse imagined his mother eating regular meals, enjoying dominoes with her new friends, and, perhaps, finding another male companion. But then a flash clip popped into Jesse's head of Momma leading a class of geriatric lap dancers, all anxious to make extra cash doing ten-dollar table dances when their Social Security ran low.

Momma's arms were folded across her chest, and she still had on her sunglasses.

"The first floor of the east wing is our memory support unit," he said with a pause. "Then we have a fully licensed health care center that offers skilled nursing care in the west wing."

Granny Finch had spent her last six months waiting to die in the west wing. When Jesse realized he had never even visited her once, a searing shame ran from his gut to his heart.

"Do you have any questions I can answer?" Reverend Lasher asked when they finished the tour and returned to the atrium, throwing his arms out wide.

Jesse spoke before Momma could. "You know, it's a very impressive place. It's not at all what I was expecting in a nursing home."

"Actually, Mr. Few, we're not a nursing home," he said with a faint frown. "You see, nursing homes accept Medicare and Medicaid as payment. Asbury Woods doesn't. It really separates us from what most people think of as a nursing home. Have you seen a list of our monthly fees?"

"Rachel," he said, turning to the receptionist, "would you hand me a fee schedule?"

Jesse glanced down at the page, hoping the shock was not apparent on his face. He did a calculation in his head and figured that his mother would burn through her savings in less than two years. He suppressed his curse words.

"When were you thinking of beginning the admission process?" Lasher's voice interrupted Jesse's inner tirade.

"We've really just started looking."

Momma drifted across the room, pretending to look at the artwork, and sat down in a lobby chair.

"I understand," he said, nodding his head in agreement. "I'm sure you know the demand for elderly care is growing— and so is the cost. What sort of long-term planning do you have in place? Savings or long-term care insurance?"

"We've got some, but not enough." Jesse now regretted not listening to the old-fart cowboy actors plug their affordable monthly payment plans.

"How about other relatives?"

"I've got a brother and an aunt in Florida, but they're too far away to help," Jesse said, knowing he sounded like an imbecile while Reverend Lasher was clearly asking a qualifying question. But he was proud of himself for not saying asshole half-brother and nympho aunt.

"I understand, but perhaps they could all join in and assist you in other ways. Mr. Few, we feel that Asbury Woods offers a perfect balance," Reverend Lasher said, holding his hands out like the two sides of a scale, "between independent living and caring support. Here's my card. You call me if I can help, and thanks for coming out to visit. I want you to know that you and your mother will be in my prayers."

"I appreciate that," Jesse said, leaving Asbury Woods, unsure whether he'd rather ask his asshole half-brother or Jesus for help.

The drive to the restaurant was a one-sided conversation, with Jesse regurgitating Reverend Lasher's well-rehearsed presentation while Momma stared out the window. Huck's BBQ was the oldest family-owned restaurant in Lewallen, opening right after Prohibition ended. The gray cement-block building with a screened-in smoke pit on the side was a buzz of lunchtime activity on a weekday, and Jesse had never eaten there without running into a friend, neighbor, or business colleague. They sat in the back corner at a small two-top table. Hickory hung heavy in the air. Jesse ordered them each a half-rack of ribs with Brunswick stew, onion rings, and sweet tea. The server put their appetizer of hot fried pickles in the center of the table.

"Momma, you want some of the pickles?" Jesse asked over the dining room noise, forking a battered and deep-fried dill chip and blowing on it to cool it down.

"No, thank you, not just yet." Her sunglasses were still on her face.

"How do you think the Hills would like Asbury Woods?" he said, circling back around to the conversation from the car.

"You're not gonna dump me in some old folk's home," she said with a wag of her index finger.

"Nobody's said anything about dumping you anywhere. But don't you at least see the benefits of living there?" he asked, discarding any earlier pretense.

"I've got everything I need at home."

"Wouldn't you feel safer? You keep telling me about this man who's after you."

"I saw him again this morning…in the floor heater."

"The floor heater?" Momma's house had an old-style fuel oil heater and blower unit located below the floor in the hallway; it was covered by a large metal grate. As a kid, Jesse had always walked around the grate for fear of it collapsing beneath him. "So who's in the heater staring up at you? Who wants to pull you down?"

"Rex Sherman," Momma said, removing her sunglasses and leaning across the table to whisper. "The devil himself—that's who. I could see his eyes shining red in the dark, peering up from under the grate. He wanted me to get close enough so he could snatch my ankle and pull me down."

"Rex? Ricky's dad?" Jesse asked, pushing back from the table. "That makes no damn sense."

Both Momma and Jesse shifted in their chairs and peered around the dining room.

There was a well-dressed blonde sitting by herself at a two-top in the center of the room. Customers and servers swirled past her table, yet she never looked up from her plate. Jesse noticed she was eating a salad and was curious about who would come to Huck's BBQ—a restaurant renowned for fat, salt, and sugar— and eat healthy.

The waitress refilled the woman's ice water. She looked up and Jesse recognized her wistful smile; it was the pastor's wife, Mrs. Suggs. With her hair done and makeup on, she was even more attractive than the family photos. It was surprising to see her dining alone. Jesse assumed that being Pastor Sonny's wife meant her days were filled serving her husband's ministry; supporting the largest church in the area was most likely a non-stop calling. He didn't know if it would be appropriate to introduce himself. She certainly would recognize his name, but from the way she was dispiritedly sifting her fork through her lettuce, she didn't appear like a woman who wanted to be reminded of her daughter's recent visit to the police station. She seemed like a lady who had more worries than peace. Jesse imagined that Denise carried a similar empty expression before their divorce, and he questioned whether Pastor Sonny was part of his wife's solution or more a part of her pain.

The server brought their rib platters to the table. Looking down at his plate, Jesse decided he'd have to find what alternatives there were to Asbury Woods.

"Momma, I'm sorry for dragging you out on the tour." Jesse unrolled his mother's utensils from the paper napkin, set the fork and knife next to her plate, and handed her the napkin. "You're absolutely right. You've got everything you need at home."

Momma took the napkin from her son. Her appetite restored, she piled fried pickles on her plate next to her spare ribs, pouring a generous portion of mustard BBQ sauce over the top of each.

11

"DAMN IT, BOYS, WE GOT THREE HOLES TO GO HERE,"
Haymaker said, opening the cooler. "And it looks like we got us
near a half a case of beer left."

"I'll take a cold one," Schaff said, hopping up from his cart
and turning toward his partner for the round. "You want one,
Bubba-baby?"

"I don't know if I should. I've got a to-do list this afternoon,"
Bubba said, looking down at the scorecard.

"A good beer buzz is an essential part of any successful
do-it-yourself plan." Schaff thrust the unopened beer toward
his partner.

"If my wife carps about me coming home inebriated again from
the golf course," Bubba said, "I'm going to refer her directly to
you."

"You fellas thinkin' about pressin' the bet?" Haymaker slurped
the foam off the top of the can. "There ain't nothin' out here today
but plenty of God's beautiful blue skies and infinite opportunity."

"What do you say, Mr. Few?" Bubba asked. "You've been kind
of quiet this morning."

"No, thanks. I'm good just winning some of your money," Jesse said, waiting for the foursome in front to clear the tee. On clear autumn mornings, the course was jam-packed as the Saturday regulars worked to get in their eighteen holes before the kickoff of the college football games that afternoon. "By any chance, have you got a Gatorade in the cooler?"

"Do what?" Haymaker screeched from behind their cart.

"I've already had a six-pack. I'm just practicing pacing myself for next weekend. Between Bourbon Street and Kimberly, I got to be ready for anything." Jesse had been baptized in the New Orleans lifestyle when he and Schaff had made a trip to the 1981 Sugar Bowl. They had spent a country-drunk week on Bourbon Street getting pickpocketed, nearly beaten up by bouncers, and chased by transvestite hookers—it was maybe their best weekend ever. Herschel Walker and Dooley's Junkyard Dawgs won the National Championship, and Jesse made it back home with only two dollars and a new appreciation for how fast an angry man could run in hot pants and platform shoes.

"Schaff, I suspect our compatriot is scheming against us," Bubba said.

"Only six beers? Do we even allow that sort of behavior?" Schaff asked, peering into Jesse's cart for a closer look. "By the way, Claire has been asking me what I heard about your meeting with the pastor."

"Sort of fifty-fifty; my wallet and watch are safe and no biker bodyguards, but no Melanie reunion for JJ, either," Jesse said. "But I've been too busy trying to help my mom to think much about it. My aunt strong-armed me into taking Momma for a visit to Asbury Woods, which was an awkward-ass train wreck. Amie and our boy Haymaker helped me circle the wagons, but I'm afraid the Indians have more arrows than I do bullets. I plan on calling in the cavalry, just as soon as I figure out how."

"I'm tryin' to help any way I can, my man. I've been gatherin' some local Sonny intelligence. It seems that rumor about the investment fund is ringin' real. I heard he's got seed money from a group of the deacons at the church," Haymaker said, cutting the tip off his third cigar of the morning. "And I've also been ponderin' your Momma predicament, and I think I have the fix you need. You see, I heard about these old boys buyin' Russian girls on the Internet. They're supposed to be totally gorgeous, flawless like them Siberian diamonds. So I was thinkin' you could get a bodacious bargain on a nurse and a wife, to help out. How's that for brilliance?"

"That'd be tough to get by Kimberly."

"Are you actually advocating that he travels to Russia and procures a new wife to care for his mother?" Bubba asked, halting his stretches to vet Haymaker's proposition. "What about the immigration process? Lawyers? The Russian mafia? The fact that she wouldn't speak a lick of English?"

"I didn't say the plan don't need tweakin'," Haymaker said, tossing a pinch of grass in the air to check the wind.

"As always, I appreciate you guys thinking about me." Jesse put his hand over his eyes to block the sun, not wanting to think about the tangled-up extension cord Momma's life had become. "Who are these other hacks hitting a ball out of our fairway? Where'd they come from?"

"It looks like Bert and his banker buddies," Schaff said.

"Yeah, they're wearing butt-ugly britches; it's Bertram's plaid-pants gang."

Jesse and his three buddies stood in the tee box, watching the intruding golfers in the fairway flail around like dirt farmers with pickaxes.

"They golf like they're planting cotton," Jesse said. "Hey, Bubba. Regarding bankers who are crappy golfers, Haymaker and I got to meet with those guys soon, like this week soon. Have you finished looking at my numbers?"

"Yes, sir," Bubba said. "For both your mother and you, and we have it all put together for you to review."

"You know, it's almost like someone dumped a dozen different million-piece puzzles on the floor, and they're expecting me to put them together. I stopped doing puzzles after kindergarten when they got more than six pieces and weren't made of wood. Can we sit down one night this week?"

"Sure, but my schedule is sort of tight."

"The numbers are a big slice of me solving my problems. Plus, it would help to know my budget for my Russian wife. I wouldn't want to get stuck with a homely Ukrainian gal."

With the next hole finally open, Jesse cranked his tee shot deep down the middle of the fairway, in the perfect position to go for the green in two and eagle. "That shot calls for a cold beer."

12

NORMALLY, THEY WOULD HAVE HAD A CLIENT REVIEW meeting at Bubba's office, but the only time they could get together was on Wednesday evening during Bubba's son's soccer match. Babineaux had given Jesse directions on where to meet him, but he'd only half-listened, assuming that because he'd been to the Lewallen County Sports Complex countless times, it would be obvious where to find his CPA. It wasn't. He thought Bubba had told him to meet him at the field closest to the parking lot and that Paul Junior's team would be wearing bright-orange jerseys. He didn't see Bubba on the sidelines, the kids on the field were half the size of Bubba's boy, and neither team was wearing orange. The chaotic screaming of the fans gathered around the dozen games added to his confusion. He hadn't been to the soccer fields in two years since Amie was fourteen or fifteen, shortly after his divorce when he was trying to prove to Denise that he could be a regular dad, not an absentee father. After twenty minutes meandering through the morass of games and fans, Jesse finally found him.

"He's getting behind you, Paulie. He's getting behind you," the CPA shouted as Jesse approached. Bubba was sitting by himself on the far end of the sideline with an empty lawn chair next to him. The fleet-footed blond on the other team picked up a pass and dribbled toward the goal. "Don't let him get behind you."

"I was wandering, lost in some divorced dad nightmare," Jesse said, taking the seat next to his friend. "They've changed this place since when-the-hell-ever I was here last. How's it going?"

"Paulie's guy is getting behind him," Bubba said.

"I gathered that."

"The kid is pushing him, but the refs won't call it. He's already scored two goals." Bubba cast a hand up in the air. "And holy cripes, there goes a third."

"That's not good," Jesse said, noticing the ice chest on the other side of Bubba. "What's in the cooler?"

"What?" Bubba said, unwilling to take his eyes off the game.

"The cooler. What's in it? Cold beer?"

"Unlike Mr. Hay, I've got Gatorade," Bubba said as the whistle blew for halftime. "Geez, you think I'd bring beer for the kids to drink?"

"I guess not, but it'd stop Blondie from pushing on Paulie."

"Tighten up," Bubba said as he got up to take the cooler over to where the team had gathered for the halftime break, leaving Jesse to consider the foolishness of his suggestion.

"Okay, so what's my financial forecast?" Jesse asked as Bubba returned to his lawn chair.

"I looked at your mother's information, and we got our hands around that. We also took an updated snapshot of your position. It all depends on which way you want to go. You were making great money a few years ago. I mean big dollars—almost baseball player money."

"I remember those days."

"So now the money is good, but it may not be..." Bubba paused and kicked at the grass.

"Be?"

"Enough to keep you from making some tough choices."

"I can make tough choices," Jesse said, sitting up straight in his chair. "What do I need to do?"

"First of all, you and Haymaker have to do something about the investment property you're holding, the supposed industrial park better known as an old textile mill. They got your personal guarantee and your personal investment account as collateral on the loan. You've got to sell it. Give it back. Talk to the bank. Something...anything."

"Easier said than done." Early in 2003, after receiving a very nice bonus, Jesse and Haymaker began buying houses, fixing them up, and reselling them. The profits were large and fast. Haymaker had a talent for bird-dogging the opportunity, and Jesse provided the capital. During the real estate bubble, they became deal junkies. They graduated to flipping commercial buildings, raw lands, and finally in 2007, they bought the old mill, where for a hundred years, the textile industry had produced women's undergarments. But in 2000, they'd moved bra and panty production offshore and shuttered the plant. Jesse had gotten a tip from a customer that the state planned to convert the two-lane rural highway that passed in front of the old mill into the new four-lane outer loop around Atlanta. But shortly after they closed on the property and signed the loan papers, the economy crashed, the highway funding evaporated, and the deal junkies had to quit cold turkey.

For the past two years, his generous divorce settlement and payments on the loan had nearly depleted Jesse's cash; it was like having to pay off your drug dealer after you recovered in rehab. "But apparently, I'll get my chance. Haymaker said they sent us a meet or talk-to-our-lawyer letter, so the two of us will be down there tomorrow. What else?"

"Buddy-roe, I know you love your house. I love your house, but that option adjustable loan is fixing to reset, and it's going to bust your tail. You should consider selling it."

"Nope, not selling the house," Jesse said, slumping back in the chair. "Besides, I'm upside down if I could find a buyer in this feeble market."

"How about selling some of your toys then? That would at least spin off some cash."

"What toys?"

"You know what I mean—the Harleys, the Jet Skis that sit most of the time, more guns than the National Guard Armory, the car."

"My Mustang Mach I?"

"Yes, the Mach I."

"Pinch your lips."

"I'm just fulfilling my fiduciary responsibility as your accountant and friend."

"Then you should have had some beer in that cooler."

"I'm trying to help."

"I know you are and I do appreciate it. I'll see my investment partner-in-crime at the house," Jesse said, getting up to leave as the second half began. "We've got a little ciphering to do."

The referee—a young man not much older than the boys playing—passed by on his way to the field. "Hey, Mr. Ref, you got a sec?" Jesse asked.

"Uhhh," the young referee said.

"You're Harrison, aren't you? I'm JJ's dad," Jesse said, giving his son's pal a smile and a friendly handshake.

"Oh, yeah, Mr. Few. What's up?"

"That blond-haired kid on the green team is fouling my left midfielder constantly. How about giving him a yellow card—or even a red?"

"Sure, I can do that, no problem-o. I'll get him in check."

"Thanks," Jesse said, giving a thumbs-up to a laughing Bubba and walking back to the parking lot.

When Jesse got back to the car, he had two voicemails waiting; he listened to them as he drove home. Jean-Paul wanted to set up a meeting next week to review the headcount numbers for their Florida operations—which meant more layoffs. Next, Kimberly asked what she should bring to wear to dinner in New Orleans, but she was really checking to see if he'd done what she told him to. "I hope you've made reservations 'cause I hear the most romantic places get booked." He decided to wait until the morning to return their calls, and he tried to enjoy a peaceful ride out to Hull-Henry Road.

He'd bought his beloved five-bedroom home right after his divorce. It was a red-brick Georgian with large white columns, and it sat on fifteen acres in the remote eastern part of the county. He had a small pasture in the front and dense woods in the back. The house was equipped with an office he spent too much time in, an overstocked gun room, a rarely used gym, a game room that Jesse was glad couldn't talk, and a home theatre where Haymaker liked to watch his Blu-ray porno flicks. Wanting to make JJ and Amie eager to come over for their weekend visits, he built a heated pool and

Jacuzzi in the backyard, which is where he found Haymaker when he got home.

"What's up, my man?" Haymaker shouted over Lynyrd Skynyrd's "Sweet Home Alabama" blaring from the outdoor speakers.

"You are, brother." Jesse smelled the sweet odor of the joint that Haymaker was smoking while he soaked in the hot tub.

"And gettin' higher," Haymaker said, taking a toke and backing it with a swig straight from a bottle of Jack Daniels. "Damn it, boy, that's good. Come on in and join me."

"I know you're naked in there, so I'm just going to pull up a seat up if you don't mind," Jesse said, sliding over a patio chair. "But I will take a hit of the whiskey and that funny cigarette you're smoking."

"Gladly." Haymaker stretched to pass the pot and the bottle to Jesse. "And I'm as naked as Noah in here, but I can't see nothing down there 'cause of the bubbles and my gut."

Jesse took two quick drags off the joint, the smoke expanding in his lungs. He blew a couple of smoke rings and then took a drink of the Jack Daniels. The whiskey burned as he swallowed it, but the fire obliterated his tension. They sat for a few minutes without talking, passing the pot and the bottle back and forth. They both got quiet again listening to Skynyrd tear through a bluesy jam of "T for Texas."

"I had a sit-down with Bubba," Jesse said.

"How's my favorite munchkin accountant doin'?"

"He's wearing out the worry beads."

"About what?"

"For a start, the old mill we were planning to develop into an industrial park. What's the banker's mood going to be like tomorrow?"

"More sour than normal, from green apple to lemon. We're just comin' off a ninety-day extension and haven't made a payment since I can't recall. But now's the time to buy, not panic sell. I found a steal on a bunch of storage units and these townhouses. Now ain't no different than bettin' on the golf course—press the bet, double down."

"I don't know about all that, but this meeting could be ugly."

"Maybe, sorta after-midnight and out-of-town ugly, but I'm cogitatin' on a plan, so stay tuned. But look here, I did have some success snoopin' into Sonny's background, preliminary fact-findin' with a few more of my key folks. The real sizzle is the investment fund he's workin' on is over in the backwoods of 'Bama. The word passin' to me is the pastor brewin' this kinship with some shit-kickin' sheriff who's like the Don of the Dixie Mafia, the Ayatollah of Alabama. You give me the high sign, and I'm ready to do some in-depth private detective surveillance. I know just where to get the gear, too."

"You can hold off for now. I've got no plans to ever allow the sun to set on me in the state of Alabama. Let me ask you a question. Are my guns worth anything?" Jesse asked. "What if I had to sell them?"

Mr. Billy had given Jesse his first shotgun, a Remington .417, when he had turned thirteen. Jesse had always owned a couple of shotguns for bird hunting, but like all male bonding outings, it took on the measuring-stick aspect and pride in owning the ten-thousand-dollar handcrafted, custom shotguns at the corporate dove hunts. At the gun shows, Jesse got a thrill in being the one guy in a hundred who wasn't satisfied in merely holding the machine gun pistols, but who actually laid down the cash and left with a TEC-DC9. That turned heads like leading Kimberly through a crowded bar.

Ultimately, beyond the machoism, his gun collection developed into an answer for Jesse's "what if" questions. What if my car breaks down in the wrong part of downtown Atlanta? What if I see a young mother and her baby getting carjacked? What if the global economic collapse brings about the apocalypse? Jesse answered his uncertainty with a pistol for the car and added a few of different calibers and sizes to stash in various places. Then, because on some Saturdays in the winter it was far too cold to golf, he spent weekends gradually amassing AR-15 rifles, a Kalashnikov AK-47, and a few other semi-automatic rifles that could easily be converted to fully automatic. That way, he was ready when Haymaker asked what if we squeezed off a few rounds from a Bushmaster AR-15 and watched a watermelon explode.

"Absolutely, shit, yes. Thanks to Pelosi, Harry, and Barry, you're sittin' on a lode of gold just on your AR-15 cache alone. You can name your price on the...umm...secondary market. All we'd have to do is take a trip to the next gun show. I got a few connections."

"I'm not surprised."

"You want me to launch my feelers?"

"I don't know. Let me ruminate on that for a bit."

"That's definitely an ass-scratcher, for sure. You want some nachos or somethin'?"

"Not me, brother. I'm going to bed before I pass out. Don't boil yourself alive in there."

"Aw, man, I thought we'd fortify ourselves with a snack and crack open the old digital black book, maybe phone a couple of friends. Take the hot tub for a spin."

"Not tonight. We've got to get up early to meet Bertram. Besides, I'm leaving for New Orleans tomorrow after that. First time I've been back since the divorce and Hurricane Katrina." Jesse's eyes were glazed over.

Denise and he had religiously attended the annual Jazz Festival held late each spring before the humidity grabbed hold. It was always a romantic escape for them both, giving them a chance to experience the mild—beignets and chicory coffee—to the wild, like Denise getting a red rose tattooed on her ankle. Jesse would wake up early, leave his wife asleep, and walk the empty streets of the Quarter, soaking in the different vibe it offered at that time of day, free from the dark tumult. It was like watching an overactive child sleep; only then could you recall what makes them special, what makes them beautiful. It wasn't late at night when he felt the city's ghosts come to life; but it was at dawn when he felt the pull of all the spirits that had walked along that bend in the river.

"Hey, Jester," Haymaker shouted as Jesse walked away. "When you and Kimberly get hitched, can I be your best man? You know I could throw an ass-kickin' bachelor party. Bring over some of them Russian girls."

13

THE PLAID-PANTS GANG—THE FOUR MEMBERS OF THE Dwyer Banking Company's loan committee—appeared to have all been bred in a laboratory by "The Bank." Their first and last names were interchangeable: Bertram Russell, Jackson Reed, Edward James, and Porter Palmer. Their dark hair, all receding and graying in varying degrees, was parted to the side of their round heads, and they each had a thin-lipped smile that didn't show their teeth. Modest eyeglasses outlined their earnest stares, and somewhere they bought white oxford-point shirts and polyester striped ties at a volume discount. All four members were focused on the ranting performer sitting across the conference table next to Jesse.

"We ain't payin' all the load for you to wax these marble floors and polish your mahogany furniture." Haymaker pounded his fist on the conference table. "What makes you think you can pull this sleazy used-car crap?"

"As we clearly stated in our numerous letters, after reassessing the last personal financial statements you both provided our committee and the depreciating trend of your land holdings—especially the industrial park project—it puts the bank in an untenable position," the lieutenant henchman, Jackson Reed, said, looking to the senior member of the loan committee for approval to continue. Bertram Russell gave a nearly undetectable endorsing blink. "We must have a resolution to these issues, and based on our appraisals, we'll need either additional collateral or a rather substantial reduction in the principal balance."

"Your numbers are self-servin' and really, it makes y'all look less like Dwyer's oldest bank and more like you're runnin' some check-cashing, payday-loan scam." Haymaker had devised their hillbilly-psycho-in-a-pawnshop plan in the lobby as they waited for the meeting that they'd fended off for weeks. The idea called for him to be insanely rude and irrational—not a great acting stretch—and when he had them worn down, "We'll slap hands like the Funk Brothers used to do in rasslin', and you come leapin' over the ring rope and slay them with the big elbow of calm logic."

"It is in accordance with the signed loan documents, Mr. Hay. Have you reviewed the documents that you and Mr. Few signed?" asked Porter Palmer, the newest lackey, causing Bertram's cheek to tick and the young man to abruptly retreat.

"Our legal team is reviewing the finer print of your alleged loan document."

Jesse thought it was almost time for Haymaker to tag out when he started fabricating lawyers.

"You could always choose to refinance with another lender," Edward James, the enforcer of the gang, said. Bertram nodded. "I'm sure the bank would find that agreeable, provided it was done in a timely manner."

"Hell, we paid you back fine yesterday, you're still fine

today, and you'll be more than fine tomorrow when this little dip is over."

"The bank has been very patient in this matter. We appreciate what you've done for us, but we have to get the loan back to a satisfactory performance; it's a necessity of a safe lending business." The bankers were employing a siege campaign. Relying on the court-tested strength of their loan documents, the junior members relentlessly fired volley after volley, repeating their message, only utilizing Bertram in a desperate situation.

"Haven't you fellas forgot how much lendin' business we've done with each other over the years?" Haymaker pushed his chair back from the table and stood up. The blue, button-down dress shirt that Jesse had coaxed him into wearing was untucked and had armpit stains showing. He had slipped off his loafers under the table, and he wasn't wearing socks. Jesse detected the familiar whiff of Haymaker's feet.

"The facts are the facts, and all we're asking for is a reasonable remedy based upon the terms of the loan. You must see that." Edward James held out his hands.

"I see it more like the time my uncle bought this bulldozer," Haymaker said, leaning on the table. "He was minin' a coal pit near Hazard, and he couldn't keep the dang dozer runnin'. But the finance company kept houndin' him, even though the dozer was costin' him money just tryin' to keep it goin'. So one night, he up and parks that tractor right on the dealer's front yard, slap in-between his wife's rose bushes and the walkway. How'd you shylocks like us to do the same with these loans?"

Bertram Russell's ears turned pink.

"Daniel, please have a seat." Bertram took a sip of water and cleared his throat. "You know as well as we do that the loan is under-collateralized, and the current value of your commercial property is far below the original loan values." He paused and looked down at his files. "You have been afforded generous extensions, based on the strength of personal guarantees, but you haven't remitted a payment to the bank in over three months—not a cent. Stated plainly, your partnership, which you've both supported with individual assets, is in default. We're beyond negotiating an impasse. The bank must take a firm position. It's more than a matter of sound banking practices; we've got the FDIC to deal with."

Judging by the pink ears and the mention of the FDIC, it was time for Jesse to leap the ring rope. He wasn't sure you could reason with bankers, but he did know how to dance around the ring until he came up with an escape plan.

"Let's take a step back and grab a breath." Jesse tugged Haymaker by the elbow. "Can I make a suggestion?"

Haymaker took his seat, and the bankers' eight eyes turned to Jesse, the three junior members aiming their cannons at him.

"Certainly," Bertram said, his ears returning to their normal pasty white, now that Haymaker had sat down and shut up.

"First of all, let's see if we can define the problem and then talk about your reasonable remedy. Sound good?"

"Fine, but I thought we had done that sufficiently," Bertram said. "Mr. Reed, let's see if we can define the problem for Mr. Few."

"Jackson, put it in dollars and cents for me." Pulling out a yellow legal pad, Jesse took the top off his pen as if he were preparing to take dictation. "What do we owe and what do you think the land is worth? Real simple."

"Yes, sir," Jackson said, studying his file. "The outstanding balance is $1,724,986; based on our recent appraisal, the market value of the old mill property is $1 million, leaving the current loan-to-value ratio at 172 percent."

"Does that properly define the problem for you?" Bertram asked.

"It does, thank you, and it seems we have got ourselves a doozie of a problem." Jesse pointed his ink pen like a gun, back and forth, at both sides of the table. "We sure do."

"We?" Bertram looked over the top of his glasses.

"Yep, I said, we. You see, I don't see a solution coming from an us-versus-them approach. No, what we need is some of the partnership attitude that we talked about when we signed these deals. We were practically patting each other on the butts like we'd just won the state football championship. You remember those good old days, Bert buddy?"

"I'd say the bank has done an outstanding job of working with you on your current situation—beyond exemplary."

"Let's talk about 'the bank,'" Jesse said, making air quotation marks.

Bertram sat as stiff as an unopened certified letter on the kitchen counter. "I know how rough things are from our seats, but we don't make a living out of lending people millions of dollars and expecting them to pay it back. So when I hear you mention the FDIC, it knots me up, just a touch. You guys need any bailout money? Are you on the failure watch list?"

"Jesse, you know we can't disclose that type of information." Bertram squinted across the table, his ears now a hot pink. Reed and James looked down at their notes; however, young Palmer flinched, shrinking back from the table. Gazing off toward the ceiling, he turned pallid, as if the disheartenment were depriving his lungs and he was suffocating in gloom.

The Dwyer Banking Company wasn't large, and Jesse could only estimate the percentage of their loan portfolio that was toxic, which the loan committee—especially the senior member—would be held accountable for underwriting. The inside money was pulling out of their banking investments, and the small local banks were swiftly becoming undercapitalized outcasts. Jesse knew then that these four men were a federal consent order away from being unemployed. He could sense the force of the Great Recession pressing down on them like stone weights, meeting after meeting crushing them until they entered their plea.

"My bad and beside the point," Jesse said, "I'd need to see some detail in how you came up with your balance numbers, and we could quibble a bit with your new appraisal, but in theory, we understand the gist of the problem, our problem. Let's get to the reasonable remedy part of the discussion."

"First, we need to center our attention on determining what sort of additional collateral you can provide," Bertram said, resuming control, the three junior members taking notes. "Then on any reduction in principal you're prepared to make, and finally, on the remittance of the next payment that is severely past due."

"Bertram, by golly, you've dumbed that down enough so even I can understand it." Jesse clicked the top back on his pen and laid it down on his writing pad. He knew country club golfers didn't enjoy direct conflict—no bloodshed in the boardroom—but he also knew he couldn't tell them that they had no money to pay them, no hopes of selling the property, and bigger worries than the old mill. Defaulting on the loans meant the bank suing him for the deficiencies and possibly forcing him into bankruptcy, but he believed they'd keep kicking the problem down the road if they could. "How much additional collateral would you need?"

"It depends on what type: stocks, investments, real estate. But I'd say $1.5 to $2 million, contingent on the form."

"All right. And if we made a reduction in principal instead, how much would it take to satisfy you, the bank?"

"In lieu of additional collateral?"

"Yeah, man. You're not getting to eat my cake and buy my bakery for free."

Bertram tried to grin, the corners of his mouth barely budging. "One point one to one point two million dollars would be a sufficient reduction, in lieu of additional collateral."

"I bet it would," Jesse said, slightly increasing his volume. "Your target loan-to-value ratio must be in the 50–60 percent range. I thought we said reasonable there, partner."

"The bank is willing to entertain a counter-proposal."

Taking a deep breath and holding it in a second before letting it out, Jesse became aware of how close his partner was sitting next to him and how short the distance was across the table. He could sense the pulse of the plaid-pants gang, and now was the time to dance faster and throw powder up in the air. "What about a short sale? For say, a little above the market value but a couple of hundred grand less than the balance."

Bertram examined his file, but the junior members had given up on the pretense of taking notes. Jackson's upper lip had sprung a sweaty leak, Edward was alternating between gnawing his nails and fiddling with his calculator, and Porter had shifted his gloomy gaze from the ceiling to the floor. "Do you have anything concrete on the table? Today?"

"Yes, sir, but it's maximum hush-hush involving the governor's office and a foreign outfit," Jesse said, ignoring Haymaker's kicks under the table. "You know, tax breaks and incentives, ultra-competitive between states. We wouldn't want Alabama stealing our jobs."

"Odd, we haven't heard any wind of it, but I suppose that a sale does improve the bank's situation to a degree. Anything else to cover the deficit of the short sale?"

"Yes, sir. I'm planning on holding an auction of my house and land along with most of my personal property." Haymaker had stopped kicking him and was now sagging in his chair. "The excess proceeds from the sale will go to pay you fellows in full."

"Interesting. That has some merit, but what would you say is the potential?"

"Plus or minus $200K, but we'll need another ninety days or so to settle out the auction and nail down these foreign buyers, you know, surveys and environmental studies."

"Another extension? We'll take that under consideration." Bertram nodded deep and long. "Can you allow us a moment to confer?"

"You want us to step out?" Jesse felt his hillbilly psycho partner preparing to leap back into the ring, so he stuck out his hand, hoping he'd stay quiet.

"No, that won't be necessary. Gentlemen," Bertram said to the junior members. He gathered up his files, and the rest of the gang trailed him out of the room, leaving Haymaker and Jesse alone.

Haymaker took a bottle of water from the center of the table. Wrenching the top off, he guzzled down half the bottle.

"Too bad that's not cold beer. I could definitely use one. How about you?" Jesse said. "I could start pre-gaming for New Orleans."

Haymaker drank more water, his face breaking out in scarlet blotches.

"You think they got cameras and microphones hidden in here somewhere?" Jesse asked, never having seen Haymaker use the silent treatment.

Finishing his water, Haymaker got up from table and threw the bottle in the trash can across the room.

"I bet they've got another group of schmoes they're bringing in here next," Jesse said.

"You mean more schmoes like me?" Haymaker was resting against the far wall.

"Who said that? I never said you were a schmo."

"Didn't have to." Haymaker's face was now a purplish-red.

"Look, man, I was winging it." Jesse was beginning to worry about Haymaker's blood pressure. "I'm sorry I spoke out of school without talking to you."

"Which part are you sorry about? The scheme of lyin' about the governor and the foreigners, the auction for the house and your stuff, or givin' me the talk-to-the-hand sign?" Haymaker asked, walking back toward Jesse. "I know everybody thinks, 'There's poor old Daniel Hay, dumb, dumber, and dumbest ass, all in one sloppy package,' but Jesus, Jesse, I thought I was your best damn friend in the world, your brother from a different mother."

"You are, man, c'mon," Jesse said with an uneasy chuckle. "But dealing with these guys is like when your wife opens the credit card bill and finds charges she thinks are strip clubs, but are really hookers. So you pump sunshine up her ass and tell her a sob story about entertaining customers. She's still pissed, but she's content, because otherwise, she's gotta face reality without an umbrella, and no one wants to stand in that cold rain. I'm not having an auction, yet, and I'm not going to throw you out in the cold, you know that."

"You don't have to believe this, but I realize that every skirt I reached under, every shot of whiskey I tossed back, and every dollar I pissed away put me right where I am today." The normal color was gradually returning to Haymaker's face. "I made all those pitiful-ass choices, but I guess it's kinda like what that Chinese-lookin' dude I read about said. You know, the one who wears the robes and is leader of a country, but there ain't no country. Kinda like the Buddha version of the pope?"

"The Dalai Lama?"

"Yeah, him. Anyway, I read his *Playboy* interview in the porcelain library." Haymaker sat back down. "He talks about this invisible force deal we all got that kinda runs like cause and effect. You remember that from science class?"

"Not that I recall. I don't suppose I thought too much about it, and I really didn't know you had."

"This dude says it's our karma controllin' what type of nut-job we are and how we got stuck where we're at in life. So I decided that I created some bat-shit karma, so I do a bunch of dumbass stuff to make it all better, but this here is the real tricky part: it don't change nothin' 'cause it's still my karma. It's kinda like Southern cookin'. We take somethin' like chicken gizzards, which you normally wouldn't put anywhere near your mouth, and we roll 'em in a spicy flour mix and shake 'em up good, then we throw 'em in hot grease. When we get done, they're damn tasty, but it's still the guts of a yard bird, and they're still damn bad for you."

"Mr. Daniel Hay, you never cease to outright amaze the hell out of me," Jesse said, smiling.

"I guess that's my special recipe for Southern fried karma, like Colonel Sanders' original recipe for his chicken. Don't think it'll make me rich, though."

"And I'm truly sorry for veering off script. I went to my strength—lying for a living."

"You are my brother," Haymaker said, reaching out to fist bump Jesse just as the conference room door opened.

"Oh, excuse me," Porter Palmer said, stopping at the door. "Mr. Russell says the bank can work with your proposal." He continued in the haughty tone of a sibling tattletale. "However, he wishes to make it emphatically clear that no further extensions will be granted, so govern yourself accordingly," he said.

"Of course," Jesse said, standing up to leave. "Tell Bertram we appreciate him working with us."

"I'm bettin' the next schmoes comin' in here don't know the hillbilly-psycho-in-a-pawnshop and the lying-ass salesman routines," Haymaker whispered as they walked out of the room. "You 'bout ready for New Orleans?"

"More than ever." Jesse winked at his partner. "More than ever."

14

WHEN KIMBERLY SAID SHE WAS LEAVING HER HUSBAND, it was unexpected, but as foreplay goes, it wasn't the worst phrase ever uttered. It was better than "pull down my gown when you're done" or "don't worry about my cats; they like to watch." It didn't really squelch Jesse's mood either, because Kimberly and he hadn't been together since they had slipped away for a quick afternoon tryst three weeks ago; they were acting like two seventeen-year-olds whose parents were gone.

Jesse was waiting for her in the room when she came in from the airport. It was her first trip to New Orleans, and she had gone to the W Hotel on Chartres Street first, not the one on Poydras Street in the Central Business District. Jesse preferred the quieter CBD in lieu of the French Quarter. She was agitated when she came into the corner suite, but the size of the living room and the fifteenth-floor view of the city calmed her down.

The spaghetti straps on her chiffon dress easily peeled off, and she led Jesse into the bedroom. While they embraced, she deftly undressed him, pushing him back onto the king-size bed.

"I've got a special little surprise for you," Kimberly said, standing next to the bed, naked except for her spike heels.

"Love your surprises."

"I've got the separation papers from the lawyer," she said, rubbing her breasts with coconut oil.

"Okay," Jesse said, transfixed by her self-massage.

"I'm giving them to Nick when I get back home." She crawled onto the bed alongside him.

"Wow, that'll be umm..." Jesse said, running his hand across her smooth backside.

"I'll be ready to move in soon. I could give this to you every night," Kimberly said, beginning to trace circles with her tongue along Jesse's outstretched body. "You like that idea?"

Jesse closed his eyes and laid his head back.

Fortunately for Jesse, he'd dodged her question because the rest of their weekend together was packed in the pleasure of morning sex, naptime sex, and even midnight-by-the-rooftop-pool sex and infused with a live soundtrack of bayou blues, foot-stomping zydeco, and a three a.m. funk jam session in Uptown— all fueled by crawfish, crabmeat au gratin, and bananas foster bread pudding. Jesse felt like it was a perfect weekend, but he understood that New Orleans was a city that divided visitors, and he was in the group that adored the city, easily rolling with its nuisances.

But Jesse had been to enough conventions in New Orleans to know that there was another group that detested the city. All they saw were the shit-faced tourists and tacky T-shirt shops. They only heard the incessant chatter of the street hustlers, "Ten dollars I can tell ya where ya got dem shoes," and smelled the foul stench of the greasy, gray water filling the gutters. They had only been sprinkled with water, and they wanted no more. Jesse had to make sure that Kimberly joined his side.

The first three nights had gone well, and Jesse needed to cap it off on the last night. They would start with a round, maybe two, of cocktails. Then they would head over to the Faubourg Marigny section and grab a Creole dinner before taking in some traditional jazz. The next morning, they would eat a late breakfast and then pick up a couple of muffulettas on their way to the airport. If the drinks, food, and music didn't win Kimberly over, Jesse hoped that the antique turquoise-and-diamond earrings he'd secretly bought on Royal Street would do the trick. He planned to give them to her at the airport before they separated; he was going back to Atlanta, and she was headed to Houston to meet her boss about their new office, which was becoming as critical to Jesse's career survival as it was the fate of MGD. He also knew his ability to dodge the move-in issue would soon run short, and he would have to resolve it before they left town.

Port of Call was a restaurant on the northeast edge of the Quarter before you crossed the oak-lined neutral ground on Esplanade Avenue and entered into the Marigny. At dinnertime, a mix of locals and tourists crowded the place, spilling out onto the sidewalk. Some of the out-of-towners viewed it as a dark and cramped dive with an often-chaotic waiting list for a table. Jesse thought they had the best burgers in the city, and he liked talking Louisiana sports and politics with the neighborhood regulars. The sweet, rum-laden Monsoon was their potent answer to Bourbon Street's Hurricane, and Jesse had long tinkered with the formula of how many of the thirty-two-ounce drinks were too many. One was a good buzz; two drinks you could control with a cheeseburger and a loaded baked potato; he never remembered finishing a third, though he'd tried.

They grabbed a pair of bar stools in the corner, and Jesse ordered their drinks. He started discussing Saints football with a couple of guys next to him while Kimberly examined her cell phone. He got into a debate about Archie Manning versus Drew Brees, Jesse declaring that Manning would've won two or three Super Bowls by now, and he was halfway through his first drink when Kimberly punched him in the arm.

"Hey, get me another one of these," she said, tapping her glass with her long silver nails.

"Here, drink some of mine," he said, pouring half of his drink into hers. "These things pack a wallop."

"I got this," she said, looking back at her phone.

"Okay, whatever," Jesse said, taking up his friendly argument again while Kimberly's thumbs pounded out another text.

In a few minutes, Jesse saw the bartender set down another Monsoon in front of Kimberly, and he watched her take a long sip from the straw.

"I'm going to tinkle," she said, sliding off her seat and leaving her purse and phone sitting on the bar.

"I'll be right here," Jesse said, waiting until she was out of sight to take some of her drink. Kimberly's cell chimed with an incoming text. Instinctively, he picked it up and looked at it. The sender was shown as Marky-Mark:

GR8 news...Congratz...I got a special prize 4 U...c u 2mor. He couldn't completely decode the text, but he wasn't totally certain that she'd be sleeping alone in Houston. Clearing his throat, he closed the message, putting the phone back on the bar. Kimberly had potentially found a way to turn her boss's frown upside down and give herself some options when it came to her future living arrangements. Jesse decided to follow Grandpa Finch's advice: "You don't have to say everything that you know or believe everything you say."

When she came back from the bathroom, Jesse noticed that her black minidress had fallen off one of her shoulders, and there was more sway in her step. She landed back on her stool with a thud and promptly drained the rest of her drink.

"Psst, that weirdo is staring at my boob," she said, pulling her dress back up on her shoulder.

"Which one?" Jesse asked, scanning the crowd around the bar.

"I can't tell; maybe that one that nearly popped out of my dress, or both of them, I guess," she said, her voice matching her wavering walk.

"I'm glad we got that cleared up, but not which boob, because they're both spectacular. Which guy is staring?"

"All of 'em," she said, jumping up again. "I'm sweating to death in this corner. I'm outta here. This place is a dump."

She grabbed her purse and phone and was through the front door onto the sidewalk before Jesse could stop her. He got the bartender's attention and paid the tab just in time to find Kimberly getting into a cab on the corner. He jogged after the car and tapped on the trunk. The yellow taxi stopped, and Jesse hopped in the back seat.

"Where we headed, beautiful?" Jesse asked.

"Funky Town! Woooo…party time!" she shouted.

"So you don't want dinner?" he asked. The cab driver, a large shadow behind the wheel, was headed down Dauphine Street, back to the other end of the Quarter.

"Nope, we're celebrafrickfating."

"What's the occasion?"

"No more nooky for Nicky. I'm going to Separation City."

"By the way, that's great news. Congratulations," Jesse said.

"Oh, my God, do you see that?" On the street corner were three female impersonators with jutting Adam's apples and floral ball gowns, handing out flyers.

"I'm sure they're dancers at one of the clubs on Bourbon Street."

"Dancers? You mean strippers?" Kimberly asked.

"No, they're in a drag show, doing a cabaret act."

"How weird. I've never seen that."

"There're some that are really pretty good; it's a hoot. I don't think they do any striptease though. That doesn't really serve them well, but there are plenty of strip clubs on Bourbon Street."

"I bet you'd like to watch a little bumping and grinding. You want to go to one?"

"I've done my time in them," he said. "But I've lost my appetite for it."

"No-nooky Nicky asked me to go to a strip joint one time, but I was too chicken. You know, before I left, I actually found him, really truly found Nick coloring in one of Brandon's coloring books. All by himself at the kitchen table, coloring, at like two in the morning. Do you believe that? Coloring? I told him if he did a good job of staying in the lines, maybe his mommy would put it up on her fridge."

"I'm sure she'd be proud. It's good therapy."

"Too damn funny," she said with a laugh, followed by a belch and a shrill scream. "So you going to let Brandon hang up pictures on your fridge when we move in?" She walked her two fingers across his thigh. "You got one of those big sub-zero monsters.

He could put lots of stuff on that bad boy."

"Sure, that would be great. But wouldn't he rather stay at his own house? Why isn't Nick moving out?"

"Go figure," she said, putting her hand back in her lap. "Our little house not-on-the-prairie is being repossessed, foreclosed on, taken back. We'll be known as the depressing divorced couple whose lawn is overgrown and with a notice from the bank stuck to the window."

"That sucks, but wouldn't Brandon be more comfortable with just you? You know, the two of you? I mean, he's going to have some big adjustments to make."

"Adjustments, yeah, right. He'll have to adjust, all right, if we're living in some government-sponsored apartments. I have to take care of my baby boy now, and he'll take care of me later."

"I'm just not sure he'd like living in a new house with a strange man all of a sudden."

"You know, I saw your boss, Jean-Paul, the other week at Phipps Plaza. He's not bad looking for an older guy. I guess it's that French-Euro look. I even thought about, you know, casually introducing myself, having him kiss my hand since we're, like, such a good client and all. I could have put in a good word for you."

While Kimberly jabbered on about helping his career, the passing neon lights illuminated her face, changing her from green to blue to red, and Jesse noticed how her lips naturally turned down in a permanent pout, and her large white teeth appeared to operate independently from the rest of her, brazenly speaking on their own. He couldn't condemn her for getting cozy with her boss, but where's the line between brown-nosing and flirting? If she did move in, he knew she would soon turn her carping vision on him; it wouldn't be long before he was coloring past midnight. Much worse was the potential for Jesse screwing up a third kid. Nick would recover from losing Kimberly—possibly be happier—but Jesse wasn't sure he could bear the load of raising another man's son. Achieving a future with Kimberly made him feel like the lonesome cowboy who, after he battles the Comanche, discovers he still has to cross an endless stretch of desert before he can return home to the waiting dance hall girl, the one who may have already married the rich cattle baron. He was unsure if he wanted to risk making a play for the damsel if there were any chance he'd lose.

They got stuck in a jam of pedestrians and motorists in-between Conti and Bienville streets, and the cab stopped. Jesse leaned his head on the glass and stared out the window, watching a ponytailed kid walk past the cab with a laundry bag slung over his shoulder and a leather pool cue case in his hand. He guessed that the young man was headed up to Checkpoint Charlie's for a late-night session of clothes washing and nine-ball. Jesse imagined what it would feel like if drinking beer and shooting pool while your clothes tumbled dry were the most strenuous circumstances he had to deal with each month.

"I'm an elliptical failure," Kimberly said, choking back a sob.

"What? Elliptical? Did you mean epic?" Jesse asked, unsure of how the conversation had led her to that conclusion. "Either way, you're not a failure."

"My mother was right," she said, wiping a tear from her eye. "I'm thirty-eight years old, and I've hitched my life to a big heap of nothing."

"Don't be silly," he said, rubbing her shoulder. "You've got that beautiful boy and you've got a good job. Hell, plus you're hot."

"I think I'm going to puke," Kimberly said.

"Get out of my car if you're going to throw up," the cab driver said, turning toward them. "I have the right to ask you to leave my car if you're unruly."

"Calm down, sir. She's okay," Jesse said. "Take us to the W on Poydras, please?"

"Yeah, calm down and turn up the air conditioner. I've got a right to A/C." Kimberly pulled her hair back off her face.

The driver weaved through the snarl, and they were a couple of blocks from the W.

"It tastes like a sewer in my mouth," Kimberly said right before she leaned over and threw up on the floorboard as the taxi pulled into the W's motor lobby.

"Out of my car," the cabbie said. "I knew she was going to be trouble."

"Welcome back to the W," the bellman said, opening Kimberly's door. "Oh, no," he added as he was greeted by the overripe, Monsoon-induced vomit and Kimberly's pale expression.

"Hold on a second there, buddy. I may need your help getting her upstairs," Jesse said. "Okay, sir, here's something for your trouble," he said to the irate cab driver, peeling off a fifty-dollar bill for a twenty-dollar cab ride. "Sorry for the problem."

He gave the bellman a twenty for helping him get Kimberly back to the suite. She hurled again—mostly in the toilet this time—before Jesse pulled off her stained minidress and heels and tucked her into bed. He set a trash can next to her on the floor and put a bottle of water and two aspirins on the nightstand, then thought better of it and added two more. Her cell chimed again in her pocket book, but he ignored it this time.

After trying to fall asleep on the living room sofa, he went back to check on her. She was passed out in a curled-up ball, and he watched her rest. He soaked a washcloth in cold water and laid it across her forehead, giving her a kiss on the cheek. The plane ride to Houston was going to be rough on her in the morning. It wasn't her first hangover and wouldn't be her last, but once she recovered and learned a new market, she'd build a stack of Texas clients for them both to utilize. He'd let her skip breakfast at Mother's, and he'd go get the muffulettas on his own. When he went on his walk in the morning, he'd consider what to do with the earrings. They'd make a nice gift for Denise.

15

TRANSPORTING MUFFULETTAS FROM CENTRAL GROCERY in New Orleans back home to Dwyer was an indispensable ritual for Jesse, ever since Denise and he had taken their first trip to Jazz Fest; it was an offering to the spirit of his parental guilt, compensation allowing him passage back and forth from his everyday world to his alternative life of debauchery. Smelling the sharp aroma from the thick slices of salami, ham, and cheese, he envisioned Amie, eating her quarter-slice in the high school cafeteria. All the cool kids would be gathered around her table, begging for a morsel, while she told them how awesome her dad was because, even though he couldn't be counted on to attend her guitar recitals and he'd been screwing a married woman for four nights, he'd made a special trip to bring his children the world's most perfect sandwich.

Walking up to his old house, Jesse peeked in the canvas shopping bag he'd bought that morning. The oil from the olive salad had bled through the wax paper in a couple of tiny spots, but his two whole sandwiches were ready for delivery. As he went past the garage window, he glimpsed Jack's faded van parked where his Escalade should have been, and he felt tension spear up his shoulder blade.

After a soft knock on the door—a courtesy that still felt strange to him—his daughter answered.

"Daddeee," Amie said, opening the door wide to let him in the house.

"Hey, my precious," Jesse said, crossing the threshold and pulling her close. "Okay, let me see your hair. What color do you call that?"

"I'm doing a throwback thing." She leaned down, running her hand through her purplish red hair. "Kind of a London, late '70s raspberry sorta look."

"Looks cool; anarchy at West Lewallen High," Jesse said. "Guess what I brought you guys, made fresh from Decatur Street in the French Quarter?"

"Muffulettas, yea, yummy," she said, faking a scream. "Can we eat them now?"

"Up to you. I've brought enough for you and your brother for tonight, and you can take some to school, make all your fellow punk rockers jealous."

"Thank you. I'm like completely famished. I'm dying for a bite now." Amie hugged her dad's neck.

"Where's your brother?"

"Locked in his tower of doom and angst. If it weren't for Jack taking us kayaking on the weekends, it'd be like he was under a self-imposed house arrest."

"Kayaking?" Jesse's voice notched up higher, the tightness in his shoulder tearing deeper. "When did you start that?"

"I don't know," Amie said, with the faltering guilt of an

embarrassed admirer. "We go out on the little lake close by, usually, and once, or maybe twice, over to the big lake and back in the swamps near his cabin. It's no big deal."

"I get it. That sounds like fun." Jesse swept his hand across her forearm and pulled it back. "Is your mom here?"

"Yeppers, she's in the kitchen with Jack." Amie called out for her mother in a fake English accent. "Oh, Mummy dearest? We've got a surprise."

"What kind of surprise?" Denise shouted back.

"Come hither and I'll show you."

"Will you give me a clue?"

Jesse noticed the lilt in Denise's voice as she got closer, a tone he hadn't heard her use in years.

"It's delicious and debonair at the same time," Amie said.

"It's me," Jesse said. "The Central Grocery delivery boy, but I'm a bit off my route."

"Hey, Jesse, I wasn't expecting you." Denise reverted to her flat ex-wife voice.

"I know I should've called or texted beforehand, but I picked the kids up some muffulettas this morning, and I wanted to bring them by on my way home."

"You were in New Orleans? How was that?"

"I had a conference deal—total snore fest—but I didn't forget these." he said, holding up his canvas bag. The impulse to run out to the car and give Denise the antique earrings rushed into his head. He imagined her beaming as she opened the box and the turquoise-and-diamonds dangling off her delicate ears.

"Okay, come on in. Jack was just getting ready to grill steaks."

"Listen, I'm sorry for intruding." Any fantasy he had of a family reunion around the kitchen table left his mind. "I'll just drop these here. Don't worry about a tip."

"Stop. At least come in and say hello," Denise said, turning to Amie. "Go get your brother."

"Yes, Mummy," Amie said, curtsying with her English accent. "But I'm not sure me lord will leave the dungeon of forlorn boyfriends."

Amie bounded upstairs to her brother's bedroom and Jesse followed Denise. Entering the kitchen, he saw Jack Lafferty wearing a white apron and leaning over a platter of four thick fillets.

"Look who it is. My man, what's happening," Jack said, piercing each piece of meat with a large, two-pronged fork. "Sorry I can't shake. You caught me playing Mr. Mom."

"Yeah, nice apron. How you doing? Good-looking fillets there," Jesse said, wincing inside at each thrust of the prongs into the marbled beef. He made a note to tell Amie never to trust a man who would ruin the flavor of a juicy steak by puncturing it with a fork.

"Aren't they? I found this really neat butcher out somewhere. Where is it, honey?"

"Nasonville," Denise said, pouring herself a glass of red wine. "You want a glass, babe?"

"Thanks, bu—," Jesse said, interrupted by Jack.

"That'd be great. Is it that Russian Valley pinot?"

"Yes, it is." Denise looked at the label to confirm her answer.

"There's a butcher in Nasonville? Does he sell crack and crystal meth next to the Ground Round?" Jesse was certain the meat was stolen or tainted, probably both. "I didn't think Nasonville had a grocery store, much less a butcher."

"And that means no wine for you," Denise said, looking at Jesse and raising her eyebrows before she handed Jack his glass. "You want me to put the sandwiches in the fridge?"

"Sandwiches? You brought sandwiches?" Jack said, pulling his long, blonde hair off his face.

"Yeah, muffulettas from New Orleans," Jesse said, about to suggest Jackoff wear a hair net if he's going to prepare food. "Hand-delivered from Central Grocery."

"Down in the Quarter?"

"You bet. They're world famous—the perfect sandwich."

"That place was always good, kind of touristy; I found this deli out in Chalmette. I wanted to take you there last time, honey, but I guess we got sidetracked that morning. Crap, I can't remember the name of it this second, though. Give me a couple glasses of good grape and it'll come to me," Jack said, wandering across the kitchen to stand next to Denise. "You want me to put the steaks up? I love a good muffuletta."

They all heard Amie clomping down the back stairs.

"Mom," she shouted, walking into the kitchen. "JJ cussed at me and told me to go away before he tore my head off and did something else totally disgusting and unrepeatable."

"Just great," Denise said. "I warned you about that stupid television."

"Me?" Jesse said, pointing his index finger to his own chest.

"I'll talk to him," Jack said, starting to take off his apron.

"No, that's okay. You put the steaks on; you worked too hard," Denise said, taking Jack's forearm, pulling his apron back down. "And we still have to start the salad."

"I'll go talk to him. Trust me, I got this." Jesse took out a whole muffuletta, handing the other sandwich and the canvas bag to

Amie. "Put yours in the fridge and keep the bag for school and stuff. It's time for a man-food delivery."

"Thanks, Daddee," Amie said, taking the bag from him. "Good luck. If that doesn't work, we should cut off his cable TV and the power."

Jesse winked at his daughter and headed up the back stairs.

Approaching JJ's bedroom door, Jesse tried to remember the last time he'd been in his son's room. It was easily over three years ago, and he couldn't recall the circumstances, most likely to look for something JJ had borrowed without permission.

"Housekeeping," Jesse said into the doorjamb, using a high-pitched Latina accent, knocking repeatedly.

"What?" JJ asked through the door.

"It's the housekeeping lady. You ready for a turn-down service?" Jesse had swapped mid-sentence to an Asian voice.

"Dad?"

"Sure, you want to be my daddy? You a bad boy?" Jesse said, going back and forth between Latina and Asian. He heard JJ stomp across the hardwood floor, unlock the door, and stomp away.

Jesse opened the door and let himself in JJ's bedroom, squaring it to the way he remembered. The walls were the same light bluish-gray, and the mural of the spacecraft cockpit still covered the wall next to his bed. The furniture had been changed to a black lacquer, and his wall posters had swapped from the Simpsons and Batman to Shelby Mustangs and Megan Fox. The focal point of the room had shifted from a desk set and bookshelf, covered with school pictures and team trophies, to the sixty-inch LED TV that Jesse had given him for his last birthday; it dominated the space. In front of the television were two black beanbag chairs, and JJ was planted in one of them, playing a war video game.

"Hey, bud, what are you playing there?" Jesse asked, trying to orient himself to the shooter's viewpoint on the big screen. The room had the sour odor of a men's locker room.

"CoD MW2." JJ didn't look away from the screen, nimbly working the controls, giving extra body language to help his character's moves.

"Of course, silly me." Jesse looked around the room, contemplating where to sit. The bed and the floor were littered with dirty clothes and towels. Detecting the outline of JJ's body on the unwashed sheets, he felt an itchy twinge. He picked up the beanbag chair next to JJ and shook the dirty clothes off, plopping the chair back down and then himself into it. "Nice setup you got here. You hungry?"

"I don't know, not really."

"Well, Jack is grilling some steaks, but if your sister and mom get violently ill tonight, call Poison Control. Would you do that for me?"

"Sure, whatever."

"I brought you a whole muffuletta here. You mind if we take a short break here and scarf down some sandwich together?" Jesse asked, waving the sandwich under his nose, warding off the reek of the room. "I'm starving."

"Thanks, but you go ahead," JJ said, still stuck on the screen.

"Okay, don't mind if I do." Jesse began to undo the tape. He noticed a *Canoe & Kayak* magazine poking out from a pile of mismatched socks. "Hey, Mr. Hay has got this extra set of golf clubs, practically brand new. They got these new hybrid heads, cutting edge, really forgiving. You wanna go with me out to the driving range sometime?"

"I guess, yeah, all right," JJ said, pausing his video game. "So how'd your meeting with Pastor Sonny go?"

"Not bad; he's concerned about a couple of things, but it still went pretty all right."

"When do I get to see Melanie again?" JJ put down the controller.

"He and I decided it would be a good idea to wait until after your court date. We think you need to focus on getting that behind you," Jesse said nonchalantly, as if he were reporting the results of a customer meeting back to Jean-Paul. "Actually, he's really worried about who your judge will be. Sonny says, based on what he's seen, that makes a big difference in the outcome of your case."

"Sonny? He's such a lying poser, a motherfucking hypocrite." JJ folded his arms and kicked the controller away with his foot.

"Hey, enough with the mo-fo word. Your mom's going to wash both our mouths out with soap. Besides, that's a bit harsh," Jesse said.

"Harsh? How about this?" JJ reached up to his nightstand and grabbed his cell phone. He pressed a couple of buttons and held the screen up to his dad.

Jesse took a bite of sandwich and read the message on the screen.

The Lord brings the punishment of the sword
so that you may know there is judgment. I hope
you get your sword up the butt!!!

"What?" Jesse said, choking down his sandwich. "Is that a text? Who sent you that?"

"I heard about your meeting, so that night, I tried to call Melanie, but she didn't answer. About a minute later, I got that sicko text message."

"I don't get that," Jesse said. "Are you sure it was from her dad?"

"Who else? It's a different number and all, but it's got to be from him."

"What do you mean it's a different number?"

"This is from a 678 area code, and the others were 770. I was waiting 'til I saw you, figuring you could text back or call it."

"You want me to call him?" Jesse asked, dissatisfied with his own answer.

"Yeah, I mean, you talked to him and all, and Jack said he'd get up in Sonny's face if he bothered me again. So shouldn't you be the one to call him instead?"

"I'm not sure. I know that you finagled that continuance delay deal, so your court date seems like a long way off, but I think you need to get that mess handled, and then worry about Melanie. Besides, she's got her own issues."

"What issues?"

"Her dad says she has an anxiety sickness, nervousness."

"I knew it…I just knew it," JJ said, tossing his phone onto the bed. He slid farther down in the beanbag chair, allowing it to swallow him. He found the video game controller and hit play, firing off shots at his next enemy.

Jesse stared at the television. JJ wasn't irrational to assume that his father would have at least as much courage as the animated GI blasting his attackers. A return phone call wouldn't hurt. Jesse doubted whoever sent the message would answer.

"Let me see that phone number," Jesse said.

JJ paused his game and showed his dad the number. Without overthinking it, Jesse entered the number and hit the green call button. Instantly, the name "Bucking Becky" appeared on his screen, along with a picture of the newly divorced youth and social media minister hoisting cocktail glasses at the bar with her friend and Haymaker the night Jesse picked her up. The phone nearly squirted out of his hands, he hit the red end button so fast and hard.

"Tell you what, let me do this after I finish my muffuletta or alone later on. Which reminds me," Jesse said, "I brought you something special back from New Orleans; it's a present for Melanie. I'll get it before I leave; it's in the car. But don't tell Mom. I want you to give it to her the next time you see her, a reunited-and-it-feels-so-good gift. Don't give up on me yet. I might be down but I'm not out."

16

EARLY ON IN JESSE'S CAREER, HE'D LEARNED THE varied roles of a sales manager: the captain steering the ship, the coach motivating his players, and the fireman coming to the rescue. Missed deadlines, irate customers, and malcontent employees all flared up in four-alarm flames requiring a blast from the fire hose to douse the emergency. Crisis management was part of his business life from the first day, but now he had to play fireman in his personal life. However, his problems couldn't be solved with a soothing phone call, a credit on an invoice, or a team meeting. He needed time to consider his options. He needed what his salesmen called windshield time.

The following week, Jesse took a mid-autumn road trip through north and central Florida, giving him six hours driving alone to reboot. He told Jean-Paul that he was evaluating the sustainability of their four Florida sales offices, which was a nice blend of truth and lie. Along an isolated section of I-10 devoid of fall foliage, Jesse evaluated his inventory of worries. He'd bought ninety days grace from Bertram and the bank, which put them at the back of the bread line. Kimberly would be busy with her separation and setting up MGD's new office with Marky-Mark. He could dodge her for a bit; caller ID and an overfull schedule could be a godsend. Besides, it would take her a while to cultivate any new prospects for them to work in Houston. The text from Bucking Becky was strange. Sonny could have been using Becky's phone, it may have been church property, or it could have come directly from her, which would explain the rhythmic thumps against Sonny's office wall. Either way, he had to keep JJ from agitating Sonny, but still make his son believe he was helping him get back with Melanie.

Fortunately, tightrope walking was a required talent in sales. Momma was what Mr. Billy called a low tide problem: "Everybody and everything looks swell during the high tide, but when the tide changes and the water goes out, you find out who's been swimming in the buff." Haymaker was driving by regularly, checking to see if the paper was picked up and there were no strange cars near her house, and Amie was stopping in a few times a week to be sure that she was eating and taking her medicine. Given Momma's dance routine, Mr. Billy's analogy was disturbing, but Jesse knew the water was receding and his mother's real problems would be exposed. Keeping her at home long term with the proper care would necessitate professional help, and that required money. Eager to gather some support, Jesse arranged for a late afternoon visit to his aunt on the way between his stops in Jacksonville and Orlando, hoping for her backing in his evolving plan to care for Momma.

Now sitting in his stocking feet in his aunt's formal living room, waiting for her to return with his Arnold Palmer—a half-and-half mixture of iced tea and lemonade—he recalled the joke that Mr. Billy would make whenever they visited his aunt and uncle's old house on the St. Johns River. "You boys don't touch a thing—nothing. Don't even let your rear ends settle hard in your chair. Lizzy is making me put down a $250 deposit just in case you break something." Only his dad thought it was funny, and Momma would shoot him a glance, inspecting Jesse's fingernails and poking him in the kidneys so he wouldn't slump.

Her new two-bedroom garden home maintained the style that made him want to sit up straight and make sure his nails were clean. The living room set was done in a French-vanilla finish and covered in a pastel-blue floral tapestry upholstery. Jesse remembered the oil portrait of a young Elizabeth White hanging above the mantel, keeping an eerie eye on him just in case he spilled anything on her plush alabaster carpet. *Fox News* was playing on the porch, and he could smell the peanut butter-toffee cookies that she was baking for the church cookie swap.

"Here you go," Lizzy said, entering the room and handing Jesse his drink. "There's a coaster on the table if you need one. I trust you didn't have any problem finding me."

"No, ma'am, not at all," Jesse said, heeding her warning not to leave any water marks. "This place is even better looking than it is on the billboards."

El Pueblo was a newly constructed retirement community hidden among the acres of scrubby palmettos and thin pine trees that filled the middle of the state. Its six square miles were populated with fifty thousand randy retirees empowered with a super-highway of golf cart paths, daily sunset cocktail parties, and an abundant supply of erectile dysfunction drugs. El Pueblo had one of the highest rates of sexually transmitted diseases in Florida.

"You sure you wouldn't rather have a cocktail?" She took her seat in the chair opposite from Jesse. She sat back, barefoot in a pink scoop neck T-shirt and white, terry-cloth capri pants, a glass of red wine at her side. She had looked haggard after her husband's death, and Jesse noticed that she had her neck jowls and baggy eyelids worked on before she had started her life anew in El Pueblo. The auburn-red coloring in her bob-cut hairdo was the only holdover from her previous look. Her round face was now drawn and brown like restored parchment.

"No, thank you. I've got some driving to do."

"We could put vodka in your Arnold Palmer. One of my guy friends calls that a John Daly," she said, laughing at her own joke.

"That sounds good," he said with a polite chuckle. "But I'd better not."

"I've got more wine in the kitchen if you change your mind. It's a very nice merlot that I heard about at my monthly neighborhood supper club. They usually get that cheap stuff from the box, but that gives me a headache, so me and a friend sneak in our own. My cardiologists said drinking a nice glass or two of red wine every day was good for you."

"Is that right?" Jesse said, noticing the thick surgical scar from her heart bypass surgery rising up between her breasts, slithering over her freckles.

"Sure. The anti-oxygen-dents, or whatever, are good for your cholesterol and your arteries."

"You certainly seem like you feel good."

"Thank you. I do feel well, but I'm sure you didn't come down here just to check in on me. You must have more on your mind? Your momma?"

"Yes, of course. Have you talked to her lately?"

"I have. She still calls me quite often, but I've not been available so much lately. Things stay busy here. I try to talk to her in the mornings—she does better then."

"That's interesting," he said, nodding his head in agreement.

"We made our little visit to Asbury Woods."

"How did it go? Did she like it?"

"Not really. In a word—no. She's—"

"Did you take the right tour? Who gave the darn thing? Did they scare her?" Lizzy leaned in toward Jesse.

"Bottom line, she doesn't want to live there—in a nursing home," Jesse said. His aunt vexed him with her single-mindedness and focus, caring more about having her world her way than being amicable.

"Who does? Nobody dreams one day of spending their life in an old folks' home—they want to be here." She raised both arms above her head and made circles in the air, like a sorcerer conjuring forth a demon.

"Yeah, well, I've got another idea, a better plan."

"What kind of plan?" Lizzy took a drink of wine and cupped the bottom of the glass with both hands, rolling it back and forth, the stem twirling like a wand.

"I was thinking about trying to do some type of—I don't know—home health care thing. She doesn't really need constant care. I see getting somebody to help her a few times a day with the stuff that she needs."

"I'm over seventy years old and live in a retirement community in Florida. For God's sake, dementia is as common down here as the flu. Your mother, my sister, has early-stage Alzheimer's," Aunt Lizzy said, staring into Jesse's eyes. "It's only going to get worse. She needs professional attention, which means more than some part-time malcompoop you hire from the yellow pages to stop by whenever and rifle through her jewelry. It's dangerous for her to be alone."

"We...I could get her a full-time live-in companion if that's what it takes."

"Sure you could. Does Gennifer still have the means to afford that? I know Billy did well; he did most of the right moves like your Uncle Archie. Archie had tremendous foresight and someday, hopefully not soon, you'll appreciate it."

Jesse took a gulp from his drink before answering, thinking it would be a sign of weakness if he asked for the vodka now. "She has some money left, in a brokerage-type account, but..."

"But what?"

"Not as much as I thought."

"I see," Lizzy said, setting her glass down and folding her arms across her chest. "That puts a gaping hole in your scheme, doesn't it?"

"Unless I can come up with my own funds or money from other sources," Jesse said.

"I certainly hope you don't think I can afford to provide for this fiasco you're cooking up. Archie left me with a well-thought-out system. I can't fool with it just because my sister wasn't prepared. I knew she'd get bamboozled somehow."

"I think it's the best plan for her," Jesse said, unwilling to debate his mother's role in the recent stock market crash. "It's what she wants."

"Son, she doesn't know what she wants or needs. You have to be serious. What you're thinking about doing can't be done. You've got to find people to interview, check if they're qualified and honest, work out their schedules, make sure your mother likes them, which won't be easy, and then, by golly, pay them—a lot."

"I never said it was going to be easy." Jesse sank back in his chair, deciding he had more chance of her agreeing to a winner-take-all chugging contest than he had in getting her approval for his plan.

"I want to let you know something," his aunt said, changing to her cloying tone. "There's a friend of mine whom I see sometimes, and he used to be an attorney in Cordele, very successful, and I've asked his opinion."

"Okay," Jesse said, assuming this was a different friend than the John Daly joke guy and the wine-smuggling guy, and that all of them were spending plenty of romantic time with his aunt.

"He checked with his old law partners, and I've definitely got a basis for an incapacity claim and can get power of attorney or even become my sister's guardian or something. I'd hate for it to come to that, but I'm prepared to do it if the situation warrants."

Jesse knew from closing sales for twenty-five years that he had to endure the silence that occurred right after Lizzy finished. It was socially awkward but the next person who spoke owned it. They were buying what the other person was selling. Either they bought your product or you bought their reason for not buying.

Lizzy raised her glass of wine, swirled the remainder, and then lifted it to her nose, evaluating the aroma. Jesse listened hard for the sound of the television and could hear the commentator lambasting the government. The silence lasted long past embarrassing and straight into inconvenient as Jesse realized he'd have to deal with the possibility of late afternoon thunderstorms snarling Orlando's rush-hour traffic. He switched directions.

"Has Momma told you who the man is she keeps seeing?"

"Not that I recall," Aunt Lizzy said, still swirling her wine.

"Rex Sherman, Ricky's dad."

"That's odd. Why him?"

"That's what I was wondering, too. I thought you'd have a clue."

"I'm clueless," she said, tucking her legs underneath her and holding her glass out like a queen no longer amused by the court jester and expecting the royal sommelier to fill her goblet before it was empty. "But it's just another reason why she needs the right care. She needs protection."

"Agreed, and she believes she needs protection from a man that's long dead—a ghost."

"So what are you going to do?"

"Right now, I'm going to say thank you for letting me drop in. It was good seeing you, as always," Jesse said, getting up from his chair. "Then I'm going to Orlando tonight and Tampa tomorrow. I may even pay Ricky a visit while I'm there. And when I get back to Dwyer, I just might hire a friend of mine, sort of a freelance private detective, to do an investigation into Rex Sherman. See what we find."

"Do what? My word, you can't be—" Lizzy said as she lost her grip on the wineglass and it tumbled out of her hand, the very nice non-box merlot escaping all over her white rug.

17

JESSE'S GUTS WERE SHRIVELED UP TIGHT. HE'D CALLED Ricky, asking to meet him for lunch before Jesse flew back to Atlanta, and told him they needed to talk about caring for their mother. The call was the first time they had spoken since Granny Finch's wake five years ago when they had ended up in a drunken wrestling match on the front yard of the funeral home. Before making the call, Jesse had hesitated, but he needed money to care for Momma like he planned.

Sitting in the parking lot of Prime's, a five-star steakhouse near the Tampa airport, he felt his insides betraying him like they always did before a confrontation. He had fired dozens of people and dealt with difficult customers, but none of those situations involved his mortal enemy. Ever since he was four years old, after Ricky had rolled him through a fire ant bed, he dreamt of beheading him with King Arthur's Excalibur sword.

Jesse had arrived early and was debating whether to wait inside or meet Ricky in the parking lot. Last night, he had gone shopping at the Neiman Marcus outlet and had bought a new Armani light-blue dress shirt and a pair of black oxford lace-ups. Now

Jesse imagined Ricky writhing on the ground as he kicked him over and over with his new half-price shoes, unconcerned about scuff marks. He inspected himself in the rearview mirror. His short, brown hair needed trimming, and the back of his neck looked shabby, but at least it was too short for Ricky to pull. He climbed out of his rented white Mercedes, glad he had gone for the luxury collection. He paced the sidewalk in front of the restaurant, checking his Blackberry. Jesse weighed the silver rectangle in his hand, flipping it over. He contemplated canceling the whole meeting, his stomach churning. His problems were starting to resemble the Whac-a-Mole arcade game. Just as he tried to smash one back down in the ground with his mallet, another one would pop up. A lurch in his intestines told him it was time to go inside.

Walking in through the heavy glass doors, he noticed he was the first customer of the day. Prime's was the same expense-account steakhouse he'd eaten at in every major city in America: white tablecloths, black-and-white checkered tile floor, and accents of mahogany and brass. He made a dash for the men's room.

The turmoil in his stomach temporarily addressed, he washed his hands and looked around the bathroom, wondering where he could hide a revolver like Michael Corleone did in *The Godfather*. He went to the bar, picked a stool facing the door so Ricky wouldn't be able to sneak up on him, and ordered a vodka on the rocks.

The cocktail started to ease his tension, and Jesse worked on convincing himself that this was like any other business lunch. But just as he relaxed he saw his half-brother walking across the restaurant toward him.

Ricky's bloated melon face hadn't changed since their funeral melee. His cheeks were dented with acne scars, and dark circles and bags pulled down his brown eyes. Only a thin strip of brittle, silver hair ventured forward across his skull. He still had his neatly trimmed mustache and goatee. He was wearing stone-washed jeans, and the first two buttons of his lime-green shirt were undone, a holdover from his disco days.

"How are pencil sales?" Ricky asked as he got closer, the same annoying jab he had used since Jesse's first job out of college.

"Not bad." Jesse stood up to shake hands. He was a good head taller than his older brother. "You need a box of number two's sent over? I'll get you the family discount."

"What you drinking there? The Frogs let you guys have three-martini lunches?"

"You want one?"

"Too early for me," Ricky said. "Besides, I'm running batting practice this afternoon."

"Batting practice?" Jesse asked, tempted to make a fat joke.

"Yeah, I'm coaching my kid's fall ball travel team. We made the play-offs."

"That sounds great, a real accomplishment," Jesse said. "And again, I appreciate you meeting me on such short notice. How's business?"

"Unbelievable." Ricky picked up the knife, drumming it on the bar top.

"Really," Jesse said, annoyed enough by his brother's nervous tapping to want to snatch away his steak knife and plunge it into his neck.

"We sat back on the sidelines for a bit when things got over-heated and watched others chasing the market. Now we're in a bargain world of short-selling chumps and FDIC auctions."

Knowing Ricky loved to talk about his wins in the real estate business, Jesse let him chatter on about business and how well his kids were doing. Besides coaching his oldest son's baseball team, Ricky was helping out with the youngest one's soccer team. Jesse was thankful that he never asked about JJ or Amie.

Ricky continued on through their steak salads about how miserable his ex-wives were and how nice it was to be able to send one of his Costa Rican girlfriends packing whenever he got tired of her. They were done with their food, and Ricky was repeatedly glancing at his watch.

"You talked to Momma lately?" Jesse asked. "How do you think she's doing?"

"Okay, all things considered. She's packed a lot of living into her days," Ricky said, giving his watch another hard look. "She calls the house all the time or leaves a message with one of my girls at the office. She ain't got the number for this." Ricky held up his cell phone.

"I think her mind is slipping, and she needs some help. I believe she has Alzheimer's," Jesse said. "She doesn't want to be forgotten in some old folks' place. It scares the crap out of her. I want to see about getting her someone—a private nurse—to, I guess, live with her."

"That ain't entirely for you to say now, is it? You don't have control over Momma's house or her money, and you ain't getting it from me."

"Okay, what's your idea? You'd stick her in some nursing home?" Jesse pointed a finger toward Ricky, trying to remain calm but wishing he could smash the side of his brother's head with a mallet like it was a mole popping out of its hole. He couldn't resist imagining what an AR-15 would do to his fat melon skull.

"Calm down; don't fight the circle of life. This is a big business, and I'm sure there are a lot of great places she can stay and get help. It's whatever she can afford."

"You sound like Aunt Lizzy," Jesse said.

"Lizzy is a smart old broad. She can hire her a high-dollar lawyer, declare Momma wacko, and do whatever she thinks is best, without even leaving her golf cart. Meanwhile, you'll be standing at the curb looking inside. Piss her off at your own risk; just remember, she can't take Archie's money with her when she goes, and we're the only blood she's got."

"Sure, sure," Jesse said, tossing his napkin onto the bar. He wasn't shocked that Ricky was mimicking his aunt's tightfisted rationale like he was her flunky parrot. His half-brother had always been her favorite. They were closer in geography and disposition. The prospect of a bequest in Lizzy's will assured Ricky's allegiance, but the gilded promise of an inheritance seemed like a morbid fantasy to Jesse. He decided to see how far the collusion between the peculiar pair stretched. "Let me ask you something. Why would Momma be scared of your dad?"

"No idea. I stopped thinking about him a long time ago." Standing up to leave, Ricky stopped. "Here's what I can tell you about my dad. One Saturday afternoon—I must've been around twelve or thirteen years old—we were over at Grandpa Finch's house. Me and him were watching the Army-Navy game together. I thought it was cool, you know, just the two of us, while you were playing with paper dolls. Grandpa loved college football, but he hated Army. Anyway, for some little kid reason, I guess 'cause the game was in Philly and my dad was from there, I asked him about my dad being a big hero in the Korean War and how he died. I'll never forget it; Grandpa looked at me real hard. His whole head was like a solid rock, but I could see the bags under his eyes twitching, sorta trembling. Then he got up and walked out of the room, never said a word; just turned off the TV and left me sitting there."

"Not a word? Now I've got even more reason to look into what happened to him."

"Suit yourself. Appreciate the lunch. Be sure to slide it on your expenses."

"No problem," Jesse said, pulling out his corporate credit card. His sour stomach was calm. He'd only committed murder in his heart; no blood was spilled on the bar. After two days, he was certain that his aunt and half-brother followed Grandpa Finch's creed about not saying everything you know. A generation or two ago, a family code was established not to discuss Rex Sherman, which only meant that there was a lot to talk about.

Standing in front of Prime's, checking his phone again, he heard horns honking and turned to see a bright yellow Ferrari pull out in front of two other cars. It had to be Ricky speeding off to batting practice. Jesse understood he'd never have a chance to coach Amie's soccer team or produce the perfect father-son talk, but he was resolved to keep delivering his kids soggy sandwiches. If he needed, he'd take up kayaking.

18

SOON AFTER HIS LUNCH WITH RICKY, JESSE INVITED
JJ to the driving range. He watched his son mangle another
shot down the driving range at Quail Woods Country Club.
For the past decade, Jesse had tried to teach JJ how to play
golf; it was a father-son ritual. In the past, their visits to
the range fizzled after two or three tries, but this year, JJ
was enthusiastic about his paternal golf lessons. Jesse didn't
question the reason; he just enjoyed the additional time with
his son and the extra chance to practice his own game. On a
clear, bright Wednesday afternoon, there were just the two of
them on the range, tall strands of pine trees running along the
boundary, intercepting errant shots and providing an alcove
for the neophytes.

"Did you know blacking out once makes you an alcoholic?"
JJ asked his father.

"Remember, see your hands strike the ball," Jesse replied.
"Don't just 'keep your head down.' Pick out a spot at the back
of the ball and watch the clubface hit it. That'll stop you from
topping so many shots."

"I mean, if having just one blackout says you're an addict or whatever, man." JJ dribbled another ball a few yards off the driving range mat.

"Don't squeeze the club so tight; it's not like you're choking it. More like you're holding a bird in your hands trying not to hurt it, but not letting it fly away."

"So I'm afraid I've got it—I'm an alcoholic. I need to go to rehab or something," JJ blurted as if he were the little boy confessing to playing with matches and catching the woods on fire.

Jesse took his attention off his son's horrid golf swing and looked at him directly. JJ was still growing his patchy goatee, and his Adam's apple was protruding out farther than Jesse remembered.

"Okay, first of all, you're under twenty-one and can't drink. Secondly, who told you all this about blackouts?"

"I was researching AA online and stuff," JJ said, shanking a shot sideways off the toe of the club. "The lawyer guy y'all hired said it'd be a good idea for me to go to a few meetings, and online would be cool. He could use it for ammo in my case, and I'm more than willing to trade drinking for the possibility of getting back with Melanie."

"Okay, anything that helps makes sense, but let's wait a second before checking you into rehab."

JJ stepped back from the practice tee.

"You know, before all this started, I thought heartbreak was something invented to sell tickets to chick flicks and download sappy songs. That it wasn't a real pain. But this really, I don't know, sucks." JJ wiped his sweaty hand on his pants. His words sped out fitfully. "I mean like physically, it's almost as if there's some part of me that's been amputated. My mind won't stop torquing me all out of shape. I gotta do something to see Melanie again."

"Hey, go easy on yourself." Jesse didn't know if the stiffness in his back was from hitting too many range balls or hearing the misery in his son's voice, but he knew what JJ was feeling. A couple of weeks after Denise gave him the separation papers and he moved out of the house, he remembered being hit with what felt like the flu. He thought he was immune to the lovesick blues, and the most troubling part was that the remedy was out of reach. Someone else controlled the cure. "What club are you hitting?"

"I don't know. The first one I grabbed. These are Mr. Hay's clubs." JJ handed the club to his father.

"This is a one iron. Why does Haymaker have a club that even God can't hit?" Jesse swapped clubs and put another ball on the rubber practice tee for JJ. He wanted to save his son from endlessly inventing reunion scenes, tormenting fragments of fantasies that chased Jesse as he waited in airport lounges, sat on runway tarmacs, and tossed and turned nights away in indistinguishable hotel rooms, needing sleep but shunning the vivid dreams of reconciliation with Denise. "Here, this is a five iron. You can almost play a whole round using just this one club."

JJ tried again and hit his best terrible shot of the day. "I give up," he said, letting out a quick, thin laugh.

"The worst part is that her dad threatens me about 'repenting or burning in hell.'" JJ mocked the pastor's pompous voice. "But before all my troubles, Melanie told me her parents were fighting about divorcing."

"You're pulling my leg?"

"Nope, and I'd love to tell the whole town what dumbasses they are for falling for that poser's bullshit act."

"I feel sorry for her mom." Every time Jesse heard of a long-time married couple divorcing, admitting defeat, a stab tore at his gut. Mrs. Suggs wouldn't be like the typical forty-something starting over, no preacher's ex-wife sitting at a bar nursing a white wine spritzer. There were friends, like Denise's, telling her with supportive faces that finally shedding her life coupled to an aloof partner would empower her, strengthen her. They'd pat her on the back and say in the long run, it would be for the best. Then they'd go home to cook their husband's favorite dinner or rifle through his drawers; either way, they were right.

"Don't feel too bad; not being married to a douche bag could actually make her mom happier."

"Who knows, you could be right about that." Jesse walked over to JJ's golf bag, pulled out the one iron again, and pushed a few range balls onto his practice tee.

"You know what Mr. Jack said I should do?"

"What's that?" Jesse asked, resisting the snappy reply of "speaking of douche bags."

"He said I need to go on a walkabout or kayaking safari with him, something about forging a new trail. That's what he did after his first big heartbreak, like I should totally blow off school and work. He thinks I'm missing an opportunity; youth is wasted on the young, he says."

"I don't know if I'd skip bond or abandon college and my future just yet." Jesse crushed a shot over the two-hundred-yard marker. He was pleased with his iron game but disappointed that JJ would consider Jack's hippy drop out advice.

"Maybe, but holy fucking shit, I have to do something different. Somehow, I'm missing out." JJ shoved the golf club back into the bag, folded his arms, and watched his father.

Jesse launched a few more crisp iron shots and then stopped. The maintenance crews were done for the day. There was no muffled rumbling of lawnmowers or buzzing gnaw of trimmers, just the spring gusts chattering at the tops of the pines. Since JJ had said the mo-fo word in front of him, now all other curse words were permissible. His son needed a plan, and certainly not from some folk artist.

"What about going to church?" Jesse suggested.

"Church?"

"That's it. You could start going to church every Sunday morning and Wednesday evening." Jesse knew his idea sounded outlandish. He'd always taught his son that Jesus was like the next-door neighbor you waved to whenever you saw him in the front yard, but you never bothered each other unless there was an ice storm or you needed your car battery jumped. "And you may as well go to the most popular church in the county, First Dwyer Baptist."

"With Melanie's dad there preaching? That's crazy."

"Hold up, listen for a second. People attend church for all sorts of reasons other than worship," Jesse said, as if eagerly pitching a diabolical solution to a pesky problem at work. "There'll be a thousand people there, but you let a mutual friend know you're going. You sit in the balcony in the back row. Pastor Sonny will be so busy, he'll never notice you. Make sure you dress to blend in, shave your goatee, and maybe wear fake glasses or something. Then you can find a way to slip out during the service, or after, and spend time with Melanie.

You've got a couple of months before your hearing. You ought to be able to see her now and then. How's that for brilliance?"

"It's insane as crap, but that sounds like it's actually doable, worth trying, anyway." JJ extended his fist. Jesse grabbed his son's arm and pulled him close for a hug.

19

THE ONLY TIME THE HOUSE PHONE RANG AT JESSE'S house was when someone was calling to ask for money. He never picked up calls from toll-free numbers or out-of-state area codes, so he was surprised when his caller ID showed *Roberta Lee* phoning from a local number.

"Hello," Jesse said, tucking the phone under his ear.

"Yes, sir, hey there, hold on a second," an older man with a husky voice said on the other end. "Is this Mr. Jesse Few?"

"Can I ask who is calling?"

"I need to find Mr. Few."

"Who's calling?"

"This is Virgil Lee. My wife and I found his mother."

"Is this some sort of weird prank? I've got your name on my caller ID." Jesse pulled the receiver out from his ear and straightened his back.

"Well, no, sir. I think we...she's out here at our house right now, washin' up a bit."

"Really?" He paused, reconfiguring his thoughts, now that he had prepared his mind to receive the worst. "Where are you?

How did she get there?"

"It's kinda a funny thing, it was. We was comin' back from sellin' a few baskets of collards up to the produce stand lady and all when we come upon a car on the side of the road broke down with a flat. Then about a short piece after that, we seen your mother walkin' along with only one bedroom slipper on. Roberta hollered at me to pull over."

"Is she okay? You're sure it's Gennifer Finch?"

"Yes, sir. She said her last name was Sherman, but she gave us your name and number. I'd say she's a tad flustered, and somehow she got skinned up in a few places, but she's holdin' her own."

"I don't know how to thank you," Jesse said, leaning against the wall for support. "I guess I need to come get her and bring her car back."

"I swapped the tire."

"I appreciate that." Jesse put the phone back under his ear, grabbing a pen from the drawer. "Can you give me your address, and I'll get someone to give me a ride out there?"

"Yes, sir. We're out in Nasonville. It's called Main Street out here, but it's really just Highway 17 out from Dwyer. We're at 7331 Dwyer Highway, on the right as you come to the top of the hill."

"Again, sir, thank you very much. Tell Momma I should be out there in thirty minutes or so."

"All righty then. Bye-bye."

~~~

It took Jesse longer than he expected to round up Haymaker and get ready. It was close to an hour before Haymaker dropped him off in front of the Lees' house and headed back to Dwyer for a date with a promising divorcee who had just moved in from Birmingham.

He had driven the Dwyer Highway to Nasonville hundreds, if not thousands of times and had never even noticed the small white house set back from the road with peeling, dull, white paint and a rusted metal roof. An American flag hung off the front porch, and a medley of empty chairs were lined up to watch the traffic zipping past.

As he walked up to the porch, he calculated the time in his head and figured he could show his appreciation with a fifty-dollar bill and be on his way home with Momma and her car in fifteen minutes or less.

Before he could get to the front door, it swung open and a large man in bib overalls came out.

"Mr. Jesse, is that you?" asked the elderly man, approaching Jesse across the porch.

"Yes, sir, it is," Jesse said.

"Pleased to meet you. Virgil Lee," he said, extending a big, callused hand. Under his overalls, he wore a faded, red T-shirt that looked like it might have been sewn together from several pieces of old cloth. He had on a pair of worn-out, black work boots with the steel toes exposed. His white hair stuck out from under the sides of his weather-beaten cowboy hat. Gray stubble covered his face, but his blue eyes were bright and clear. "Come on in the house."

Virgil led Jesse past the darkly lit den and into the brightly lit kitchen, where Momma was sitting next to a round woman at an oval Formica table. They were both peeling potatoes onto a newspaper.

"Lookee who I got here, ladies," Virgil said in a voice loud enough to be considered shouting. "Mrs. Gennifer, you recognize this young fella here?"

"Hey, Momma, you doing all right? You look good."

"Oh, Man-o, you found me. You won't believe the adventure I've had today," Gennifer said, standing up to give Jesse a hug and then sitting back down to resume her potato-peeling chore. "I was just helping Roberta fix supper."

"That's nice. They sure helped us out a bunch," Jesse said.

"This is my wife, Roberta, Mr. Jesse," Virgil said.

"How do you do, ma'am," Jesse said with a nod.

Roberta Lee looked up at Jesse through her thick cat-eye glasses and smiled. There were two silver rhinestones on one side of the black frames and none on the other. She and Momma were wearing similar light denim dresses; Roberta's was fully stretched out at the seams while Momma was swallowed up in hers.

"You're going to let us stay and enjoy these mashed potatoes, aren't you?" Momma asked.

"Of course, you two have gotta join us for supper," Virgil said, slapping Jesse on the back. "We don't usually eat meat on Saturday night, but Roberta flat insisted on fryin' up our Sunday chicken this evenin' for Mrs. Gennifer."

Jesse looked over at the stove and saw chicken frying in the black cast-iron skillet; the crackling reminded him of Granny Finch.

"Gosh, Mr. Lee. You and your wife have gone to such trouble. I don't want to put you out any more than we've already done."

"Virgil, call me Virgil. You ain't puttin' us out. Besides, I'm chargin' the battery up on your ma's Cadillac, and it won't be ready for a couple of hours. It's a miracle that dad-burned thing started in the first place."

"I sure do appreciate all this. If Momma is helping cook, is there something I can do to pitch in?"

"Tell you what, come on out on the back porch and help me churn some ice cream."

"Homemade ice cream?"

"Sure enough," Virgil said, pulling a silver canister from the refrigerator. "This custard ain't been in the icebox as long as Roberta likes it to be, but it'll do just fine. Come on, follow me."

"Lead the way," Jesse said, once again following Virgil, this time out the kitchen door onto a screened-in back porch. Virgil flipped on the light switch, and the yellow bug light overhead covered them in a golden-ocher glow.

"Out here's what they call nowadays—my man cave," Virgil said. Mr. Lee's man cave was only slightly bigger than Jesse's walk-in closet in his master bedroom, and it was enclosed in a clutter of opened boxes, broken tools, and stacks of old catalogs. Tacked on the wall was a 1987 Snap-On Tools' calendar with a big-haired blonde in blue jean shorts and a flannel shirt stretched across the hood of a vintage pickup truck. Hanging next to the calendar was a Gold Star Service Flag.

Virgil reached into an upright storage unit and pulled out what Jesse thought was a wooden bucket. "It's jim-dandy out here in the spring and the fall, and it always gives me a spot I can go off to and dream a little. How about fetching me a bag of ice out of that freezer there, Mr. Jesse."

Jesse held the bag of ice while Virgil Lee put the canister of custard into the pine bucket and attached a white motor to the top.

"I got my rock salt, and we're a-makin' ice cream that easy. Pull up a seat while we let science and the motor do the hard part."

Mr. Lee settled himself in a worn-out living room recliner that swayed from side to side as he adjusted himself, and Jesse sat down in a green metal lawn chair, the only other available seat, beside a crooked tower of magazines. They listened to the hum of the motor and the crunch of the ice. Virgil occasionally commented on the weather and his vegetable garden.

"The lady up there—where we sell our baskets of cabbages and collards—is always quizzin' me to be sure my vegetables are organic. She wants to make sure we ain't sprayed them with no pesticides. I say, 'Oh, yes, ma'am,' like I'm not fudgin', but if it comes from the ground it's organic. Forget her on findin' out what's in a few shovels full of chicken shit and my homemade bug killers."

"Mr. Lee...Virgil, I don't know what Momma was doing on the side of the road, but I really appreciate you and your wife helping her out."

"Don't think nothin' of it; you're quite welcome. Roberta wouldn't have it no other way and I wouldn't neither." He sprinkled rock salt on top of the ice, careful not to let any settle on top of the canister. "I tell you, we was all lucky we found her. I don't know what spooked her. I guess it was the blowout on the tire, but she was mighty jumpy when we came up on her."

"I can't imagine where she was driving to; usually she just goes to the grocery store or to the...run a short errand. I haven't considered it too much, but I guess I'm not really comfortable with her driving."

"I'm seventy-eight years old. I worked for the power company for nearly fifty years and I can tell you firsthand—gettin' old ain't for the faint of heart or the weak. Like the saying goes 'If I'd have known I was gonna live this damn long, I'd have taken better care of myself.'"

"I never pictured her not being my mother, that there'd come a day when she couldn't do it herself," Jesse said.

"You know, I used to get madder than a mosquito in a mannequin factory at the way life was a-doin' me. I mean, not just me gettin' old, but seein' all the problems that Roberta had to go through herself. She had a bad scare with the woman cancer. And my youngest daughter was all messed up in the wrong crowd—a bad bunch from down the road a bit—and goes to stealin' from Roberta and me. It just sent me into a blasted tailspin of wantin' this somethin' or other and wishin' for all kinda stuff. I was makin' a mess of things, and heck, a dog don't even mess in his own pen the way I was."

"I'm with you," Jesse said, rocking back in his chair.

"You know, some days I don't know brown gravy from white gravy, but that strugglin' feeling don't ever stop for most folks. I'm tellin' you, I tried to see all the B.S. happenin' to me almost like manure fertilizin' my heart, changin' my crazy monkey mind for the better. I started comin' out here in the mornin' and late at night and sorta steerin' my thoughts—my imagination— toward more useful, practical notions."

"How'd that do for you? Did that help?"

"Readin' a cookbook don't make you no fancy chef. I had to start believin' with my hands and my feet, and even on my knees. I guess it came down to me lovin' folks that were assholes— pardon the French—helpin' out my sister-in-law when I didn't want to, and forgivin' and forgettin'. I even had to give a pass to the Man Upstairs for lettin' one of them IEDs kill my only grandson in Iraq."

Virgil reached down and shook more rock salt onto the ice; the container whirled about the bucket while the brine solution helped to gradually transform the mixture of scalded milk and sugar into smooth homemade ice cream. Jesse let the revolutions of the churn guide his thoughts to the open range where two cowhands, one old dog and one greenhorn, swapped stories by the campfire, grateful for the lull, telling tales they wouldn't share anywhere else.

~~~

Full of Roberta's fried chicken, mashed potatoes, and ice cream, Momma and Jesse headed back to Dwyer.

"That was certainly nice of them to have us for dinner. Roberta is some cook," Jesse said.

"Connie Francis," Momma said, half-dozing in the passenger seat. "I woke up from my nap, and I clearly heard her singing 'Arrivederci, Roma.' I was trying to find where the music was coming from. That's how I got out here."

"That's okay, Momma. It's fine now."

"When you boys were babies, I'd put y'all down for the night, and Preston would put her record on the stereo. Rather than go out, we'd slow dance in the front room, and he'd whisper in my ear. He was real shy, bashful even with me, his wife, but he loved that album—the one with her on the cover where she was dressed as a gondolier with Venice in the background. Did I ever tell you about how handsome your father looked driving his gold Cadillac convertible?"

"Yeah, you've told me that." Jesse looked over at his mother and was pleased to see a slender smile on her face.

"That was the car that he and your Grandpa Finch drove to Philadelphia to...to see the Army-Navy game back in '54. He kept the program from that game for years. Preston said the car didn't have a heater that worked, and he'd never been so cold in his life. Remembering that trip always made him shiver, both of us."

Jesse had never heard that story before. "Didn't you live in Philly then with Rex?"

A pair of overloaded log trucks passed by, going in the other direction, rocking the Cadillac. Jesse thought they were headed to PM's mill in east Alabama, some small town that traded jobs for the industrial stench of pulp. When he was a trainee, Jesse had spent a week at the mill, so he knew how paper was produced. But for him it didn't really exist until he could sell it to customers by the truckloads. He never considered the truckers who hauled the trees, the land the trees came from, or the loggers who sold the trees to the mill. Momma's life before he was born was just like the wood that became paper.

"I was back home by then. So this afternoon, I started walking around the house, looking for Connie Francis. I couldn't find the stereo in the living room, but I knew the music was coming from somewhere. I checked in the hallway and the spare bedrooms, but I couldn't find the record player anywhere. I even stuck my ear to the door of the master bedroom."

"You should've called me, and I'd have helped you figure it out."

"I was going to. I went off to the kitchen intending to call you and see if you'd help me find my Connie Francis records."

"I'd have been glad to do it."

"But before I picked up the phone, I decided to have me my whiskey sour. I opened the refrigerator to get out my cherries, and as I was closing the door, I smelled something peppery. It almost reminded me of Aqua Velva aftershave. It nearly singed my nostrils."

"Funny how our brains and our senses work together like that."

"But what was strange is that Preston had always worn Clubman Pinaud. It was more polished like he was—it suited him more than Aqua Velva. You know, GIs used to drink that stuff in the Army."

"I'd never heard that."

"And then I screamed and dropped my jar of cherries, right on the kitchen floor."

"What? Why'd you scream?"

"'Cause of Rex. He was standing there in the back doorway. His hair was all slicked back in that ducktail he had, but his face...it was all oily and glowing, flushed-like. He was wearing a dirty T-shirt and torn trousers, like he'd just come in from work."

"Momma, you know it's just your mind playing tricks on you. You're all right with me." He didn't have to look to know that her smile was gone.

"He called me an 'old cow' and said I 'made a mess,' that I busted my cherry on the floor. That laugh of his...he started taking steps toward me."

"You ca—"

"He had his black cord in his hand, the old gnarled one that used to fit the toaster I broke. He told me I 'need a lesson.' So I rushed out the front door toward the garage. But when I was peeking back, I tripped over a root or something in the front yard, and I fell right onto the edge of the driveway, skinning up my palms and knuckles. I got back up, but I was so dizzy that I could barely stand up. Still, I kept going to the carport, when I felt this chill sweep over me. I didn't have to turn around 'cause I knew Rex was closing in on me."

"My God, Momma, I'm so sorry. I'll take care of you and make sure you're safe. From now on, I'll always be here for you, right? You know I love you?"

"I love you, too, Man-o."

They rode in silence for a few minutes, and finally, Momma fell asleep.

All he had learned about Rex in the last few weeks streamed through Jesse's mind and filtered out not as solid statements of facts but as shifting fragments: Rex and Mom in Philadelphia with his black cord; his grandfather and father's Army-Navy game trip; Momma's horrific visions of Rex's return. Jesse couldn't be entirely certain the danger was all in Momma's muddled mind and there wasn't someone still out there. He knew he'd most likely gathered all the clues that Aunt Lizzy and Ricky were willing to give, but on the right morning, he'd ask his mother again. Once Haymaker finished his sleuthing on Pastor Sonny, Jesse might ask him if he had any connections in the Department of Veteran Affairs.

Watching his mother sleep in the passenger seat reminded Jesse of the story he'd heard in Vacation Bible School when he was a boy. Some precocious camper asked the teacher what dying was like and the teacher said, "It's like riding in the car with your mom and dad late at night, and you get so tired that you can't stay awake. Then the next morning, you wake up safely in your bed and don't remember how your parents carried you in from the car and tucked you in. You're just there with Jesus." Jesse wondered if in the morning Momma would think she was in heaven when she woke up in his guest bedroom.

20

FOR JESSE, FROM THE END OF OCTOBER UNTIL JANUARY
was an Americana opiate, as if getting fat and going broke
was tranquilizing. Workaday households stayed stoned on
inappropriate costumes, football, high-fat food and high-risk
office parties, foolish spending, and topped it all with two days
of binge drinking and still more football. Nothing created better
camouflage than the holidays. The bankers were unwilling to
disturb their year-end books. Kimberly was counseled by her
lawyer to let Nick move out and hold on to their house as long
as possible. JJ was busy with final exams and a retail job, and
Momma watched every seasonal special from *It's the Great
Pumpkin, Charlie Brown* to *Dick Clark's New Year's Rockin'
Eve.*

His mother had moved in two months ago, and they'd only had
a couple of caretaker catastrophes between her and Haymaker.
He'd ended a client meeting abruptly last month after Hay had
called Momma's favorite soap opera heroine a "dried-up slut" and
she'd retaliated by locking the sliding glass door when Haymaker
went outside for his afternoon toke. Jesse negotiated a truce over

the cell phone once Haymaker apologized through the glass door and promised to make her a whiskey sour. He'd never admit it to his aunt, but she was correct—finding qualified help was difficult. Jesse, Haymaker, and Momma had met with ten or more candidates, and none of them passed the muster—too lazy, too sketchy, too snippy, or all three. Good people who had good positions didn't change employers during the holidays. But by the first two weeks of January, exhaustion prevailed, remorse and credit card bills arrived, and PM held budget meetings.

Early on a Friday afternoon, Jesse was sitting in the corporate conference room, and he was supposed to be paying attention to what Liliane Bollore was saying about overtime and payroll expenses at their north Florida plant. But he couldn't stop wondering if this was the longest he'd gone without getting laid since Amie was born seventeen years ago. That had been six weeks. Now it had been over three months.

The apple-biting brain in his pants was advocating an immediate hookup with Kimberly—right now, this afternoon—but the slightly less reptilian mind between his ears was reminding him that based on how their relationship started, it practically guaranteed that it wouldn't end well. The cerebellum was recommending to continue deflecting her text messages with excuses about his work schedule and not endangering her divorce proceedings. Rationally, he knew it was smarter to choose Internet porn and any attractive woman, over thirty, before Kimberly, despite his lust and the necessity for MGD's new Houston office to boost his sales budget. The crash of Liliane's fist on the table promptly refocused Jesse's mind.

Liliane was the craggy chief financial officer of the North America Paper Division whom the Paris headquarters had put in place to watch Jean-Paul and the Americans. She was currently questioning Millard Marks, PM vice president of North America Paper Production, on his employee cost—plant by plant; it was a brutal review. Liliane was an "expert-comptable," the French equivalent of a certified public accountant, and also an "avocet," the dreaded accountant-lawyer combination. She was asking him questions that she already knew the answers to, and Millard, a south Georgia man from two acquisitions back, was stumbling badly. Fortunately for Jesse, he had already undergone Liliane's inquisition at the last meeting.

For the past year, Liliane had been PM's leader in lowering costs to match their rapidly dropping North American revenues. Liliane's own "March to the Sea" had slashed through the South, closing two plants in Georgia and permanently displacing families. She was eyeing more, so Millard's stubbornness in deciding on whether to lay off either nine or ten administrative people was not serving him well. Everyone in the room, except Millard, knew his headstrong opinion came not from any sound business reasoning, but from his sexual indiscretions with the accounts payable clerk. They all knew Liliane had seen the emails between the two and the photos—*quelle horreur*—and was hoping not only to reduce the head count by ten in Baldwin, but also to replace an older, overpaid, chauvinist VP with someone younger, more pliable, and definitely cheaper. That's what the cutback culture had become at PM.

At first, they targeted the people who already had written warnings in their employment files, like trimming back the dead branches to allow the healthier ones to grow; it was a benefit of tough times. Next, they increased the frequency of random drug screenings, which brought the head count down even further.

But when these techniques weren't producing the results they needed to show Paris, they didn't hesitate to sharpen their bayonets—except they weren't layoffs; instead, they implemented "reductions in workforce."

Jesse had delivered the bad news to so many coworkers and colleagues that he'd become disengaged from the process. The first few times it had bothered him, but he went through the steps to rationalize his guilt—"they'll be better off for it" or "they brought it on themselves." Yet, he knew ex-employees, their spouses, children, and grandkids, would loathe him for generations to come. However, there were no sympathetic news stories about how apologetic the remorseful decision makers felt, and they weren't added to anyone's prayer list.

Still, the attrition didn't stop, so now Jesse was musing about his sexual needs when Heather, his assistant, came into the conference room and slipped him a note: *Please call Denise ASAP.*

Jesse read the note and felt a pang sting him above his eyebrows. As much as he wished this were the remedy for his libido emergency, he knew it wasn't. During their twenty-year marriage, Jesse would never have considered leaving a meeting to make a personal call, but he waited for Jean-Paul to ask a question, pausing Liliane's slaughter, and slipped back to his office to call his ex-wife.

"Hey, thank you, thank you for calling me back so quickly," Denise said when she answered her cell phone on the first ring. There was edge in her voice. "I hate to bother you at work."

"It's just a budget meeting. Everything okay?" Jesse asked in his business call calm.

"Has JJ called or texted you today?"

"No, why would he?"

"How about Melanie's dad?"

"Pastor Sonny? Lord no. What's going on?"

"I just got a nasty visit from Sonny. Apparently, it's Melanie's eighteenth birthday today, and he found JJ parked in front of their house, waiting to give her a gift. Sonny told me that if he ever found JJ around his daughter again, he was going to get a restraining order and see that his bond was revoked."

"Jumping Jesus Jones, can he do all that?"

"You tell me. His hearing is coming up soon, so I don't think we really want to find out."

Jesse sighed and leaned back in his chair, staring at the ceiling. "What did JJ say?"

"Not too much. Something about a special present for her and that Melanie is an adult now, so there's nothing he can do to stop them from being together."

"I'm not sure now is the ideal time to play Romeo," Jesse said, his chest tightening when Denise mentioned the gift, afraid that it was the antique earrings from New Orleans. "How's he doing otherwise?"

"He was doing better—busy with school and work, going to AA meetings at some church, every Sunday morning and Wednesday night."

Jesse took a long pause.

"You there?" Denise asked.

"I'm here," Jesse said. "That's positive, the meetings."

"They were. But for some reason, he stopped going after he got his tires slashed at school."

"He got his tires slashed? Cripes almighty." Jesse rocked back and forth in his office chair, hoping the pastor hadn't unleashed his security team on JJ. "Does he have any idea who did it?"

"I have no inkling. He's hardly answering any of my questions. He actually told Jack about his birthday gift idea. I'm beyond having any clue of why that boy does what he does."

"What can I do to help?"

"I've taken away his car keys until after his hearing, so he may call you, whining. Don't give in. It's time for some tough love."

"Of course. I'm rock solid here."

"Jesse, this isn't like buying him a toy after I said no. Don't make me the bitchy mom; please, just don't," Denise said, pleading for Jesse's dubious support as she had for twenty years. "I've got to run JJ to work. Let me know if he calls you."

"Will do," Jesse said, easing the phone back onto its cradle. He closed his eyes and slowly counted to one hundred, imagining that he was out on Virgil's porch, enjoying the afternoon sun and a bowl of homemade ice cream.

Over the years, Jesse had seen coworkers leave the office early for their children's broken arms or their spouse's flat tire. Jesse didn't have an urgent crisis, but he was desperate to avoid the claustrophobia of the conference room and skip the afternoon carnage. Jesse sent Jean-Paul an email explaining that he had to leave because his mother's doctor had called about an emergency, and he headed home. Fortunately, today he was ahead of rush hour, and when he walked into the den, it was empty and quiet. But then he heard the whirring of the blender and the crushing of ice coming from the porch.

"Daddy is home," Haymaker said as Jesse stepped through the sliding glass doors. He punched the "off" button and pulled the pitcher off the blender. "You're just in time for daiquiris. I was feelin' a little homesick for the corner daiquiri store, so I decided to whip up a batch or two."

Momma was sipping from a nearly empty daiquiri glass and sitting in the chaise lounge with her feet propped up. She was wearing two cardigan sweaters over her white housedress, and she had on a pink Atlanta Braves baseball cap.

"Hey, Momma," Jesse said, bending down to give her a peck on the cheek. "You look like you're having a nice afternoon."

"I just love these strawberry things your friend is making," she said, pointing her glass toward Haymaker. "But some music would be nice, don't you think?"

"I'll see what I can do."

"Let me top you off again there, Mrs. Gennifer," Haymaker said, heading toward Momma with his fresh pitcher. "I kicked this batch up a bit with some of that Nicaraguan rum we scored when we were down in Cos—"

"Hold on a second there, cabana boy." Jesse grabbed Hay by the arm, reversing his course. A large glob of pinkish-red drink spilled out of the top of the pitcher, splashing onto the patio.

"Whoa now, horsey. We're losin' our frozen concoction there," Haymaker said as Jesse led him back toward the blender. "But no worries, Jester. There's plenty in this batch for us all to get a taste."

"I'm sure there is, but didn't we talk about monitoring Momma's drinking a little bit better, especially with all her meds?"

"We did, but it's also Friday, and everybody is workin' for the weekend. You want me to fix you one of my fruity-tooty-knock-you-on-your-booty specials?"

"No. Well, maybe a small one later on, but not just yet. I'm worried about how the alcohol affects her with all her medicines." They both looked over at Momma, who was tipping the bottom of her glass up to get the last drop of her drink.

"I understand you bein' worried about her, but what harm is it goin' to do her at her age to knock back a few drinks in the evenin'?"

"Plenty. It makes her loopy."

"How about we switch her to some of that medical marijuana then? I was thinkin' about mixin' up a tray of pot brownies for my divorce support group anyway."

Jesse stared at his friend for a second and smiled, shaking his head. In his blue flowered shirt and beige shorts with sweat dripping down his forehead, Hay looked like he could be working at a pool-side bar. He knew Haymaker was simply playing to his strength. "Bless your party-loving heart; you are something special. Fix me one and top off Momma's."

"You got it, boss," Haymaker said, pouring Jesse a drink. "Let me get Mrs. Gennifer's music taken care of, too. I made a new playlist for her on my iPod, and she's been askin' about it all afternoon."

Haymaker scrambled around for a few minutes, pouring Momma a fresh daiquiri and going inside to turn on music. After he finished, he pulled up a patio chair and sat down next to Jesse while Momma sipped on her libation and listened to "The Girl from Ipanema," the soothing Latin backbeat providing the perfect Friday afternoon poolside song.

"How's that drink taste, Big Un'?" Haymaker asked. "I was figurin' we could have a couple of toddies, grill some steaks, and head over to T's later, unless, that is, you got somethin' lined up with your little blonde friend."

"Kimberly? No, not tonight," Jesse said, not in the mood to explain that he'd been avoiding her and her texts. "I've talked to a new temp agency, and I think I'm close to getting us some part-time help."

"That's cool. We made it through today, and you know me. I'm no Scarlet Nightingale or Nurse Ratched for that matter, but I'll do whatever I can to pitch in."

"Momma didn't mention anything about a man, a stranger, or anything?"

"Not once, and I've been keepin' the doors all locked and bolted like you said, and I've got all the car keys put up."

"Any calls from my aunt?"

"Sir. No, sir."

"Amie hasn't called the house, has she? She was going to sit with Momma on Sunday."

"Can't say she did," Haymaker said, shaking his head. "But we did get a piece of news delivered—certified mail—and it ain't good. Bertram had their lawyers drop the demand letter bomb, so it appears we got thirty days to get right."

"They took the ninety-day extension business serious. What are the options? One more round of hillbilly psycho and the lying-ass sidekick?"

"Highly doubtful, I've got a better chance of sleepin' with my pissed-off ex-wife than we do wigglin' another extension out of the plaid-pants gang. And if you don't have the cash, I say it's time to tap out the partnership. We start transferrin' assets now, it won't be quite so fraudulent when the bankruptcy papers slide across the trustee's desk."

"Declare bankruptcy?"

"Hell, all your top athletes and movie stars do it, and I'm already morally bankrupt, so what's the big difference?"

"The difference is we personally guaranteed the loans and fraudulent transfer of assets is just that—fraudulent and criminal." The sudden smack of uneasiness that began earlier with

Denise's phone call overran Jesse's body again. He took a small sip off the top of his daiquiri, careful to avoid gulping too fast and adding an ice cream headache to his problems. "I can't afford for my company to find out. The French would have a dim view of the whole situation. I'm sure Denise and the kids would be real proud of me, too."

"Ten-four that. My sleazy divorce lawyer buddy owes me one. I'll see if he can send some type of bunko comeback, but I think we're just whistlin' past the gallows on this one."

"Most likely, but we haven't lost yet, and in today's society, anything is possible," Jesse said. "Adding to the misery index, my monthly mortgage nut just readjusted; damn payment went up nearly 50 percent. Bubba still thinks I should sell the house."

"Nah, man, that's like sellin' your convertible just because it's wintertime," Haymaker said, speaking with an off-center crispness, transmuted by rum into an expert on endless topics. "What you need is one of them strategic defaults—stop payin' the mortgage and pocket the dough. I guarantee it'll take them a couple of years to evict you. Meanwhile, you're scoopin' up undervalued assets like that package of townhouses and storage units I was tellin' you about."

"That's a sinister idea," Jesse said. "But I just can't bring myself to do it."

"I feel you, man, but if you don't think the fat cats from Wall Street to Motown didn't run the numbers before they decided to let Mr. and Mrs. Taxpayer bail their asses out, you're dead wrong."

"Yeah, maybe. We ready for the gun show this weekend?" Jesse asked. "I've got a kind of catalog put together with pictures and stuff for most everything."

"That'll be handy, and we need somethin' to show your average Joe gun buyers, but to get the large Benjamins, we need to deal with the—how do you say—fringe element that don't take to federal stamps and paperwork."

"How fringe is this element?" Jesse glanced over at his mother; she was asleep with her empty glass laid across her chest.

"Fringy as a mo-fo, truth be told." Haymaker filled up their glasses with the rest of the daiquiri and muffled his voice like he was an underground arms dealer speaking on the hush-hush. "Let's see, there's the rednecks from up around north Alabama, and there's the anti-everything, conspiracy types from Michigan or the Idaho area, those sorta places. Then, just to make it interestin', there's the thug-life crews that have made the ATL their home base now, most of 'em comin' in after Katrina in '05. Top that off with assorted Mexican gangs runnin' illegals, dope, and putas. Then sprinkle in the Asian punks in their pimped-out Civics who turned Chamblee into Chambodia, and you got yourself a prime cash-money sellin' bidness opportunity."

"Are you sure? Man, that sounds way too far out for me. How are we—you—going to get in touch with these people?"

"I got some contacts, guys who know other guys, that sorta thing. By the by, we can also do some swappin' for some surveillance gear, if you're ready to get a look up Pastor Sonny's robe."

"Let's not poke that bear too hard just now; we're in that low-key period between JJ's arrest and his court date. He just raised holy hell with Denise about JJ trying to give Melanie a birthday present."

"Sounds like that bear has already been walloped pretty good already. I'm tellin' you, that dude is doin' somethin' slippery. I'm hearin' all sorts of loco stuff about shady Ponzi schemes and gang members he stills knows."

"You don't think he'd send somebody after JJ, do you? Threaten him sort of?"

"Preacher man is singin' from his own wacko hymnal. Who knows what darkness is in that man's heart. You about ready for another batch and a bowl of—"

Jesse's cell phone rang, interrupting Haymaker.

"Maybe this is Amie." Jesse glanced down at his phone. "That's weird," he said, before answering. "Hello, this is Jesse Few." He walked to the far end of the pool to take the call. After a couple of minutes, he came back to Haymaker, who was working on another pitcher of drinks.

"We got us a sitter?" Haymaker asked, mixing in a spoonful of concentrated strawberry mix.

"I don't know...no, it wasn't her. It was Ricky."

"Your brother? What did that ol' jackass want?"

"Bad news...incredible, really...hard for me to even process right now, but my aunt passed away. Aunt Lizzy died today," Jesse said. He looked down at the daiquiri from the earlier spill. The red splatter stood out against the white concrete, glistening in the last of the afternoon sun. Sugar ants were starting to run a trail through the drying mixture, searching madly, some drowning in the melting ice chips while others plundered the morsels of the sweet drink. He thought the scarlet stain would be a permanent reminder of his aunt's death, that every time he saw it, he would have a random memory of her life. But he realized that the next hard rain would wash most of it away forever, and what little that'd be left would turn black with grime. Honking geese flying overhead snapped him back, and when he turned around, his mother was standing close by.

"What about Elizabeth?" Momma asked, stepping even closer. "What happened to my little sister?"

21

"JUST LIKE THAT," RICKY SAID, SNAPPING HIS FINGERS, the loud pop filling the small room. "She's here one night, and then before dawn, some old dude finds her dead on her sunporch." He mindlessly fumbled with one of the many funeral home brochures on the table next to him. "Mm, I guess that little bypass job wasn't holding up as well as she hoped."

"That's so sad," Jesse said, raising his eyebrows and tilting his head toward Momma in a vain hope that his half-brother would understand his shut-up-you-idiot look.

There had been no consoling Momma last night, and she had insisted on them leaving for El Pueblo before sunrise. She had to be there, with her little sister, to take care of everything. It had been a hard drive, but they had made it in time to meet Ricky at the funeral home right after lunch.

"Evidently, this fellow who found her was a neighbor," Ricky said, continuing on in much more detail than he had over the phone. "His wife is in some kinda vegetable state 'cause of a stroke or something."

"I want to make sure that we have her portrait here for the viewing," Momma said quietly from her seat next to Jesse on the sofa, a wad of Kleenex clenched firmly in her hand.

"What's that?" Jesse asked.

"The portrait that Archibald had done of her. I know that's how she would want to be remembered."

"I know the one," Ricky said, reaching out and giving his mother's forearm a gentle pat. "She really looked beautiful in it."

"Sure, I remember it, too," Jesse said, putting his arm around her.

"Y'all may have been too young to recollect, but she lived with us one summer in College Park. It was just the four of us." Momma dabbed her nose with a tissue. "I think you were both in diapers still; it was before I met Mr. Billy, right after Preston had that horrible accident on the ice. She took care of you two while I worked at the department store, just like y'all were her own baby boys."

"I don't recall that house," Jesse said. "I forgot that we ever lived in College Park."

"I remember it," Ricky said. "It seems like there was a park or swing set nearby."

"There was. They belonged to that private school next door, and we would take you boys over and push you for what seemed like hours." Momma let out a heavy sigh. "Gosh, that seems like it happened to another person in a different life, but yet it's almost like we're still out there somewhere on the playground, right now."

"She wanted a little girl of her own so badly. She was absolutely heartbroken when they finally learned about Archibald's situation. She said it was because of the war. It was right about then that Archibald had her do the sitting. He wanted an oil portrait of her, professionally painted. She was so proud of it, and he was, too—proud of her."

"Those two took us to every tacky tourist trap in Florida." Jesse softly chuckled. "We went to Marineland, then that old, run-down alligator farm. Every year, we had to go visit the Old Jail in St. Augustine and get our picture taken in that cell. You remember that?"

"Sure, putting on those phony prison costumes," Ricky said. "But my favorite was them mermaids at Weeki Wachee Springs. I loved them costumes."

"You two were always special to her. She doted on you both. It wasn't always easy for her but she had a way of letting you know." Momma twisted the tissue tightly around her finger. "You know, she came to see me yesterday afternoon. I recall being in a lounge chair around a pool somewhere. I remember her sitting down on the edge of the chair and it coming up in the air a bit with her weight. I was afraid I'd go soaring off into space, but she put her hand on my leg and I felt safe again. She smelled sweet, almost like peppermint." Momma's words stumbled out, trembling.

"She started putting on her bathing cap, tucking her hair under it like we would do when we were young. She told me that she was going swimming—down in the deep end, past the drain. There was a cave. A clear white light. A shining silver temple. She wanted a glimpse. She told me that she'd find me again. She kissed me on the cheek. Then she was gone."

"These places got to be recession proof, don't you know." Ricky picked up a casket brochure, rolling it up like a telescope.

"Where's the damn funeral director?" Jesse asked, standing up to pace the teal arrangement room. "I thought they said around one o'clock."

~~~

Aunt Lizzy had preplanned an excellent send-off for herself. They had a viewing on Sunday night in El Pueblo for her newfound local friends. Her portrait was on display next to the head of the coffin. Several silver-haired single gentlemen came to pay their last respects. Jesse noticed Mister Cordele Lawyer Man's knees buckling a bit when he passed by the open casket. The memorial service was held Monday at her old church in Jacksonville, and even though Lizzy had not lived there for a few years, a large crowd filled the pews, thanks to the timely two-day placement of the obituary as she had directed. At the graveside service, "Amazing Grace" played on bagpipes as the hearse arrived, and the pallbearers transferred her casket.

They held a covered-dish luncheon in the parish hall after the burial, and afterward, Jesse took sanctuary on a bench in the church's memorial garden. An older woman in a black cocktail dress came around the corner, carrying a cigarette and a lighter.

"Oh, I'm so sorry," she said, turning around to leave.

"You're fine," Jesse said. "There's plenty of room and air out here for us all."

"I'm not even going to enjoy it, but I'll do it anyway. I'm Anna Ritchie," she said, extending her hand. "You're one of Gennifer's boys, aren't you?"

"Jesse Few," he said, standing up to shake her hand. "Yes, ma'am, Elizabeth was my aunt."

"I thought I recognized you." Only a few black streaks remained in her short, silver hair, and years of smoking had added gravel to her Southern accent and creases on her face. "I met you, gosh, more years ago than I want or care to even think about, when you and your brother would come down for the summers."

"Wow, time does fly," Jesse said. "That makes me feel old."

"Tell me about it. Were those your children at the service?"

"No, ma'am. Those are my brother's kids, from Tampa. My two are back in Atlanta." Denise had told Jesse it was fine if JJ and Amie flew down to at least attend the graveside service, but Jesse had decided it wasn't necessary. They didn't need to miss school, and he needed to focus on helping Momma. "Just my mom and I came down from Atlanta."

"I know we're all gonna miss the old gal. I never met anyone like her, but she sure wouldn't want me boo-hooing about it."

"She was tough." Jesse had met many of his aunt's friends the past few days and heard stories about her life, poignant memories about college and charity fundraisers that he never would have heard anywhere else.

"Let's face it—Liz was a bitch with a capital B." Anna held her cigarette before her lips and stared beyond the memorial garden to the A-frame sanctuary roof, hoisting the gray steeple and weather-beaten cross, which rose above the palm trees. "But God bless her soul; she helped me through raising my three girls, their weddings, and my divorces. I think we tried every fad diet that was ever published. She was always there for her friends. I'll miss my traveling buddy. She told us you are quite the golfer. Could you beat her?"

"Never played with her," Jesse said.

"Never?"

"No, ma'am, never." Jesse looked away from his aunt's friend and scanned the purple and white plants blooming in the winter garden. "Never played with her once."

"You missed something. You know, I'll never forget it. I was playing with her the day she got her only hole-in-one," Anna said, her smoky coarseness delivering an improvised blues elegy. "Archie had gotten her this new set of woods for her birthday, and she just couldn't get used to them. She was cussing Archie, threatening to throw the clubs in the lagoon, but that gal never gave up on anything. Then, on the next-to-last hole, a little par three over the lagoon, she decided to give them one more try. Wham-o, bam! Two bounces on the green and, pretty as a princess, right into the cup. We each gave her a hundred dollars, and she bought us all a new pair of golf shoes."

"That sounds incredible. I'd really like to have seen that." Jesse felt like he should apologize for never taking the time or caring enough to play golf with his aunt.

"I wished she'd lived longer, but I pray she died happy."

"Amen to that," Jesse said, turning back to watch Anna Ritchie stamp out her cigarette in a patch of sandy ground.

"I'm sorry for your loss. Have a safe trip home," Anna said, before returning inside and leaving Jesse alone in the garden.

Noticing the lipstick-stained cigarette butt sticking out from the upturned black soil, Jesse wanted to call his aunt's friend back and confess to squandering the moment to laugh in Lizzy's new living room and drink her non-boxed Merlot. Telling her that he'd numbed himself to her existence, but somewhere, deep inside, he still relished the grace of lying on the cool tile floor in her old beach house, watching Neil Armstrong take the first step on the moon and being unaware of red MGB strangers.

22

TWO WEEKS LATER, RICKY CALLED JESSE WITH MORE
news about Aunt Lizzy.

"I'm the executor of Lizzy's estate. We need to meet about the
will," Ricky said as if he were ordering the valet at the country
club to pull his car around. "I assume the Frogs will let you break
away from counting toilet paper sales for a couple hours so we
can have a sit-down with her estate guy in Jax."

"Of course, if I need to," Jesse said, the sibling agitation turning
his cheeks red.

"Oh, you need to, all right. I'll set it up and tell you when and
where. Can you handle that?"

"Sure, I'm just ... " Jesse said, hesitant to admit to his older
brother that he'd never considered his aunt's will. He understood
Archie had a plan for her, but he didn't know that Ricky and he
were part of the plan, too.

"Don't worry, baby brother. This just may turn out in your
favor after all," Ricky said.

~~~

By Thursday, they were in Roberts, Carter & Tanner's conference room, waiting to meet with Aunt Lizzy's estate attorney. Jesse had flown down that morning from Atlanta and had told Jean-Paul that he had a meeting with one of their customers—allowing him to cover the trip on his expense report—but he wasn't sure he'd actually have time for an unscheduled client meeting.

"So, Jesse, you know why the St. Johns River flows north, don't ya?"

Jesse didn't respond. He'd been baffled when Ricky had told him about the meeting with the lawyer, but he didn't expend too much thought on any activity involving his half-brother.

"'Cause the Georgia Bulldogs suck," Ricky said, cackling with laughter. "You remember those weekend house parties Lizzy and Archie would have for the Florida-Georgia game?" Ricky paced back and forth in front of the large picture window.

"Yeah, the world's largest outdoor cocktail party," Jesse said.

"When was the last time you guys won that game?" Ricky stopped his pacing and then quickly did a few deep knee bends. "The Gators have been kicking that Dawg tail so much, it's almost kind of an anticlimax these days."

"It does seem that way," Jesse said, trying to figure out why Ricky was full of more nervous energy than usual, almost giddy even. He sat by himself at the long glass conference table surrounded by black office chairs. The lawyer appeared, sparing Jesse any more brotherly small talk.

"Good afternoon. I'm Tim Tanner," the man said as he walked into the room, shaking Ricky's hand first and then greeting Jesse as he rose from the table. "You're fine, don't get up."

"I'm Richard Few, the executor, and this is my baby brother,

Jesse," Ricky said, in a flat baritone that sounded like he was reading the evening news.

"I was sorry to hear about your aunt's passing," the lawyer said, sitting down across the table from Jesse and folding his hands across the top of the files he had carried in with him. Tim Tanner was a tall, slender man with a full head of black, curly hair and a well-trimmed beard that gave him a scholarly look. However, the oxford blue tailored shirt and the French cuffs made it clear that he wasn't a college professor.

"Thanks, we appreciate that," Ricky said, taking a seat at the head of the table between Jesse and the lawyer. "She was almost like another mom to us. I was especially close to her, being here in Florida."

"She was certainly special," Jesse added.

"She was that, and your uncle and she took great care to put together an estate plan that took maximum advantage of the dynamics in the development of the tax laws over the years," Tanner said, reaching into his file and handing Ricky and Jesse each a legal-size piece of paper. "For the sake of ease—and in an effort to fully illustrate the entirety of the various provisions in Mr. and Mrs. White's estate—I've taken the liberty of drawing up this diagram. You'll want to examine it first, so please go ahead and digest it, if you will. Then I'll walk you through an analysis."

Jesse looked down at the paper that Tanner had slid across the desk to him. It was a confusing network of flow charts with puzzling arrows and dotted lines zigzagging across the length of it. Jesse studied it quietly for a few minutes. In the bottom right-hand corner, where all the lines led to, were two stick figures, one with Ricky's name beneath it and one with Jesse's name.

"It seems pretty straightforward to me," Ricky said, taking off his reading glasses and sliding the paper back.

What the fuck? Jesse thought. *This crap looks like hieroglyphics to me and makes as much sense as a treasure map drawn by a drunken, one-eyed pirate.* He was sure that Ricky was bluffing his ass off. Both Tanner and Ricky paused, looking directly at Jesse.

"Yeah, I'm ready for a little walk-through," Jesse said, barely raising his head up to meet their eyes.

"Excellent. Let me begin," Tanner said. "The Whites' estate can be considered to consist of three distinct asset types: personal property, life insurance, and investments."

For the next fifteen minutes, Tanner explained the structure of Archibald and Lizzy's complex estate, and Jesse's attention span struggled like it did in college French class. The split-dollar life insurance policies, probate process, and estate tax exemptions zipped over, under, and through Jesse's head. He was more prepared to conjugate verbs than he was to grasp the terms Tanner bantered about, but like any good salesman he could rapidly add numbers without a calculator: $500,000 in personal property, $2.75 million in her investment account, and a $1 million life insurance policy. Trying not to imagine over $4 million stacked up on the conference room table, a tingle formed in Jesse's belly and was beginning to fan out toward his groin, but he still wasn't sure if the sequences in the diagram came to him.

"As you can see by the illustration, Archibald and Elizabeth bequeathed all the assets of their trust, their insurance, their investments, and their property to their nephews, Richard and Jesse Few."

The thrill wave that had started in Jesse's belly and balls now ran straight through his chest and into his heart.

"Richard, let me explain your role as executor. Typically, if we run into any formidable complications, it's during the probate process, creditor claims, or pending lawsuits. I can't imagine that being the case with your aunt and uncle." Tanner took several minutes to tell Ricky what his duties were and how probate worked. Jesse knew he should have been paying attention, but he felt like running down the hallway, pumping his fist, and putting his head down on the conference table and bawling.

"Do either one of you have any questions?" Tanner asked.

"Not here. In my view, you've honored their legacy really fine," Ricky said, turning to Jesse. "How about you, little brother?"

Jesse's mind reengaged, and his first question was: How do you send a Harry & David fruit basket to dead people? Then another question popped out of his mouth without him considering it first. "What about Momma? Our aunt's older sister? Our mother?"

Ricky followed the words out of Jesse's mouth across the table, pivoting to look at Tanner.

"That's an interesting matter," Tanner said, again folding his hands across his files. "I think I've got some leeway to answer your question to an extent. Mrs. White and I had some recent conversations regarding the matter of her sister, your mother. When it came to alterations in her estate plan to make certain provisions for her sister, we discussed several options, but the issue was unresolved at the time of your aunt's death."

The charge of euphoria was still circulating throughout Jesse's body. There was so much Jesse needed to do with his half of the money, but he didn't give a crap what the dotted lines and stick figures said. Somehow, his mother was going to be the first one he helped.

~~~

They ended their meeting with a list of information that Ricky and Jesse both needed to provide Tanner, and afterward, Ricky asked Jesse to talk with him alone before he left. They decided to grab a couple of sandwiches at the deli in the office tower lobby.

Jesse watched his brother empty two packs of mayonnaise onto each half of his low-fat turkey sandwich.

"I've got a proposal for you," Ricky said. "I'll give you my half of Lizzy's personal property—the house in El Pueblo, all that stuff—and you'd use it to take care of Momma. There may even be a little upside in that for you."

"So you knew she—they—had their will done this way?" Jesse asked.

"Yeah, for the most part, anyways."

"The most part?"

"When Archie asked me to be their executor, he told me a few things." Ricky dipped his turkey sandwich into more mayo.

Jesse considered the macabre proposition that Ricky had just made him, and then studied his older half-brother and the big glob of mayonnaise he had on his cheek. He would have liked nothing more than to pummel him right there in the lobby for asking him to wager on when Momma would die. But for two hundred and fifty thousand dollars, he could be done with the son-of-a-bitch for good. He wondered if he'd ever feel the same remorse about his broken relationship with Ricky that he now felt toward Aunt Lizzy. Probably not; he was more likely to feel guilty for not giving a good shit if his brother were dead or alive.

"That sounds like the best thing for us to do. Of course, we'd have to get something in writing, put it on paper." Jesse handed his brother a napkin. "You got something on your face there."

"Thanks," Ricky said, wiping off his cheek.

"Not a problem. By the way, there's something I've been meaning to ask you about."

"What's that?"

"Momma is scared shitless of your real dad, Rex—claims he's almost chasing her like a stalker. She said he had a toaster cord that he used to beat her with. You got any clues about that?"

"Not a bit, but like I'm sayin', that's why you need this cash," Ricky said, diverting his eyes from Jesse and stuffing the last mass of rye bread, turkey, and mayo into his mouth.

"Did Momma ever take you to his grave? Where's he buried, by the way?"

"Arlington or Philly; I've got no idea," Ricky said. "I was a little kid when the whole war-hero accident stuff all happened."

Watching Ricky rip open a bag of chips and pour the remaining greasy crumbs into his mouth, Jesse remembered the burning smell of plastic as Ricky melted his favorite army men with his Creepy Crawler set, and Ricky sitting him on top of a burning pile of leaves, howling as the steel-blue smoke swirled around him. Perhaps Ricky's proclivity for random, red belly torture and vicious nut punches was inborn with Rex's sperm. Jesse had raged for years to swing the sharpened edge of the Excalibur sword across his brother's neck, which only fostered his bitter suspicion that providence killed Rex in a Jeep crash; retribution wasn't that simple.

"Hell, I need to find out where he's buried," Jesse said, "and make sure he's still damn dead."

23

JESSE'S RICHEST CLIENT, A SOUTH DAKOTA PUBLISHER
of porno magazines, told him once that there were two types of
fuck-you money. One was dubious. It meant you had enough cash
to grumble "fuck you" after you hung up the phone, followed by
a namby-pamby email. The other was the genuine fortune that
empowered you to unleash a "fuck you and shove it" face-to-
face with a mutineer's swagger. Deciding if he had a legitimate
shot at leaping off the corporate treadmill was harder for Jesse
than he expected. Two million dollars tax-free seemed like
fuck-you money—even the dubious type—but Jesse's finances
had gone way off the track. His personal assets resembled a
sunken train wreck. In the two weeks since his meeting with
Tanner, he'd been calculating the different possibilities.

PM's employee handbook was kept in a four-inch ring binder
and updated quarterly. As preparation for their "reduction in
workforce" campaign, Liliane had made sure all the senior staff
were trained in the company's retirement policy. That half-day
session was reinforced by reviewing it personally with the two

dozen or so people Jesse had personally cut; discussing the benefits of the company's prescription drug program was a reprieve after you eviscerated a person's career. Being fifty-five years old and having twenty years of service made an employee eligible for maximum retirement benefits and fully vested in any stock options. Jesse was six years from fifty-five, and because of the loss of tenure through two mergers, he was five years short of his 100 percent vesting. If Jesse left today, he'd lose the health insurance that still covered Denise and the kids, and he'd piss on nearly one million dollars worth of options. After he'd written all the scenarios up on a whiteboard, he'd almost concluded that he'd ride the hamster wheel at PM another six years and retire with full benefits at fifty-five, the double nickel.

Jesse had given Tanner's office the last piece of information that they had requested, and he was expecting the five hundred thousand dollar life insurance proceeds to settle into his brokerage account in the next few days. He hadn't talked with Bubba about the inheritance, as bad news flared up his CPA's hemorrhoids, but good news only made him search for impending catastrophe and gave him diarrhea. But he and Haymaker had spent hours pondering the possibilities. He'd given Hay permission to start remodeling his mother's house in downtown Dwyer, making it more suitable for the elderly and a live-in caretaker. They hadn't yet decided how to appease the plaid-pants gang. The local bankers still had Jesse by his fiscal short hairs, but he'd put in a contract with ten thousand dollars of earnest money—his last chunk of reserve cash—on Haymaker's townhouse and storage unit deal. According to his investment partner, the deal was "a whole herd of cash flow," and they savored being the hunter again rather than the prey.

His intention was to spend the afternoon locked away in his office confirming his numbers. Since it was PM's annual budget season, everyone would assume that he was merely working on his next iteration for Paris.

Coming back from a client luncheon, Heather handed Jesse a phone message from Kimberly—claiming to be a dissatisfied client—and told him that Jean-Paul wanted to see him immediately. He pitched Kimberly's message in the trash. Going toward the corner where the executive suites were located, Jesse expected the meeting to be another discussion on his sales budget.

When he reached the admin's desk, she got up to announce him. Jean-Paul and Liliane had adjoining offices and shared a French administrative assistant. Walking into his boss's office, he was surprised to find Liliane seated next to Jean-Paul at his small conference table. Jean-Paul usually spared him the grief of negotiating with the stubborn controller during the preliminary rounds of budget preparation.

"Good afternoon. Thank you for coming by so soon," Jean-Paul said. "Please, have a seat. Everything is good? Yes?"

Jean-Paul's formal tone and Liliane's presence made him sag, praying he wasn't going to have to provide them more names for layoffs.

"Yes, sure. Everything is fine," Jesse said, waiting to sit down. "I didn't bring my budget folder. Do I need to go back and grab it?"

"No, that won't be necessary," Jean-Paul said. "Go ahead and take a seat."

"Okay, yes, sir." Jesse eased down into the stiff-backed office chair, dreading the deceitful process that made him feel like a McCarthy-era informer.

"Jesse, we have some serious topics to discuss with you this afternoon, and maybe even some tough questions for you."

"I understand," Jesse said, fidgeting, uncomfortable with the hardness of the seat bottom. "I'll do what I can."

"As you know, Millard has left the company."

"Yes, sir," Jesse said, well aware Millard's career crashed when Liliane uncovered he was banging an accounting clerk, sending her naked pics through the company email, and then refusing to put her on Liliane's layoff list.

"So, you see, there is an opening for the director, the head of manufacturing."

"Right, right, yes." Jesse was starting to relax, thinking that they were going to ask him his opinion about a possible replacement.

"It has been decided to combine the oversight of both the manufacturing and your sales and marketing role. We'd like you to consider this new position."

Jesse now sat up straight and moved to the edge of the chair.

"That's very flattering and most definitely appreciated. It'd be a tough task, but it could be done."

"That's good." Jean-Paul turned to Liliane. The craggy CFO pressed her lips together and shifted her body in an angle away from the table.

"Unfortunately," Jean-Paul continued, "in examining our profit requirements and the need for a global synergy of resources, we need to eliminate some positions, head count, definitely in your sales group and then the manufacturing group, once you assume control in your new role."

Unfortunately for Jesse, as soon as he heard the word "unfortunately" he knew eliminations were coming; it was the canned layoff phrase. No wonder the corporate fishwife was in here.

"That truly is unfortunate. I don't really know what to say," Jesse said, the sudden knot in his lower shoulder blades sinking him back. There was no point in arguing, because there was no changing anyone's mind. Besides, the mind that would've needed changing was eating *foie gras* in Paris right now. "What sort of positions?"

"It hasn't been officially determined, but we need to start by cutting one more regional sales manager and go to two," Jean-Paul said.

"There's a package?"

"*Oui*. Yes. Of course." Jean-Paul handed Jesse the boiler-plate termination letter and release along with an outline of the severance being offered.

Jesse had looked at so many of these over the past couple of years that it only took him a couple of minutes to scan the document and find the highlights. It was generous, but he couldn't sit across the table from one of his colleagues, another Ralph Rigget, and shatter his world. Paris saw his workmates as names and numbers on a page, but he knew about Ralph's college tuition payments and his wife's biopsy. He wanted to see if he could get any more added to the package; after all, Liliane wasn't going to cook him and eat him just for asking.

"Quite frankly, this is a bit disappointing, considering the number of years they've served the company," Jesse said. Knowing the Frenchman's fear of American lawyers, especially discrimination lawsuits, he added, "And their age."

Liliane looked at Jean-Paul, and then she finally spoke.

"What about the reports? The expenses?" Liliane said, a rise of anger in her voice, tapping a file she had lying on the table.

"His two Florida trips?"

"*Ça ne fait rien,*" Jean-Paul curtly said to her, causing her to throw up her hands.

Jesse realized that Liliane had come prepared to fight him on the layoffs, and she'd brought a weapon of her own. She didn't have the same ammunition that she'd used against Millard—naughty emails to a chubby accounting clerk—but she had Jesse for padding his expense reports. Jesse didn't fully understand what Jean-Paul said to her, but he hoped it neutralized her enough before Liliane tried to club him in the head and stuff him in a boiling pot.

Sitting in the executive suite, a corner office far removed from the thousands of workers who relied upon PM to feed their families, the stress squeezed Jesse's brow, the heaviness making it feel like his eye sockets were bulging. He wanted to be finished traveling every week but never really going anywhere, working hard each month to make or miss a sales goal only to have it reset at the start of the next month, and most of all, he was done operating the guillotine for PM's reign of terror. Now was the time to peel off the hood of the corporate executioner; he was ready to revolt.

"*No mas.* I can't decide how to split the baby one more time. I'm done serving cake and lopping off heads," Jesse said.

A vacant look was their reply.

"Sorry if I confused you, but I think I have a reasonable option, which I'd like for you to consider," Jesse continued, grabbing the reins of the conversation. "Doyle and Dawson are good, solid producers. Because of the cutbacks, they're out there working the territory themselves, selling and producing week in and week out. You know Stan Banfield, our southeast regional manager?"

"*Oui*, of course," Jean-Paul said.

"He's my best guy, top-notch, Wharton MBA, the whole deal. He's got more manufacturing experience than me. He came from that side of the business. I've got him listed as my successor. I think you should give him the job, the new role over sales and manufacturing."

"I don't understand," Jean-Paul said, leaning across the table toward Jesse while Liliane relaxed in her chair, folding her arms.

"Jean-Paul, I'm sorry, but my passion for this stuff has faded. I'm reducing myself from the workforce," Jesse said, a warm lightness now pouring over his head and flowing throughout his body.

"What are you saying? Are you sure?"

"Yes, I guess I am. How do you say it? I'm *fini*," Jesse said with a content smile.

"Can you give me another option? Would you reconsider? Take some time off? A sabbatical, maybe?"

"I don't think so. I'm a million miles past the place that a sabbatical can cure."

"But Stanley? Is he the right man?"

"Like I said, he's got the resume. He'll be cheaper than me, especially after that big raise I was going to ask for. Plus, you won't have to relocate him."

"I suppose we could consider him, *oui*."

"I have six weeks of vacation banked, so give me the same severance package here," Jesse said, pushing the termination letter back across the table to Jean-Paul. "But start it after you pay for my six weeks of vacation. And keep paying my health insurance premiums for another eighteen months. I'll help Stan any way I can. That sounds fair, doesn't it, Jean-Paul?"

"*Oui*, very, *très bon*," Jean-Paul said, sticking out his hand. "I'm so sorry it ended this way. I've enjoyed working together." Shaking Jean-Paul's hand, Jesse gave a short nod to Liliane. Fuck-you money or not, he was now unemployed.

24

TEN DAYS OF GAINFUL UNEMPLOYMENT MADE JESSE feel like he was going through menopause: mood swings, night sweats, and memory lapses. Every morning he got up—either earlier or later than normal—dressed for work, minus socks, and commuted downstairs to his home office, pretending to finish up a few projects for Jean-Paul, but spending more time preparing for his upcoming fantasy baseball draft.

After he told Bubba about his inheritance and his unplanned retirement, Bubba had convinced Jesse to sign up for a mini-triathlon, claiming that training would take the edge off his transition. He'd run for something besides an airplane, for the first time since high school, spent more money on a bike than he did his first car, and undergone a stroke assessment at the YMCA with Doreen, the cute and sassy swimming instructor. He still wasn't sure where he summoned enough courage to wear a Speedo in public.

The benefit of his self-inflicted career crisis was that when Amie invited Jesse and Momma to attend her senior recital and the party afterwards, he told her that he'd actually be able to attend. He was looking forward to it, despite it involving an encounter with his ex-mother-in-law.

Yet none of this activity was making his new routine seem normal; it was like the clock was stuck. At least when he dialed in for his conference call with Ricky and Tanner, it provided him with a concrete objective and a sense of sanity to the day. Jesse understood conference calls.

After a few minutes of Ricky's awkward banter, Tanner moved to the purpose of their call. "The life insurance proceeds have been paid. Were there any issues with that?"

"None here," Jesse said. The money had settled in his brokerage account the Monday after he quit his job, and he anxiously checked the performance of his stocks every thirty minutes.

"Not a problem on this end; it's out on the street," Ricky said.

"Very well. Moving on," Tanner said, "I'm in receipt of the executed copies of your formalized equalization agreement."

"That's good to know," Jesse said. Soon after their meeting in Jacksonville, Ricky and he signed their deal to give Jesse all of the proceeds from the sale of their aunt's personal property in exchange for him supporting their mother. The fact that his half-brother, as executor, was responsible for inventorying and selling the property made Jesse wary. "How's the inventory list coming?"

"I've been done with that for a long while," Ricky said. "Just waiting on the probate thing to be over so I can start selling the stuff. Don't get all antsy-pantsy."

"In regards to the matter of the probate, we've placed the Notice to Creditors," Tanner said, "and we received several demands for payment."

"What sort of demands for payment?" Ricky asked.

Jesse listened, clicking through spring training reports on his computer, searching for fantasy baseball sleepers.

"There are a few that are for unpaid household services—pool cleaning, air-conditioning repair—which are fairly common; however, we have some that are rather substantial."

"Just how substantial we talking here?"

"We haven't verified the proof of debt, but there's a $62,000 claim for unpaid medical bills from a plastic surgeon in Orlando, and Archie's business partners have a $300,000 claim for unreimbursed life insurance premiums, which I must say, I warned your aunt about."

"That's gonna make a dent in that personal property cash," Ricky said, adding his chronic snicker. "But it ain't too bad. We got the investment dough."

Jesse squelched a "fuck you, Ricky" in the middle of their phone call, letting somebody else make the prick's day. The way he figured it, he was still collecting $1.5 million and shedding his half-brother. The creditor's claims on the estate would put a crimp on any reasonable plan to salvage their old mill loan; it would mean choosing between rescuing a dying deal with Bertram and the plaid-pants gang or joining the Great Recession scavengers and closing on Haymaker's storage unit and townhouse package.

"We've also received correspondence from a local personal injury attorney." Tanner stopped and cleared his throat before resuming. "Evidently, several months before your aunt's passing, she was involved in an altercation at the golf course, and allegedly, she ran over an individual, a jogger, with her golf cart. The plaintiff is an oral surgeon from Chicago who was visiting his parents, and apparently he's filed a five-million-dollar personal injury lawsuit against Mrs. White and now her estate."

Ricky embarked on a tirade against ambulance-chasing lawyers and personal injury swindles. Jesse exited the fantasy baseball site and sat up straight in his chair.

"Richard, I truly understand your sentiment," Tanner said after Ricky ended his rant. "Nonetheless, factually speaking, probating her will has opened up her estate to the plaintiff's attorney, and in your role as executor, you have certain fiduciary responsibilities. Given the current situation, I strongly advise waiting two years before distributing any further funds to her heirs, which includes not only the personal property but the investment account, too."

"Did you just say wait two years?" Jesse asked, clenching his teeth and his butt cheeks.

"Yes, Mr. Few, I did. That will allow sufficient time for the insurance company to settle the claim, feasibly within the half-a-million-dollar policy limits, and the statute of limitations to pass. Any action other than that would only exacerbate the potential charges of inappropriate conveyance."

Tanner went on explaining insurance defense, policy limits, and something called subrogation, but Jesse was scrambling—his life of semi-retirement had crashed after ten days. There was no chance of returning to his old job after Liliane filled it with a cheaper replacement, and he'd be forced to complete a resume for the first time since college graduation, when he had a scraggly beard and woke up each morning with bong hits rather than Starbucks.

The call ended with Tim Tanner promising to send them a letter outlining the unforeseen hold up in their aunt's estate, and Jesse tumbling through his desk drawers for the stack of business cards he'd gathered over his career. The options did laps around the inside of his skull. Sending out a resume in this economy was futile. When he was at PM, he got so many unsolicited applicants, he stopped opening them. There was always consulting. Jean-Paul could be his first client. The slang for "bankrupt" burst into his mind like hurdles around a track: dead broke, flat broke, stone broke. He needed aspirin and maybe a run, a long run, to like Cancun.

The doorbell rang, and he knew he'd have to answer it. Momma and Haymaker were watching *The Price is Right*, impervious to his unfolding disaster. The pace of the day was beginning to resemble work. Jesse hoped it was more files from Jean-Paul, and not more bad news from Tanner, Bertram and the bank, or his mortgage company, wondering how a piss-poor salesman was going to afford the payments on an eight-hundred-thousand-dollar loan.

Opening the front door, Jesse expected to see a chunky guy in a brown uniform holding out a pen with a package tucked under his arm. Instead, he saw a pair of oversize tortoise sunglasses and taut, tan legs flowing out from under a white miniskirt.

"Surprise," Kimberly said, taking off her sunglasses.

"Damn, girl, this is a surprise," Jesse said, steadying himself with the door. "I was going to call you, but I wasn't sure it was cool, mid-divorce and all. How are you doing?"

"I'm just peachy," Kimberly said. "I hate ambushing you like this, but I heard about what happened at PM and I thought, 'Oh my God, how weird.' I was worried sick. I haven't heard from you in almost forever. Are you okay?"

"Just great, and I know I should've called. I really was, but I had to turn in my company cell phone. Not having it anymore is almost like going into the witness protection program."

"So, seriously, what are you going to do? Do you have another job?"

"Actually, I'm starting my own consulting business. I think PM is gonna be my first client, which is weird itself." Jesse detected her orange-blossom fragrance, and her black stretch top was reminiscent of the outfit she'd worn on their second date. The lunch they'd never finished. That afternoon in Buckhead, when they peeled off clothes in front of the window, naked, twenty stories above the traffic on Peachtree Street. He felt the pulse of an erection. "You see, my aunt died all of a sudden, and I've been taking care of my mother here at the house."

"Your mother lives with you? I didn't know your mother was living."

"Yeah, she was living in downtown Dwyer when she got sick, but it's getting better. I'm getting it under control."

"I guess there's another whole side to you that you kept from me." Kimberly advanced toward the threshold, progressing closer into Jesse's space, and shifted from catty catching up. "So you weren't going to call me or text me? Just throw me out with the white trash?"

"No, of course not. I hate it, but I've had a lot of stuff going on," Jesse said, opening the door wider, after he considered hiding behind it. "I'm sorry. What do you want me to say?"

Kimberly stepped into his living room. "I want you to say that I mean something to you besides a part-time piece of ass. Try saying you love me."

"Hey, sweetie, it's not about you; it's me, my problems." Jesse moved toward her, straight into her blast.

"You son of a bastard, you didn't just say that." Kimberly held her hand up to stop him. "Like this is some kind of high school breakup and you're going to ask for your goddamn CDs back. I gave up my marriage for you. I've got a son to take care of, and you painted yourself up to be some big wheeler-dealer who had it all figured out."

"Things change, people and situ—"

"You know what your, and every other old geezer's, problem is?" Kimberly said, glowering and pointing a finger at him. "You pop your little blue pills and have your little sunset moments, thinking you're back in the game, but you don't want women your own age. No, you want to get rid of their flabby asses or floppy whatevers and go after the young ones. The thing is, we don't really exist to you. We make ourselves so shallow and easy, and we treat each other like bitches to compete for you. But at the end of it, we're nothing to you but a leftover toy from last year's birthday party."

Fighting the impulse to bolt out the door and go for a run in his khakis and dress shirt, Jesse simply let her vent, defying the reflex to question how it felt tossing Nick aside or if she enjoyed seeing Marky-Mark in Houston.

"Guess what?" Kimberly bit her lip, holding back the tears. "You'll never be young again, no matter how many pills you take or hours you spend in the gym—your butt is drooping just like all of us, every damn second. You know I'm right, don't you... you...you...pussy weasel?"

Sweat and tears fused on Kimberly's cheeks. Her trembling chin made Jesse wish he could annul their afternoon tryst at the Ritz, or ignore her flattery the first night they met at the museum, never playing the game of schoolyard boy-girl chase. But he knew that was as useless as fixing their failed romantic partnership or expecting to receive her forgiveness.

"Look, Kimberly, I deserve everything you said, but please—"

"Shut up, you ass wipe." She turned and strode out the door, hollering over her shoulder. "You're done in this business. I'm so telling your old boss about our little *liaison*. You better get used to handing out shopping carts at Walmart."

Jesse watched the sway of her miniskirt as she strutted away, wondering how close he'd come to burying his Denise dreams and who would forget whom first.

Kimberly backed her car up a few feet and tore through the lawn, swerving past the magnolia tree, peeling out onto the road. Jesse was relieved she didn't give him the finger and do doughnuts in his front yard, but he didn't doubt her intention of speaking to Jean-Paul. Implicitly threatening the French about their relationship would be simple. His consulting business exploded on the launch pad, but this day was feeling more like a typical workday: lost deals, irate customers, and failed ideas.

His cell phone chimed for an incoming text message; it was from JJ:

Ok if Mel comes 2 the recital??

JJ's request seemed benign; it was a free world as people loved to claim.

Sounds good.

That was the least complicated thing he'd done all morning. At least someone was happy.

25

TWO YEARS AGO WAS THE LAST TIME JESSE ATTENDED a party with Denise's parents. He'd come home after a grueling road trip to a house full of her relatives there for her father's eightieth birthday party; the party was a surprise to them both. Jesse was sullen the whole evening, and when Mary Hill, Jesse's former mother-in-law, nagged him for hogging the cashews, he screamed, "Who wants a handful of my nuts," flung the bowl across the room, and stomped off to the bedroom. The party after Amie's recital was going only slightly better.

Denise and Jack attended the recital along with Luke and Mary Hill. Jesse and Momma sat in the back and didn't see JJ and Melanie in the school auditorium. After the recital, they all gathered at their old house, and when JJ showed up with Melanie, wearing the Royal Street earrings, Denise pulled Jesse into the kitchen for a secret trial.

"Denise, look right here at his text message," Jesse said, holding up his cell phone as evidence. "It just says recital. That's it. How was I supposed to know he meant party, too?"

His ex-wife's normally full, curvy lips were flattened out

thin, transforming her "don't be a dumbass" frown into her furious scowl.

Jesse recognized that enraged expression from the night of Luke Hill's party. After the guests had left and she'd cleaned up the cashews, Denise and he had a bitter fight, and later, lying in bed, they decided to separate, sobbing in each other's arms. Tonight, he doggedly continued his defense. "Besides, it's not like we're harboring an escaped convict or aiding and abetting a murderer on the run. Plus, our son really appreciates catching a break for once."

"I bet he does. He's been a real a-hole ever since that creepy thing happened with his tires and he stopped going to those meetings." Pressing her scowl tighter, Denise snatched a wooden spoon from the drawer, slamming it shut. "He still has to go to court, you know. You and he act like the attorney made that go away, but he didn't because he can't. I'm sure Melanie's father has the date circled on his calendar even if you don't. What's the pastor going to do if he finds out she's lying and we were in on it?"

"Technically, she's not lying. Melanie is also Amie's friend, so it's not like she's being totally dishonest about being at a friend's house."

"Oh, I forgot I was dealing with an expert on the subjectivity of truth."

"I'm going to ignore that. Let's not blow this up. This is a big deal for Amie." Jesse had never been prouder of his daughter. She played two guitar solos, flawless versions of Pink Floyd's "Wish You Were Here" and Duane Allman's "Little Martha," before two hundred silver-haired and pimply-faced listeners, accomplishing a feat with a poise that he never could have dreamt of doing. "And JJ and Melanie are talking to your dad, making it easier for him to ignore your mother. I'm simply trying to make it a pleasant evening for everyone."

"Whatever," Denise said, turning around to stir the potato salad, meaning the judge had ruled and the verdict was in—Jesse was guilty of being a jerk, a repeat offender. "Jack is out on the porch grilling. The sooner we eat, the faster she gets home. Why don't you go check on your mother and go see what trouble mine is causing?"

Now the sentence had been handed down—ex-mother-in-law service, worse than solitary.

Jesse took a large drink of wine and sidled his way out of the kitchen.

In the living room, Momma was sitting quietly, and Jesse took a seat next to her. He'd taken her to the beauty parlor to get her hair done, and she was having one of her good days. JJ was cuddled next to Melanie on the sofa, enjoying a good-natured conversation with Luke Hill about the Braves. Amie was waiting for her boyfriend and hovered between the living room and the front door. Mary Hill was patrolling the room, pretending to sort through magazines as she indiscreetly scanned a stack of papers someone had left on the coffee table.

"Did y'all hear about those tornadoes in Texas this morning?" Mary Hill asked, pacing over to the window. She separated two slats of the venetian blinds. "Luke, would you just come and look at this black cloud?"

"Honestly, I'm all too familiar with black clouds, and I don't think I need to see another one," Luke Hill said from his seat on the sofa across the living room. "I'm talking to my grandson and his pretty girlfriend."

"That's one hellacious-looking storm headed this way," Jack said, coming in from the deck with a platter of grilled chicken. "I got done just in time before supper and I both got whooshed away. I thought I saw a couple of hens blowing past the house. Almost plucked one out of the air—talk about your free-range chicken." He laughed at his own joke and headed toward the kitchen.

"Very funny, but there could be a twister fixing to hit." Mary Hill yanked on the draw cord, trying to pull up the blinds.

A cell phone started ringing, an old car horn tone, and Melanie pulled away from JJ, reaching down for her purse on the floor. She peeked at the screen, hit the mute button, and dropped the phone back in her purse. Nibbling her chipped and peeling manicure, she glanced at JJ.

"Don't tell me," JJ said. "It's the family Pharisee tracking you down."

The old car horn sounded again, and Melanie hushed it without checking the screen.

"We might need to take cover," Mary Hill said, now ricocheting around the family room. "Shouldn't we turn on the news, go to the basement, or something?"

"When I was a young girl, whenever it was really storming badly, my mother always made us open all the windows in the house." Momma set her wineglass down and leaned closer to Melanie. "She was always frightened, but my daddy never was scared of anything. And I remember my sister, Elizabeth, liked to go outside and look at the sky change from blue to gray to black and then back again."

"Raymond isn't here yet," Amie announced, coming in from the kitchen. "Mom thinks that we should probably hold dinner."

"That settles it. Come on, Luke. Grab a couple of those throw pillows for cushioning, and let's go to the cellar, just to be safe," Mary Hill said, shaking her head. "Aren't y'all coming?"

The pinging sound of hail and hard rain hitting the glass began, and the chimes on the porch clanged loud and long.

"I haven't heard of any warnings. Most of the time, this passes by in thirty minutes." Jesse was determined not to let Mary Hill's panic wreck their family gathering. It was always the first steer startled that caused the stampede. He tried to be a man who never whined about life being unfair, despite how arbitrary the results seemed. But he couldn't help but feel a sting noticing how Mary Hill had aged differently—better—than Momma. From what Jesse observed she was more agile, physically and mentally, than his mother, even though they were nearly the same age. Regardless of her emotional tendency to be pessimistically petty, she probably had a higher quality of life than Momma. A few minutes separated on different floors from Mary Hill was a good idea. "If we hear a noise like an approaching train and see a house fly past, we'll take cover."

"Amie, darling, I'll put two of these over my ears, and one over your grandmother's face; that ought to protect us all," Luke Hill said, taking a few of the small pillows off the sofa and trailing his wife as she disappeared down the basements steps.

Melanie jumped as a burst of wind battered the side of the house, making it groan. Her cell phone sounded again, a soft sound of piano keys. She pulled her phone out of her bag, read an incoming text message, and dropped the phone back in her bag.

"What is it now?" JJ asked.

"That was my mother," Melanie replied. "Daddy is freaking out."

"That's just great," JJ said, his Adam's apple bobbing back and forth. "What's he gonna do, send Blade after me again?"

Jesse was unsure of who Blade was, but watching the tense exchange between JJ and Melanie reminded him of being on an awkward double date.

"You know, I had all those cheese and crackers earlier, so I'm really full. I don't think that I really can eat dinner." Melanie twisted her long blonde hair into a knot and pulled her ponytail tighter.

"Those are the most beautiful earrings I think I've ever seen," Momma said. "Where did you get them?"

"Thank you, Mrs. Gennifer," Melanie said, tilting her head, showing off the teardrop turquoise stones surrounded by cut diamonds and set in yellow gold. "Your grandson, the romantic, got these for me, just because."

JJ squirmed in his seat, the earlier glee robbed from his face.

"Those are nice," Jesse said, lightly punching his son in the arm. He was glad to see Melanie showing off the gift he'd intended for Kimberly during their New Orleans rendezvous. Perhaps JJ could accomplish with the gift of the earrings what Jesse couldn't. "You've got very refined taste."

"They set off your eyes perfectly," Momma said. "Almost like they were made for you."

"I think they were, in another lifetime. They speak to me in French sometimes. I wish I could understand them," Melanie said. "I wonder what's going on with that storm. You think it's okay to drive?"

"I remember one time during a storm, when Mother made Elizabeth and me get in the closet. We were little girls. We still had pigtails in our hair," Momma said. "I was so scared of the wind. I remember Elizabeth telling me to hold her and everything would be fine. She made a rhyme of it; 'Hug me tight; it'll be all right.' Elizabeth was always so brave, so strong."

"Mrs. Gennifer," Melanie said, almost whispering, taking Momma by the hand. "Your sister wants to tell you something— you know, from the other side."

Jesse stifled a snort and leaned back.

"What? What is it?" Momma fixed herself on Melanie's eyes.

"She says she saw the shining light; it was beautiful, and now she's fine. She's at peace and don't worry about her."

"Can I talk to her? Can I tell her 'I love you'?" Momma asked, tears rolling down her cheek.

"Always. She knows and she loves you, too." Melanie put her other hand over the top of her and Momma's hands.

"You hear that? She's at peace," Jesse said, smiling and patting Momma's knee, hoping that their spontaneous séance helped his mother, somehow. "That's good to know."

"Your aunt wants to tell you something, too, Mr. Few." Melanie turned to Jesse.

"Okay," Jesse said, clearing his throat.

"She wants you to know that she'll always be grateful to you. You saved her, she says."

"I'm not sure how I saved her, but I'm thankful for her enabling me to help Momma."

"No, not your mother. You saved your aunt. You saved Aunt Lizzy. She's telling me there were so many other choices you could have made, but you didn't."

"I'm not sure what to make of all that." Jesse nodded his head. Melanie had obviously heard enough from Momma and JJ to assemble an ambiguous clairvoyant experience. At least it gave his mother an opportunity to soothe her grief.

"Mrs. Gennifer, there's someone else there, but I don't like him, the way he feels. I'm sorry." Melanie turned back to face Momma. "I don't want to talk to him; he's so red with rage."

"It's Rex. Get away from him, if you can, sweetie," Momma said, pulling Melanie's hand to her chest, her voice quivering. "I've been trying for as long as I can remember—too long."

"I want to, but he's yelling at me. It's like he's trying to grab me all over," Melanie said, her face contorting.

"Dad?" JJ said, turning to Jesse.

Jesse strained to hear his mother's reply.

"It's all my fault. I sent them. I prayed they'd find him." Momma let go of Melanie's hand and closed her eyes.

Before anyone else could speak, Amie walked into the living room.

"Raymond is here, so Mom is serving dinner. After all, this is *my* soirée," Amie said. "Granny Hill and Grandpa came out from hiding. She'd just as soon get carried to the Lord in a swirling cloud than die of starvation."

"Amie, I really appreciate you having me, but I've got to go." Melanie stood up and smoothed out the wrinkles in her dress. "I'll speak to your mom on my way out. Mr. Few and Mrs. Gennifer, it was nice seeing you. I hope I didn't upset anyone."

"Oh, no, we're fi—" Jesse started to say.

"You're eighteen now. When does your damn daddy stop ruining our lives?" JJ asked, interrupting his father, the cords in his neck stretched taut.

"JJ, please, don't make it any worse." Melanie grabbed her purse, clinging to it tightly.

"Worse? It can't get any worse for us. I'm done with all this sneaking around bullshit."

"What am I supposed to do?" Melanie asked as if she were lost and asking for directions home.

"Make up your mind; it's that simple." JJ rushed toward the front door. "I'll meet you by your car."

"In the middle of a downpour?" Melanie hurried after him.

Coping with a breakup was an inevitable fact of young adult life. Jesse realized JJ was learning that genuine heartache wasn't like a country song, it didn't end in less than three minutes. The earrings and his suggestion of the clandestine church meetings only proved his parenting skills were amateur. Not all fatherly advice was worth the cost, and he was culpable for prolonging his son's misery. After watching him struggle with Melanie, Jesse wasn't certain whether he was teaching JJ how to ride a bike without wearing a helmet or keeping him on training wheels far too long.

The front door banged closed, shaking the house harder than the spring thunderstorm.

"Oh, my," Momma said. "What was that all about?"

"That's a long story, Grand," Amie said, extending a hand to help her grandmother up. "And I'd tell you at dinner, but my mom would probably give me the evil eye. You think JJ is getting pelted by hail?"

"Yeah, let's see if we can find another discussion topic," Jesse said, following Momma and Amie into the dining room. In truth, Jesse realized the kid next door showed his son how to ride a bike while he was out of town, and if he inadvertently taught JJ anything, it was from observing his relationships with women and the manipulative choices he made. Unfortunately for JJ, practicing life lessons wasn't constrained to the safety of the driveway, and he was risking an eruption from Melanie's father, who could only be deceived for so long. Wishing that the pining young couple would discover new infatuations was an impractical solution. Haymaker would suggest flying in a Russian girl to seduce his son, but Jesse needed him to investigate this Blade character who JJ mentioned. The best hope was that JJ would resolve his court case before he went crazy or Pastor Sonny struck back.

26

JESSE'S DECISION TO BANKRUPT THE OLD MILL partnership and auction off his house was like getting vaccinated for an overseas vacation. You rolled up your sleeve, turned your face to the wall, and winced through the pain, knowing that enduring the prick of the needle allowed you to lounge on an exotic beach with an umbrella drink in your hand without the threat of contracting typhoid fever and dying in a foreign hospital. With a twenty-five-hundred-dollar check to Haymaker's divorce lawyer and a few scrawls on the papers, their partnership filed for bankruptcy, parked their loan in the bank's mahogany boardroom, and jilted the old mill, leaving it betrayed and abandoned—again. The next time he saw Bertram at the golf course, it would be embarrassing for them both, but there was no inoculation for social discomfort. That situation would require gumption.

The company auctioning off his house and the majority of his man toys preferred that Jesse be dead—"estate sales always attract a greedy crowd." Instead, they settled on him moving out. His gun collection and Haymaker moved into one of the vacant townhouses their new partnership, Scrounger LLC, acquired, and Momma and he moved back to her freshly remodeled home in downtown Dwyer.

Beyond the quartz countertops and stainless steel appliances, Jesse had decided to widen the doorways and modify Momma's bathroom, understanding that his mother's health would continue to decline. They were getting used to different surroundings and a different routine. He hoped that today wasn't typical because by the time he had put Momma in bed and kissed her on the forehead, he was exhausted. But for the past two hours, every time he had been about to fall back asleep, he'd hear creaking rafters and a humming refrigerator, and he'd be wide awake again.

At his old house out in the country, when Jesse lie in bed in the middle of the night unable to sleep, he could hear the faint whistle of the freight trains in the distance. It was a soothing, pensive call that reminded Jesse that life's troubles were far away, out of reach. At his new house with Momma in downtown Dwyer, the railroad tracks were a quarter mile away. The shrill burst of the whistle screaming in the dark, cutting through the night, created sleepless nights. Flopping around in bed like a fish on the dock, Jesse pictured the train making circles around downtown and the cruel conductor blasting the train's sadistic trumpet to make sure everyone else in Dwyer was awake.

He lie there wondering how he went from living in a small mansion and screwing in his hot tub to living with his mom and sleeping by himself, like he was a horny teenager again. All he was missing from his new room were the *Playboy* magazines Mr. Billy used to give him, the Farrah Fawcett poster on the wall, and the stolen copy of *Fear of Flying* he kept hidden in his drawer. Maybe, Jesse thought, the post-orgasm release that always made him drowsy after sex would help him fall asleep, but he couldn't get the right fantasy going in his mind. He hadn't fully recovered from Kimberly's ambush. Nearly sleeping, he was having the vague sketch of a dream about seeing Doreen, the dark-haired swim coach from the YMCA, walking on the beach.

Close to Jesse's age, Doreen's auburn hair, brown eyes, and dark tan reminded him of the perfect cinnamon bun. Jesse enjoyed watching her on the pool deck, showing the class the proper stroke technique or exhorting Jesse to finish those extra laps. Over the past few weeks, Jesse and Doreen had begun chatting regularly after his workout, and he had told her a little about his situation with Momma. In his dream, she was hunting for seashells, and as he got closer, he noticed her long, white dress rippling in the ocean breeze. He could see her tan lines underneath.

The first shriek from Momma's room snapped him upright in bed.

The second shriek and the crash sent him fumbling for his shorts and T-shirt.

Bolting down the hallway toward her bedroom, he flung her door open. In the odd amber glow of the streetlight shining through her window, Momma was cowering in the corner, her cries filling the master bedroom. Her bun had come undone, and her stark-white hair was sticking out all over. The bedside lamp was on the floor. He approached her in the corner, and she flinched; whatever had scared her was as real to her as the hardwood floor under his bare feet. She stopped screaming and looked up at him. For a few seconds, they didn't recognize each other.

"Momma," Jesse said softly.

"Preston? Is that you?" Momma asked, drawing back into the corner. "Where have you been? I thought you said he'd never bother me again. You promised me."

"It's me. It's Jesse."

"Stop him. Please don't let him get me." Her voice was feeble and hoarse from the shrieking.

"It's okay," Jesse said, reaching his hand out to her. It might have been the sparse light or the daze of sleep deprivation, but he felt others present in the room. "I won't let anyone get you."

"It's Rex, the devil," she said. "He tried to get in the bed with me, get up under my nightgown. He said he was tired of waiting, so he was taking back what was his. He told me to lie still and just shut up if I knew what was good for me."

"He's not here now," Jesse said, extending his arm farther. "He's long dead and gone."

"No, he's not gone. He's still got his black cord."

"Sure he's dead, fifty years ago, in a Jeep accident after the Korean War." Jesse took two steps closer, and it was as if he advanced to the edge of a chasm. He quickly closed his mind, shutting it out.

"You're wrong. Preston broke his promise...he's not dead."

"I don't think so, but I believe we should be sleeping—not debating—at this time of night," Jesse said, kneeling down and rubbing her shoulder. "It's just us moving you from my old house back to your house; it's got you out of sorts tonight."

"I wish that were so," Momma said, leaning her weight onto her son.

"Let's you and I go see if there's any good old black-and-white movies on." He raised her up off the floor and gave her a hug, gently rubbing her back. "We both could use a little Bette Davis or Joan Crawford right now."

Jesse led Momma into the den. A tension headache pinched the back half of his skull. Jesse understood that it was going to take more than a chair-height toilet and a walk-in shower to renovate Momma's crumbling mind, and he didn't know if he'd ever resolve her mysterious visions of Rex and his black cord. Flipping through the channels hoping to find *Mildred Pierce* or *All About Eve*—not *What Ever Happened to Baby Jane?*— Jesse recalled the sensation he'd felt in Momma's bedroom: two identities emerging from the void, one wicked and one loving. If Rex were the devil, that would make Preston her guardian angel, and the father-son bond meant Jesse had inherited the promise his birth father had made. He was bound to battle the same demon.

Another train passed by, and the bellowing horn penetrated the windows, invaded every room in the house, and burrowed deep into Jesse's mind. Momma was curled up, asleep on the sofa. Jesse could hear her delicate snores across the room. He wanted to reach for her, to be as near to her as her breath, but his arms betrayed him. They wouldn't leave his side. Closing his eyes, he finally dozed off.

27

AFTER TAKING MOMMA TO THREE DIFFERENT DOCTORS, Jesse had decided they were the same as automobile mechanics—show them all the same problem, and they all have a different fix. Her internist hedged and weaseled around any diagnosis, deferring to specialists. The young geriatric specialist hinted at a diagnosis of mild cognitive impairment, a relatively new term, but wrinkled his oily nose when Jesse asked if he was 100 percent certain. The neurologists offered up a distracted smile and a diagnosis of either the early stages of dementia or just plain old age, like Jesse and Momma were airline passengers choosing between the dried-up beef or the rubbery chicken. None offered a solution other than the drugs she was on, and none could explain the visions of Rex.

After three drives to Atlanta, three long waits, and three co-pays, Jesse still didn't have a clear understanding of the enemy that was devouring his mother. He hoped Doreen, the swim coach from the YMCA, would be his ally in the battle. She'd invited him to stop by her herb shop a couple of times, and after his frustrating appointments with the doctors and the latest Rex scare, he decided it was time to pay her a visit.

The old train depot she had converted into her store was just a short walk from Momma's house. Jesse felt eighth-grade-dance nervous as he pushed open the front door. He paused for a second, adjusting to the dark and a flutter he hadn't felt in years. Some type of Middle Eastern music that Jesse had never heard before was playing in the background, and perfumed incense was burning to cover the moldy smell.

"Hey, swimmer," Doreen said, walking out from the back. "It's good to see you. Welcome to the Herb Depot."

"Thanks. You've got a nice place here." As Jesse's eyes became accustomed to the light, he checked out the brown-eyed beauty in her flowing purple dress. Trying to play it cool and not get caught gawking, he looked up, pretending to admire the ceiling. "Wow, are those the original beams? I bet those have been in place since at least the turn of the last century. Amazing. How long have you been open?"

"Yeah, we really love the energy of the space. We opened two years ago, right after Thanksgiving. How's that for great timing? I always thought the economy was for other people," Doreen said, with a surprising dollop of cynicism. She came around the counter to straighten out a display, and her arms were moving non-stop like they did on the pool deck. "My partner says that we just need to trust our intuition—go with our gut."

"There's a lot to be said for that attitude," Jesse said, curious who this "partner" was. He'd never seen a wedding ring at the pool, but he'd never directly asked, either. He was trying to check out her ring finger, afraid that following her fluttering hands made it seem like he had a nervous tic.

"I guess. Right now, she's on a pilgrimage to Nepal with her husband, so I'm sure she'll come back with a whole new attitude and lots of wild ideas."

"Wow, Nepal. I haven't been there," Jesse said, the word "husband" increasing the tingling in his stomach. Since his divorce, and shamefully before, he'd been meeting women in cocktail lounges, airports, or the yellow pages—never in herb shops in the middle of the day. There was something different about Doreen beyond her spicy appeal that made him lose his James Bond-Casanova confidence, if he ever really had it. "I don't suppose they have to worry about getting a chair by the pool."

"Not hardly," she said, still buzzing about the store.

"So I've taken my mother to three different doctors, and to be honest, I couldn't compare them to witch doctors; that wouldn't be fair to natural medicine. Maybe like those oddball mechanics from Mayberry?"

"You mean Gomer and Goober, the Pyles?" Doreen asked with a wily grin. "They were cousins. Most people forget that. How old is your mother again?"

"She's eighty-two." If you'd asked Jesse that six months ago, he'd have had to stop, think, and then guess. But after the last couple of weeks, he'd memorized her birthday, her Social Security number, her allergies, and more intimate details about her medical history than ever. The lumpectomy she'd had twenty years ago but never mentioned to Jesse—information that Momma couldn't keep straight anymore—was only a small portion of the new weight Jesse carried.

"That's about when my father-in-law was diagnosed."

"Really," Jesse said, guilty of being more concerned about the existence of in-laws than their medical condition. He checked her ring finger again, and it was tan and bare.

"I guess, technically, he was my ex-husband's father. So does that make him my ex-father-in-law? Anyway, whatever. Excuse me." She walked past Jesse and brushed her hand across his back as she slid past him to get to a shelf. "Does she drink tea?"

"Every morning; she drinks it rather than coffee." Watching her study the items on the shelf in her loose-fitting long dress, Jesse felt a spark of pleasure flashing back to his dream of her fluttering beach dress.

"Lemon balm tea helps in calming nerves," Doreen said, picking up a greenish-yellow box. "I know my father-in-law would get really anxious and upset sometimes, especially when we changed his routine or at a certain time of day. I'd fix him a cup of lemon balm tea in the afternoon; it seemed to help smooth out the rest of the day until bedtime."

"I've noticed that with Momma, too, but she'd prefer a daiquiri or a whiskey sour at cocktail time. But let's try some of that, because we could sure use some smoothing out."

"I like you. You make quick decisions," Doreen warmly giggled, setting the two boxes of tea on the front counter.

"I always try to pay attention to the sage advice of experts," Jesse said, considering telling Doreen about the dead first husband who haunted his mother, but unsure what to truly say.

"Let's see what else we can come up with." Doreen moved back across the room to another shelf of bottles.

Jesse stood next to her, pretending to analyze the different herbs as intently as she was. Doreen selected ginkgo to help with her memory and St. John's wort to help with depression. He recognized a familiar one that he thought he'd seen Haymaker take a few times. Picking up the bottle, he showed it to Doreen. "What's this one do?"

"Goat weed?" She looked at him with a wide smile. "Goat weed? It sounds interesting."

"The other name for it is even far more interesting—horny goat weed," she said, grinning. "That makes it kind of self-explanatory, don't you think? I could give you a sample to try, if you wanted."

"No, I'm good," Jesse said, putting the bottle back on the shelf. "Appreciate the offer."

"I'll give you a rain check," Doreen said with a wink. "Back to your mother. The biggest thing you can do is keep her active for as long as you can—talk to her, take her on walks." Her velvety voice softly delivered every word. "Get her a day clock that shows the day of the week and not the hour. If you keep her engaged and involved, it'll help so much. Just spend time with her."

"I do appreciate it." Jesse was uncertain what the teas and herbs would do for Momma, but he was grateful to finally have a sense of control over what was happening to her. There was a cheerful optimism in the old train depot. He felt a slender trace of the passengers who'd passed through the station before him. They were a collection of fellow travelers, laden with bundles yet brimming with boundless enthusiasm, willing to confide their secrets to whomever they crossed as partial payment for their journeys.

"Figuring this thing out with my mother, it's made me feel, shit—helpless, I guess. Every morning, she wakes up as someone different. Surprise, I'm not your mom. I'm some crazy old woman who's stolen her body. Crap, it's been harder than solving a math problem with a slide rule. You don't know or maybe you do. I'm just trying to say thanks."

"You're more than welcome." Doreen stopped ringing up Jesse's purchases; her eyes narrowed, and her lips and cheeks beamed with grace. "It's why I'm here."

She looked back at the cash register, finishing her work.

"This is interesting music," Jesse said. A smooth baritone was reciting a lyric that Jesse couldn't recognize, and a joyful audience was repeating it; drums, guitars, and cymbals filled in behind them with an uplifting backbeat.

"It's a guy called Jai Das." Doreen handed him a CD that she had displayed on the counter.

"Cool. He's an intriguing-looking dude." A pony-tailed, middle-aged man in an orange T-shirt was on the cover, sitting cross-legged in front of a microphone with his eyes closed, seeming blissfully content.

"Very. He's chanting prayers to the Hindu gods."

"I'm not sure I could dance to it, but it kind of gets inside your head. I'd give it a ninety." All Jesse knew about Hinduism came from a few Bollywood movie clips and the polite Indian couple at the dry cleaners who had exotic pictures of crowned elephants hanging on the wall and eagerly handled his dirty clothes.

"He's holding a kirtan—a kind of concert—next weekend in Atlanta," she said, placing Jesse's items in a wrinkled paper bag.

"I'm pretty sure that I've never been to a kirtan."

"So, you know, you could. Would you like to go with me?" Doreen handed Jesse his bag of herbs and tea.

Jesse's eyebrows raised when he took the sack. He could imagine the bullshit he'd take from his golf buddies if they knew he'd been chanting to Hindu gods. If he ever went to church again, he'd probably get scolded by the Methodist preacher. He'd confided more of his feelings about Momma in thirty minutes than he ever had with Kimberly. Doreen had already seen him in his Speedo, practically naked, so Jesse figured why not finish the schoolyard game of you-show-me-yours-and-I'll-show-you-mine. Expose himself from the beginning. Besides, he could give back as much grief as his buddies could dish out, and Christmas and Easter were plenty enough to cover his ass in church.

"Yeah, I'd really like that." It wasn't a date to the dreaded eighth-grade dance, but it was the first relationship Jesse had started since he'd been divorced that hadn't begun with vodka or pinot grigio and involved the possibility of adultery or the vice squad. At least he was pretty certain that there were no awkward slow dances at a kirtan.

28

ONE OF THE ADVANTAGES OF OWNING YOUR OWN storage business was that you never had to decide what to throw away. Jesse had filled up two large units when he moved out of his old house, and now he was taking a load from Momma's house over to put into one of the smaller units. It was a mix of boxes left over from Granny Finch and some he had taken out of Momma's closet in the master bedroom. He probably should've taken most of it straight to the county dump, but when he came across a stack of Momma's high school yearbooks or his grandparents' wedding album mixed among the silver-plated teapot without a handle and the yellowed books of S&H saving stamps, he didn't have the heart to merely toss it all out. Maybe someday his grandchildren would want to know that their great-grandmother was named the best looking in the senior class of 1949 or see the shy smile of their great-great grandfather on his wedding day.

Distractedly fantasizing about his kirtan date with Doreen, he picked up the last load. The tattered box was the heaviest so far and smelled of mothballs. Jesse opened it up to see if he could lighten it up before moving it. Inside on top was a small green lockbox. Curious, he picked it up and shook it. Hoping it was forgotten stock certificates or an original version of the Constitution, he pulled out his pocketknife and easily popped open the lock; inside were several photographs and a worn manila envelope.

He thumbed through the old black-and-white pictures. Each one was of the same person, a young woman. Most of them were close-ups taken from different angles, and all showed cuts and bruises on her body. She looked like she'd been in a car accident, but Jesse didn't understand why someone would take pictures to preserve such an unpleasant event. The last photo was taken from a distance and showed the woman holding a baby in her arms, with a large bandage over her nose and a black eye. Jesse studied the woman and the background. Behind her was a boxy sofa that looked retro now but was probably fairly new at the time, and the woman was wearing a scarf to cover her hair curlers. Her face was slender, almost gaunt, emphasizing her high cheekbones and angular nose. Her eyes were hollow and spent, as if they'd been scorched. Then he recognized them both: his grandparents' living room was the backdrop and the young woman was Momma. He didn't recall ever hearing a story about her being in any kind of accident, but clearly, at one point, her nose had been broken and her body severely battered.

He opened the envelope and pulled out the paper inside. At the top it read, "Decree of Divorce." Scanning the document, he noticed the date of November 26, 1953, and the plaintiff, Gennifer Finch Sherman, and the defendant, Rex Clark Sherman. He flipped to the last page, saw Momma's signature, and fixed on the two brown spots dotting Rex's scrawling mark. A squeamish heat rushed down from the back of his throat. Jesse put the document back in its envelope, along with the pictures, and placed the lockbox on the passenger seat. He carried the rest of the keepsakes to the storage unit, pulled the rolling door down, and padlocked it shut.

Getting back into his car, Jesse considered his discovery. He realized the dates didn't match with the story he'd always been told about Rex's Jeep accident, and that he was probably the last in his family to know about the divorce, or worse. The bile simmered in his stomach. Reluctantly, he recalled Momma's first pleading phone call about the stranger in her back yard. At the end of last summer, he had few options for help, but now he could talk to Doreen about his new findings or somehow show the photographs to Melanie to see if her connection to the other side was genuine. Cranking the car, Jesse decided only Momma could tell him the truth behind the welts and the broken bones; he put it into drive.

When he reached her house, Jesse found his mother resting in one of the Adirondack chairs he had bought to go under the oak tree in the backyard. Sitting down next to Momma, he kept the green lockbox tucked under his arm. Jesse was lost on how to start an overdue conversation: a question, an accusation. He absorbed the scant afternoon breeze and the honeysuckle vines still wrapped around the fence.

"Did you get everything moved, Man-o?" Momma asked, using his childhood nickname that he hadn't heard her say in months.

"Yes, ma'am. I'm my own best storage customer," Jesse replied. Momma's hair was freshly washed and styled. She wore her tight silver ringlets like a headdress. His mind shifted to the photos of the battered woman in curlers.

"How about a cool drink? A peppermint iced tea? Isn't it nearly aperitif time?"

"Not just yet." The wrinkled face of the lady sitting next to him drew up tighter, beyond youthful and fresh to bleak and abused.

"I see you found the box that Daddy kept." Momma spoke with a certain resolve.

"I did." Jesse saw her watery eyes drain and turn frightened.

"That thing gave me nightmares, tormented poor Preston."

"You knew about the box?" Dark green and purple bruises spread across her ribs and torso. Her sharp nose, which linked generations of their family, became twisted and swollen.

"Of course, Daddy said we might need it someday."

"Why didn't you tell me?" As each wound on her battered body became sharper, Jesse's aging mother was being transformed to the abused young wife.

"Oh, Man-o. What would you've done?"

"I don't know," Jesse muttered. His earlier nausea stirred. "Something."

"I'm tired of running, done with being scared of it. I guess there's only one thing left for me to do." She reached her arms out, motioning with her fingers for her son to pass it over. Jesse placed the box in her slender hands. Easing the lid open, she trembled as she removed each photograph.

"That bastard and his black cord. I snuck out at dawn on a Saturday morning, after he broke my nose, then beat me and...I left him passed out in that smelly front room, walked through the frozen sludge with your brother on my hip. He wasn't six months old, but I know he saw it all, felt it somehow. I went down to the Philadelphia train station, neighbors gawking through the window, never helping. Devil's Pocket, for sure. I scraped up snow and ice at the train station to fight the swelling. I didn't have the money for a sleeper ticket. I didn't hardly doze off for three nights. I wore dark glasses and a scarf, convincing myself that people might think I was a Hollywood starlet trying not to be noticed. I got back to Dwyer two days before Thanksgiving, Momma and Daddy hollering like I was the prodigal son returned. But when Daddy saw my nose and my black eye, he got scary quiet.

"It didn't take him no time to take the pictures, go see the judge, come up with a story about him and Preston driving to the Army-Navy game, but I knew. We all knew. After he got back and locked it all in this box, my daddy never said a word, but Preston did. The night he proposed to me—parked out on the bluff overlooking the river—he told me everything."

Swaying in her chair, his mother spoke so rapidly that Jesse labored to track her words.

"Rex had been drinking ever since he got off the graveyard shift, just like I told them he would. So he never noticed your father's gold Cadillac convertible with the Georgia tags. Stepped into our smelly front room; found two white-hooded men hiding there. Sounds foolish and hateful now, but Preston believed being in the Klan was what you had to do back then for business, like going to the right church or club. It wasn't right, I know, but it wasn't always wrong. Daddy knocked Rex square in the jaw with a padlock wrapped in a handkerchief before Preston even raised his axe handle. Preston dragged him to the kitchen table, but as soon as Rex could talk, he went on justifying and threatening. Only made it worse. Daddy laid that padlock across his face again—broke his nose before he could go on too long."

The brutal figure of his hooded grandfather battering another man's face clashed in Jesse's mind with photos he'd just seen of the grinning bridegroom and the patient man who'd taught him how to bait a hook.

"Daddy made sure he signed that divorce decree. Told him he was from Lewallen County, Georgia, and we had our proper hearing with the judge. Rex signed the papers, blood dripping out of his nose, but Preston could see him plotting and scheming, dying to wrap his black cord around Daddy's neck, beat them both with that padlock and axe handle."

"Your granddaddy tells Rex that as far as anybody knows, he was dead. Don't write my daughter, don't call my daughter, and don't have any notions of coming south. But Preston knew. He knew in his heart that we needed more than a piece of paper to protect me. Lord, how he cried when he told me about the axe handle, splitting the air...then it stopped, the crush."

Momma cupped a fist over her shivering chin and lips. "I'm sorry. I'm so sorry. It's all my fault," she murmured.

The pictures and the green lockbox rested on Momma's lap. The afternoon sun shone on the black-and-white photographs—the only time the harsh portraits had ever seen daylight. Jesse gathered them up, stowing them in the thick grass under his chair. He stretched his palms out toward Momma, and she laid her hands in his. Rubbing his thumb along the top of her skin, he felt the fresh porcelain smoothness between the withered crevices.

"What's left? What are we going to do?" Momma pleaded.

"I love you, Momma, nothing changes that." Jesse bent down and gently kissed the back of his mother's hands. His thoughts spun into a convoluted mixture of shock at the story he'd just heard and relief in finally resolving the mystery haunting his mother. He wasn't certain what the statute of limitations was for a justifiable homicide, but he wasn't going to ask the Philadelphia Police Department, a local criminal lawyer, or even Haymaker. It would take him a long time to sort out who the true culprit of the crime was. Maybe his father, Preston, was both criminal and hero, just as Momma was both victim and the punished. Jesse didn't know if her demonic visions of Rex would ever return—or if he was banished for good—but he was certain that Momma's mind would continue to unravel; the disease would progress, relentlessly. If he were lucky, there would still be times when they would connect as a mother and her son, but he knew they would be fewer. Two or three years from now, she might get pneumonia or her heart might slowly fail, and then nature would finally soothe her pain.

His mother fell against his shoulder, unleashing trembling sobs. Jesse squeezed her tight.

29

THE OLD BOWLEGGED GUY WITH THE GNARLY ELBOWS
at the bike shop was right. The upgrades had made Jesse a
bicycling beast. He jammed his new three-hundred-dollar
Shimano pedals up and down. He was in a rhythm, the cadence
zone, and he was almost home. He looked down at his new cycle
computer. This could be his fastest time ever and his first ride
without a fall. He took in the roadside scenery, noticing that his
eyes felt less frantic and his jaw was more relaxed; even the
sprawling kudzu appeared to be in order. Now if only the bike
seat wasn't making his ass ache and the spandex shorts weren't
chafing his crotch.

Approaching a four-way stop, he prayed that it would be clear.
He didn't want to unclip his new cycling shoes from the pedals.
Jesse hadn't practiced stopping enough like old bowlegged told
him to do before taking the bike on the road. Fifty times on each
side, he'd said, but the morning air and sunshine tempered any
concerns about crashing. He started thinking about bacon instead.

Ignoring Haymaker's Moscow advice, Jesse allowed a tempo-
rary employment agency to send a young woman, Mattie, to be

Momma's caretaker. After the green lockbox, his mother had been sleeping more and was starting to occasionally lose her balance. Mattie worked five days a week, helped Momma with her medicines, and made sure she was eating regularly. She had the perfect disposition for dealing with his mother; the only problem was that most of the time, Momma insisted on calling her Polly. Mattie would be at the house now to fix breakfast, and she didn't microwave her bacon—she fried it in the pan, extra crispy.

Jesse neared the intersection and stopped pedaling. Coasting, he squeezed the right-side brake handle, remembering to be gentle and use only the rear brakes so he wouldn't pitch himself over the handlebars again. The intersection was empty and no cars were coming. He let off the brake and pumped his thighs. This was the sprint to the finish line, and all he had to do was safely dismount the bike when he got home.

Since his departure from PM, Jesse had honed his plans for the future. They'd set up the townhouse next to Haymaker, as his office and bachelor pad. A Guatemalan crew was renovating the townhouses, and Jesse was the project manager, afternoon beer-buyer, and gopher. He was averaging three trips a day to the building supply store. His PM severance was floating him until they rented the townhouses and the storage units turned around. At the auction, he'd sold his jet skis, Harley Davidson, and Mustang Mach I, but the auction only produced a tepid short-sale bid on his old house, and the mortgage company was insisting on Jesse contributing toward the deficiency before approving the sale. After chipping in the proceeds from the man toys, he was still eighty grand shy. Haymaker was brazenly confident he could easily sell Jesse's gun collection for double or triple that amount, and Jesse could pay the mortgage company their "blood money," helping him avoid the shame of "shitting the bed" by filing for personal bankruptcy.

Busy fantasizing about selecting an interior designer, Jesse rounded the curve and saw Mattie's maroon van parked safely out of the way, but blocking his driveway dismount was JJ's black Mustang. Turning in, he anxiously rotated his right foot, trying to release it from the pedal, but the tension was too tight. He was nearing the parked Mustang. If he didn't get unclipped, he was going to have to divert course and make a controlled crash landing onto the grass. Hopefully, it would be softer than last time when he face-planted into the holly bushes.

With one last hard twist, his foot broke free. Jesse mashed the brakes and stuck his free leg down as a kickstand, stopping a few feet short of the Mustang's bumper. Amie hopped out of the car.

"Hey, precious," Jesse said, fighting to catch his breath. "What brings you by? Your mom finally give you permission to drive your brother's ride?"

"No, sir, but sort of, yes," Amie said. She'd cut her hair short and dyed it a frosty light pink like a cupcake. "Anyway, we—you and Mom—got a real problem with JJ."

"What now? Did the pastor catch him playing stalker again?"

"Way worse than that. When we woke up this morning, Jack's van was missing and JJ is gone. Mom sent me over to tell you. She wants you to come over to the house as soon as you can."

"What? Why didn't you tell me sooner? Did you try his cell phone? He might've got called into work early or gone to get biscuits."

"We can't call anybody. Your crazy son dumped all of our cell phones in the toilet. And he took a bunch of clothes. And Mom's secret cash. And the pistol you left for us in the house."

"Why'd you wait? Hold on a second," Jesse said, reaching into his bicycle saddlebag to check his cell phone. "Houston, we got a 'for real' big problem."

"What's that?" Amie asked.

"Thirteen missed calls from Pastor Sonny." Jesse held the screen up to show his daughter.

"Crap, that's probably one angry father of a preacher's daughter."

"Yep. You go back home and let me change out of these stupid bike shorts. I'll grab Mr. Hay and we'll be right over. Jesus on the cross, I don't want to guess what your brother has done or what Sonny is doing about it."

HAYMAKER AND JESSE BARRELED DOWN THE BACK
roads to their old neighborhood. The adrenaline was flowing
across Jesse's skin, along the boundaries of his body, streaming
past his Adam's apple, his belly button, down to his kneecaps,
and then back up to the small patch of hair on his lower back. He
hadn't felt this nervous since he'd gotten the call from Momma
about the stranger in her backyard and he'd pulled out his pistol.

Why in the fuck would JJ bring a pistol?

Feeling the fear twist and torque his insides, Jesse wondered if
Hollywood always edited out the scene where the hero squatted
behind a cactus before riding off to settle the score.

One of Haymaker's phones rang and he picked it up to answer,
listening intently.

Jesse turned on the Cadillac's navigation system, pulling up
Dwyer and Lewallen County on the screen, highways he was
long familiar with traveling. He punched the zoom out button,
showing the surrounding counties, punched it again, showing
the state and Chattahoochee River dividing west Georgia and
east Alabama, and then stabbed at it continually, until it was

a flat map of the globe. Jesse wondered how equipped his son was to be traveling on his own. He'd spent hours riding with young sales trainees, advising them on day planners, purchasing agents, and the best strip clubs. If Jesse put the time on paper, he'd invested far more in nurturing his sales force than his own son. Jesse certainly hadn't prepared JJ to be on the lam.

"That was my inside gal pal at the GBI," Haymaker said, after he hung up. "And she had a couple of nice tidbits. Accordin' to her, Pastor Sonny might have a problem brewin'. One of his funky insider real estate scams over in Alabama has attracted the attention of the Feds. Seems somebody has been bribin' a few state folks to get a casino license. And apparently, Blade is a guy named Bernard Bernstein, and he's one of Sonny's old biker buddies from his Satan's Wolves days. He did some heavy prison time, but the Baptist got him on the payroll. Might need to practice my bar-fightin' skills, just in case I need to give Blade the El Paso left hook."

"That's why I brought you along, but here's the thing," Jesse said, pulling into the driveway of his old house. "Denise is probably bouncing off the rafters. No mention of what you heard about Sonny. Ten-four?"

"Roger, over and out. But I'd love to whip Bernie the Blade's ass."

~~~

"Does it matter if it's instant rice?" Amie asked, tightening her brow. "Because this is boil-in-a-bag with the smiling dude on the box."

"That's Uncle Ben. He's cool, and instant rice is cool, too," Haymaker said.

"Hmm, I think there's some organic, long-grain brown rice in the bottom of the pantry. Way more natural than this stuff, but only Mr. Jack eats it."

"I bet that tastes like granny's used...bunion pads, but we don't need it. This'll be good."

Haymaker and Amie—along with Jesse, Denise, and Jack— were gathered around the black lacquered dining room table at Denise's house. They were staring at three bowls of uncooked rice.

"Burying our drowned cell phones in the rice dries them out? Why can't we just use a blow-dryer or something?" Denise asked. "Why did I give up my house phone? That was stupid, stupid, stupid. Jesse, give me your phone. Let me call. Have you tried calling?"

"Fifty dozen times and straight to voicemail every time. You're welcome to try."

"Never mind. God, he'll be wanted...never get a job...never go to college." Each thought added to her burdened grimace. "Worse, he might never come back. Why don't people still take Valium?"

"It'll be fine," Jack said, stroking Denise's hair and down her back. "We're going to find him, or better yet, he'll find us."

Jesse lowered his eyes to his cell phone, checking for text messages and emails, none to help. Thumbing through his phone's apps, he realized how useless a smartphone was in the crunch of a crisis. He glanced over at Amie, pinching the bottom of her lip while she focused on the bowls of rice.

"He'll find us?" Haymaker asked. "You mean like he'll be

comin' back home or trackin' down Denise at the grocery store
or somethin'?"

"Not exactly; more finding himself." Jack nodded his head.
"They could've just gone off on a short road trip retreat, without
any pressure from family or friends. That's how I see it, for sure."

"That's not how I see it at all." Denise stood up and walked a
lap around the table. "We need to come up with a plan for finding
him before the nutty pastor does or he misses his court date on
Monday. What'll they do if he misses his hearing? When did I
become the mother of an outlaw? Sorry, Haymaker, but we need
to get new phones. I don't see the rice trick working."

"I agree," Jesse said. "Anything in his room?"

"I don't know," Amie replied, sounding startled by the question.
"I didn't look."

"I searched it, cleaned it, searched it again, and then cleaned
it again. Then Jack searched, probably better," Denise said, her
voice weakening as if she were ready to collapse. "I'm so terrible
for letting him live in that pigpen, *Good Housekeeping* Seal of
Shame for me."

"He's got the keys to the cabin, so they might've gone there,"
Jack said. "We could drive down there and look for him. What
do you think?"

"If you're talking about your place in south Alabama, I just
don't see much sense in us going off on some wild-ass chase
without a solid lead," Jesse said. Glimpsing the strain in Denise's
face, he couldn't help but think her panicky self-loathing was all
his fault. He hadn't carried his weight of their parental burden—
now or ever. The stress and sadness pooled up under her eyes,
covering her cheekbones. It was the same desperation he'd seen
on Kimberly.

When JJ was two or three, he'd been running a fever and couldn't stop coughing. Jesse remembered he sounded like a nonstop barking seal at the circus. In the middle of the night, Jesse discovered Denise in JJ's bedroom; he was coughing uncontrollably, and she wore the same expression she did now. All Jesse wanted to do was go back to sleep. Recalling what Momma had told him she'd done when he'd had the croup, he went into the bathroom and turned the shower on its hottest setting, the steam filling the room. Then he picked up JJ and brought him in, holding him on his lap for fifteen or twenty minutes while the warm mist opened his airways. JJ was safely asleep when he put him down in his bed. It was one of the few times Denise had offered him an adoring face of astonishment.

Studying the way his daughter was tapping her index finger against her cheek, Jesse decided it was time to ask her a direct question.

"Amie, do you know where your brother went?"

"Dad?" Amie's eyes ping-ponged around the table.

"Amie Barbara Few," Jesse said, raising his voice at his precious girl for the first time in a decade.

"Hey, okay," Amie said, swaying her head from side to side. "I don't know. I'm sorry, but the poor guy needs a break, and the whole story doesn't really sound that good—sort of bad, actually."

"Doesn't matter. Go on." Jesse maintained his authoritative business voice.

"Mom, you probably don't know, but when you go out traveling to the festivals to show your photographs with Mr. Jack and leave us home alone, we don't always stay home. It was JJ's idea at first—really it was—but we take these weekend road trips while you're gone."

Denise's entire face expanded in shock. Jesse passed up a grin, but he still felt taller, knowing that his kids had inherited some of his skills.

"Don't be so surprised, Mom. Didn't you ever wonder how the house stayed so clean and the groceries never got eaten? Any-who, it got too expensive to go anywhere fun like Panama City or Disney World, so we started going to Melanie's parents' place in the mountains; it was pretty cool, a little creepy. We had free run of this humongous house overlooking this bayou lake thingy. But the last few times, they took off there on their own. It got to be kind of their special place, which is completely gross and boring. It's called Morez Mountain, and it's up north, near where Alabama, Georgia, and Tennessee like all three come together."

"That makes sense," Haymaker said.

"Totally," Jack said.

"It's in Rudolph County. We call it Rudolph-the-Redneck-Reindeer County. They're probably already there by now," Amie said.

"That means we've got to leave now, pronto. If Pastor Sonny figures it out first, JJ will be cuffed in the back of a cop car again." Jesse stood up from the table. "Denise, you and Jack should stay here, I guess. Haymaker and I will go. We're a team."

"Here's the situation, Daddy," Amie said. "I can't tell you exactly where the house is or how to get there, but I could definitely show you."

"Mom?" Jesse asked, looking at Denise. "That's your call."

"It scares the mommy in me to death. What other choice have we got? I really don't need to have to decide something now."

"I know JJ." Amie got up and stood next to her mom. "He and I are simpatico siblings. I can help for real."

"I might actually need her to find this place," Jesse said, self-ishly wanting her to experience the tall, good-looking cowboy version of him rather than the scruffy varmint outlaw dad. "It sounds like Google Maps whatever won't help. I can't call Sonny and ask him."

"You promise to take care of her? Let her use your phone to call or text me?"

"Of course. First sign of anything too dangerous and we retreat. But I don't think we'll have any problems. Sonny is a man of the cloth. I can handle him."

"That's your famous last words, which I've heard from you before, too many times. I don't know...I don't know...I don't know. I never did any crap like this to my mother. Wonder whose past teenage misdeeds I'm paying for?" Denise grabbed Amie close, hugging her tightly. "I hate having only terrible choices. First of all, be smart. Secondly, stay in touch. Lastly, go get your brother and Mel and hurry your fanny home."

Jack jumped up from the table and joined in on the family hug. "It's going to be fine. I feel it."

Jesse nodded to Haymaker and pointed toward the door, bris-tling at the embrace that sent him off on his mission.

31

RUDOLPH COUNTY HAD TRIED TO SECEDE FROM THE
Union not once but twice. The first time was along with the
rest of Alabama and the Confederate States in 1861. The
second time was over a hundred years later in 1963 when
George Wallace, Alabama's infamous segregationist governor,
stepped aside at the schoolhouse door, tacitly agreeing to
integrate the University of Alabama. Rudolph County didn't
cotton to civil rights—or any other rights—for the colored
and refused to be regulated by blowhard politicians and Papist
Yankees. Eight months later, when one of Wallace's agitated
aides threatened to bankrupt the city by withholding state
funds and shutting off the water and power supply, Stumpy
Folkston, the sole Rudolph County commissioner since
returning from World War II with a Purple Heart, agreed
to drop their secession plans. Stumpy was turned out at the
next election and forced to move his family to Chattanooga.
Rudolph County couldn't stomach turncoat cowards.

Late on a tranquil spring afternoon, Jesse, Haymaker, and
Amie crossed the Rudolph County line with a loud whump. The

rumbling of the tires transitioning to the worn-thin pavement filled the car. The potholed road shook them about, ghostly faded lane markers giving meager guidance to safe travel.

"That was a helluva jolt," Haymaker said, studying an Alabama road map unfolded in his lap. "God don't want people up here. The river snakes every which way but near this place, and the giant-ass lake peters out into a muddy swamp right before it gets here. No wonder we're two hours from the interstate; gotta make it tough to reach all these French kissin' cousins and snake-handlin' banjo pickers."

The growl from the road continued as they drove closer to the small mountain peak up ahead, passing through the center of the sparse town.

"Okay, precious, you ready to give us directions?" Jesse asked.

"Most of the time, directions south of the Mason-Dixon include the Walmart and the Waffle House," Haymaker interjected. "But I ain't so sure this slice of peckerwood paradise has even got a Dollar General or a Huddle House."

"JJ always said the directions are like walking, left, right, left; it's the goofy freak-show landmarks you have to remember." Amie leaned into the front seat. "First, we're looking for the junk place."

"I assume this auto salvage yard is the junk place," Jesse said. On the left, basking in the setting sun was a crooked two-hundred-yard section of fence formed by crumpled car hoods, each section a different height, style, and color—red to yellow, yellow to black, black to blue—a spectrum of Detroit's ancient palette. Past the first section of fence was a crimson concrete block building with Sally's Salvage hand-painted in white letters across the front, followed by another section of car-hood fence.

Crushed car carcasses were stacked on top of each other, peeking above the fence line.

"If it ain't, I'd love to see the junk place. Reckon Sally uses the fence to keep a few yokels in or keep the Feds out. I bet back in the day, you could get you a new VIN plate and any odometer mileage you wanted."

"Yeppers, this is it. It's up here on the left in a teeny bit."

"This ain't the ATL; make sure you use your blinker," Haymaker said.

"This is definitely not home, Kansas, or any other bumpkin town I've ever blown through. You know, it's odd. The longleafs and ridges look the same as north Georgia, but man, they sure feel different, almost like they're jagged." Jesse put on his blinker and slowly turned left off the county highway. The muddy gravel road they turned onto immediately began to ascend and twist upwards.

"One time, we were coming down this road, trying to get home before Mom did, and we passed Melanie's father," Amie said. "He had to notice the black Mustang. It's only been in his driveway like a gazillion times. Melanie thought she saw the lady in the car with him; it was some woman who works at the church. She's like the Facebook minister."

Jesse gave Haymaker a glance; that had to have been Becky, the bucking divorcee. It also meant that the pastor might have a notion where his daughter and JJ were hiding.

"All righty, the haunted trailer comes up quick where we turn right."

"This should be good," Haymaker said, rolling down the window.

Buried deep in the foliage on the right side of the slithering road, surrounded by the white cross blossoms of the dogwoods, was a burned-out trailer slumping on its side like a contorted beer can that had been thrown in the campfire, the charred roof ripped open to the spring sky. A pickup was parked in front with an oak tree stretched across the smashed cab, the dirty, shattered windshield the lone witness to the catastrophe.

"Hell's bells, that's haunted all right. That truck ain't that old, maybe less than ten years," Haymaker said. "I know it's a Ford, but why would somebody leave a semi-nice pickup truck like that abandoned up here in the woods? Where's Sally's Salvage when you need 'em?"

"No clue, but I don't think I need blinkers up here," Jesse said, turning right. The road was washed out—less gravel and more dirt. The climb became steeper, coiling around the mountain.

"We're getting close, almost there. Look for the flag and the hands, Daddy. They're hard to see in the dark, so we need to hurry."

Jesse gunned the accelerator. The back tires of the Escalade swerved as he hit a slippery patch of clay. Searching for the next landmark, Jesse felt the returning quiver of his nerves. He pictured an unshaven cowboy trotting into town, a sweat-stained bandana tied around his neck. Jesse squelched his fear. The ascent was getting steeper, and the afternoon sky was turning into dusk, nighttime seeping onto the mountain road. Amidst the dwindling light, Jesse stopped at a small, wooden road sign. He turned into the driveway.

"That's a bit of déjà vu," Jesse said. "The American flag with the praying hands over the top is the same as the lapel pin Sonny wears all the time, except his pin has got a diamond accent in the middle instead of a silver reflector."

"Even Jesus needs a touch of corporate brandin'," Haymaker

said. "Check out the nice, slick blacktop. This driveway has better pavement than the interstates around Atlanta." The headlights illuminated a black, velvet strip forging upward between the trees. "What are we goin' to do about the gate bein' padlocked? Does that mean JJ and Melanie ain't here?"

"Not necessarily; we lock ourselves in to psych out the 'Bama-billies," Amie said. "The combination is some Biblical riddle. How many books in the bible? The old and mean part."

"Old Testament? Thirty-nine," Haymaker responded, adding, "my great-granny paid me to go to church with her."

"That's it. Thirty-nine is the first number. And then what's that real famous chapter that's always on the pamphlets church people hand out?"

"This I know because the Bible tells me so, John 3:14," Jesse said. "So it's 39-3-14. Amie, you wait here. C'mon and help me, Haymaker."

"If you're waitin' on me, you're backin' up," Haymaker said. "I'm ready to launch into full JJ extraction mode."

Jesse and Haymaker got out of the SUV. Amie leaned farther up and yelled out the car door.

"Oh, oh, I almost forgot. There are cameras everywhere, in the trees and hidden all over. Melanie and I never understood it, but JJ loved to play with the whole system-a-bob on his laptop."

With Haymaker holding up his cell phone as a flashlight, Jesse quickly spun the dial on the lock and pulled on it. It didn't budge.

"Let me clear it and try again." Jesse recited the instructions. "Spin it three times, start at thirty-nine, now to the left, past the number once, stop on three, and right to fourteen." He yanked on the shackle, and again, nothing happened. "Shit, are you sure great-granny was taking you to a real church? Maybe it was a bingo parlor?"

"The Tabernacle Pentecostal Church didn't have bingo, but they did have paddles for heathen boys who misbehaved in Sunday school. So I got my answer whupped into me. Where did you get yours?"

"The Rainbow Man."

"Dustin Hoffman?"

"No, the dude who wore the bright-ass rainbow wig to the World Series, the Super Bowl. He was always in the background, holding up his sign on camera. It only said John 3:14."

"I hate to knock you off your road to salvation, but we called that rainbow wig dude Rock n' Rollen, and his sign said John 3:16."

Without a word, Jesse worked the new combination and popped the lock open. They each swung open a side of the gate and met back in the middle of the driveway when they were finished.

"Nice teamwork," Haymaker said.

"Speaking of, how about taking over the wheel? I'm working on the final touches of my plan."

"No problems. I'm an excellent wheel man. Too bad I forgot my drivin' gloves. But related to the team theme, there's somethin' I've been meanin' to disclose, and it might be my last best time."

"Your dramatics are killing me. What is it?"

"The Escalade don't have a spare because I took it out and loaded the wheel well down."

"Loaded it down?"

"I'd planned for us to meet tonight with some hip-hop fella. You know, peddle some of your guns for the mortgage company's blood money. I packed the big-dollar ones: all the Glocks, the MAC-10, and the TEC-9 as greetin' cards, the Uzi if they wanna go old school, and those custom German machine pistols if we can get the large Benjamins. Plus, I got your AR-15s back there and the AK-47. If you're stayin' outta your own private bankruptcy, my brother, these guns are the ones to do it."

"Holy crap. We crossed state lines with modified weapons? Isn't that a federal crime?"

"Modified maybe, but we gotta be extra super careful 'cause I did have to bring some ammo. The worst part was to not have a spare for this long ride. I got all nutted up every time we hit a bump."

"Why didn't you tell me? Never mind. Let's roll. I need to rethink my plan."

Haymaker guided the Escalade through a series of switchbacks leading up the hill; along the way, motion-sensor lights spotlighted the vehicle as it passed. They reached the top of the driveway and pulled up to a stacked stone and timber mansion in the sky, the A-frame roof reaching to the darkening heavens.

"Shangri-frickin'-la-di-da and sweet baby Jesus, ain't this a long way from a manure-filled manger," Haymaker said. "Talk about walkin' on the water."

"I told you," Amie said. "Wait until you see the inside."

"Let's go." Haymaker jammed the car into park and undid his seat belt.

"Hold on a second," Jesse said. "There's no lights on, and I don't see Jack's commie van. How do we know they're here?"

"We always park in the garage. And I'm pretty sure they're here because that looks like Melanie up there." Amie pointed toward the house. "Like I said, cameras everywhere."

Jesse and Haymaker looked up and saw a young girl standing at the entry to the front door, fifty yards up a stone stair path.

"I'll just grab her and throw her in the truck while you chase down JJ," Haymaker said. "We'll leave Jack's van for Sonny and Sally's Salvage—a thanks-for-your-hospitality gift. We'll be back on the road in ten minutes."

"I doubt that'll work, Mr. Hay. You don't know my puppy-love-struck brother."

"Here's what we should do," Jesse said. "You two are dropping me off here."

"What?" Amie protested. "I didn't come this far to miss the good part."

"Yeah, my brother," Haymaker said. "You can't do this lone-wolf commando style."

"You know, this morning I agreed with you, but now I think it's the only way. If you leave me here, he's got to deal with me. We've got to deal with each other. If this becomes an oh-shit Sonny episode, this might not end as smoothly as a soap opera, and I can't risk that for Amie. Given the recent news flash from my partner, it might be best if you guys waited in a nearby spot as backup, like the cavalry."

"I still call bunko," Amie said, slumping back in the car seat and folding her arms.

"I get your point about protectin' little Pinky back there," Haymaker said. "But I hate it, too. Tell you what, little sister; we'll go sample that greasy-spoon diner I spotted."

"Give me a hug and order me a blue plate special to go. I haven't eaten all day."

All three travelers got out of the car. Haymaker and Jesse man-hugged.

"And you're sure this is a good idea? This town is as squirrelly as an acorn bar after midnight. If the shiitake hits the attic fan too hard, you call me." Haymaker gave Jesse one more hasty hug. "I can drop number one daughter off and be back up the mountain in twenty minutes."

"I can't say it's a good idea, but it's got to work. I'm not sure who said it—maybe Tom Hanks—but failure is not an option." Jesse wrapped his arms around his daughter. "I love you, precious. I appreciate all your help. Really I do," he said, squeezing Amie tightly. "I don't know where I'd be without you. Please, please call your mom from Haymaker's phone when you can. She's worried about you. Let her know you're safe as promised. I love you all."

"We love you, too." Amie gave her dad one last embrace and jumped into the front seat of the SUV.

Jesse watched the taillights trail down the driveway, disappearing into the serpentine curves of Morez Mountain. Without hesitation, he bounded up the stone stair path. As he approached the tall cut-glass door, Jesse saw Melanie in her tank top and jean shorts. She leaned inside the doorway and turned on the outside lights. Now Jesse could see her delicate smile in the spotlight and he understood why they were here. He recalled the first night he saw Denise at the Halloween party, her gentle beam shining through her Deborah Harry ruby-red lipstick and pale makeup.

"I'd tell you I just happened to be in the neighborhood," Jesse said when he reached Melanie at the door, "but that's way too corny of a line. How are you? You guys doing good?"

"Hey, Mr. Few, we're fine. Actually, I'm okay, chilly standing out here, but JJ freaked out when he saw you at the gate. He ran upstairs. I told him Amie would eventually have to say some-thing, but anyway."

"Amie said y'all like it up here."

"We do. Despite the characters and lack of charm, this moun-tain can be marvelous, peaceful, if you let it be." Melanie hugged herself tightly. Her teeth were chattering. "Did you talk with my father? Is he with you?"

"Nope, the pastor isn't with me and we haven't talked lately."

"Why is everyone so afraid of him?"

"That's an excellent question, young lady. You mind if I come inside before I answer that. You're freezing out here."

"Yes, sir. I'm very sorry." Melanie swung the door open and turned on the inside lights as she led Jesse through a cathedral ceiling foyer, exposed hand-hewn beams begging for attention.

"Make yourself comfortable on the sofa," Melanie said, pointing to a brown leather sofa in front of a two-story stone fireplace. "Let me go upstairs and bring JJ down."

Jesse had forgotten how politely polished Melanie was, espe-cially for a teenager. Her mother must have trained her to be a proper preacher's wife. Jesse also reminded himself that this was the same girl who had coaxed Haymaker into giving her tequila and who had conversations with the spirits of the dead.

Jesse glanced around the open-space living room, noting the expansive west wall of floor-to-ceiling windows. Watching the sun drop below the distant tree line, Jesse thought Amie was right, swanky-panky indeed. There were two near-empty glasses of pink wine and a board game laid out on the coffee table. Noticing the pile of clothes on the floor, Jesse realized he'd interrupted their foreplay, maybe a dirty game of strip Scrabble.

Jesse hurried over to the wall of windows, far away from the coffee table and sofa. He was sure this day couldn't get any stranger: ex-wife, ex-wife's hippie boyfriend, and now his runaway son and his psychic girlfriend playing kinky board games in her megalomaniac father's chalet deep in the land of the redneck lost. The exhaustion began settling in his shoulders. It was sunset, and Jesse didn't know where he'd be spending the night. He couldn't remember the last time that'd happened.

"Dad?"

Jesse turned around. JJ was standing behind the sofa, holding Melanie's hand. He was wearing a red Georgia Bulldog T-shirt and black gym shorts. His hair looked wet, and he had his laptop tucked under his arm. Jesse felt relieved to see that his son was fine. "Jesse Few, Jr., I presume?"

"Why are you here? Where's your Escalade?"

"Amie had to get back for school so she and Haymaker headed back. I told 'em you'd give me a ride home."

"Dad, what are you thinking? I'm not going home. I can't go back. I'll take you to the bus station or something."

"Bus station? That's the best you got to offer."

"I'm sorry, but Melanie and me, we're figuring things out. We came up here because it's quieter here than anywhere else. I guess none of the dead here are troubled, so they don't bother Mel so much."

"Son, I'm not sure I fully grasp hold of all that."

"Most people don't, Mr. Few, but that is what is so special about your son," Melanie said, not hesitating to boast about her boyfriend. "He sees the things in me that other people don't notice or think is a fault—the curse of my fragile, female mind, my dad says—but JJ treats it like it's something special, a gift. This is the best place for us to sort out our future together."

"There won't be a future if you two don't get back. And now," Jesse said, "Melanie, you asked why people are afraid of your dad. I'll tell you. He's a scary man who loves his youngest daughter very much and he has the power, the people, and the means to ruin anyone who threatens his world. And JJ, you're in his way, in harm's way."

"What can he do that he hasn't already done by keeping me from Melanie? If he wins that war, my life is ruined anyway, without her. What else do you think matters? School? Dumbass jobs?"

"Come home with me, please. Your court date is Monday. They don't send kids to the state penitentiary for a DUI. You don't know what's going to happen."

"Sure we do. You forgot the bogus drug charges and, you said it yourself, Pastor Sonny doesn't get what he doesn't want. And he doesn't want Melanie and me together. But it's not his decision. This is our moment to be together. He can't rob us of this because it belongs to us, not him, no way."

"You know your mom is freaked-out scared. You dumped her cell phone in the toilet for crying out loud. You cut her off."

"I'm sorry about that. I just didn't want them bothering us nonstop."

"So why take all these risks?"

"You didn't take any risk, did you?" JJ replied, cocking his head and staring down his father.

"What?"

"You certainly didn't take any risk. You gave up on Mom, Amie, and me without even putting up a fight. Big Daddy just left us all cozy in the house and checked on us once a week, maybe, if it was convenient. Nurtured us with a checkbook and an ATM card, believing that was the same thing as love. You didn't count on the money getting tight and Mr. Jack showing up."

"Wait a second," Jesse shouted, tiring of parental diplomacy. "You can't turn this around like some trick—this isn't about me."

"Now you understand," JJ shouted back. "All I know for sure is there's no turning back now." JJ composed his voice as if he were indulging a child's ceaseless question. "I've made sure of that. Mel and I can't give up on what we have, not like her folks did. Especially, not like you did. I'm not numb to how I feel."

"You brought a pistol with you." Stung with embarrassment, Jesse couldn't allow himself to be distracted by his son's psychoanalysis. "Why in hell's half acre do you need a pistol?"

"I already got rid of the pistol—sold it, sorta." JJ released Melanie's hand and moved to the coffee table, opening up his laptop. "I'll pay back whomever I need to, but I've gotta check the cameras just in case."

"Why in the hell did you sell it? What if you need it?"

"Ha, make up your mind. And I did need it, but for something real, not the boogeyman you imagine is around every corner."

"Mr. Few, JJ is too nervous or shy to tell you this. I don't know why, I mean I do, but we traded the pistol this morning at a pawnshop in Tallapoosa for this." Melanie held up her left hand to show Jesse her thin gold band with a petite round diamond. "We'd already finished all the paperwork before today, so we talked this lady judge into marrying us right before she went to lunch."

"I might need to sit down." Jesse plopped down in a rocking chair in front of the fireplace. Staring at Melanie's ring, he could sense the genuine bond the couple shared. By now, there was even a balance in their relationship. It was the same connection he'd given up with Denise and dreamt of feeling again. He'd taught JJ a lesson, and he didn't even know he was doing it. There was an odd mix of pride in the man his son was becoming and shame in that JJ had reached an emotional maturity that Jesse still couldn't fully grasp. He wanted to be happy for them both, but if there were no time for fear, then there was no time for joy. "I'm supposed to say congratulations, but given the circumstances..."

"I'm sorry I—we—waited to tell you. I guess I'm not sure how to tell my folks, my mom especially. Who cares what my dad thinks, right? But I'd hate to ask you to keep a secret from them, him."

"Mel, we may not have to worry too much longer." JJ turned the laptop to face her. "I'm pretty sure that your dad and his biker thug are headed for the front door now. I should've seen them coming."

32

"WHY IS IT THE GOOD GUYS NEVER LOCK THE DOORS until it's too late?" Jesse said.

From a wireless camera mounted above the front door, Jesse, JJ, and Melanie saw Pastor Sonny rushing up the stone path. A short, thick-set, middle-aged man with a sleeve of tattoos was struggling to keep up with the pastor's pace.

JJ dashed for the front door. Jesse and Melanie hurried behind him. Just as JJ reached the foyer, Pastor Sonny blasted through the door. Instinctively, JJ tried to push him back outside. Sonny locked arms with JJ and pressed back harder. They slipped to the floor with a thud. JJ was on top of the pastor, their arms flailing about.

"Daddy...JJ...stop it now," Melanie screamed, reaching to pull JJ off her father.

"Taser him, Blade...Taser all of them," Sonny shouted from the bottom of the scrum.

Jesse and Blade eyeballed each other, the stubby biker reaching with his right hand to unbuckle the stun gun from his side holster. Jesse faked a right cross at Blade's nose, who threw up his arms to block Jesse's punch. But exactly like Haymaker had taught him, Jesse stepped solidly into the El Paso left hook, banging his fist squarely on the biker's chin. Blade reeled sideways and crashed into the front door, shattering the glass. Jesse kneed him in the mid-section, hoping he hit his nuts. Blade groaned and slumped over in a small pile of glass. Jesse turned to his son's brawl with Sonny.

The pastor had thrown JJ off, and both men were on their knees, scrambling to stand. Melanie grabbed for her dad, but he shoved her back.

"Get back out of the way." Sonny stood up before JJ could and planted his foot in JJ's chest, kicking him back down. JJ's skull plunked against the hardwood floor. With his back to Jesse, Sonny readied his massive fists for a groggy JJ.

Jesse lunged for the pastor, wrapping him up in a bear hug. The pastor lashed out with his elbows. Holding on, Jesse squeezed the pastor's solar plexus with all his strength. Sonny began to spin madly around the foyer, whirling Jesse off the walls and crashing into the furniture. Jesse gripped Sonny tighter as if he were compressing himself into the preacher's heart.

"Aaarrrggghhh," Sonny blared as his frenzied spiral weakened. "Get this son-of-a-bitch off me."

Jesse was fighting to body-slam Sonny when he heard the *boosh* of a small explosion, followed by an electric whirr. He instantly felt a sharp pierce in his butt. Uncontrollably, he released his grip on Sonny and collapsed into a spasm. Staring at the hand-hewn beams in the ceiling, Jesse was straining to make his muscles respond.

"Put some cuffs on these two. Then go take care of the van," Sonny ordered Blade. "You ready there?"

"Sure, sure; that's all set."

"Good. Before you go, get these two up. Put them on the sofa until Sheriff Sully shows up."

The stubby biker put zip-tie cuffs on JJ and hoisted him up, leading him into the living room. He came back for Jesse.

"Nothing like an X2 to the ass, tough guy," Blade said, zip-wrapping Jesse's wrists in plastic handcuffs. "Behave yourself, or I'll give you a blast to your balls and carve them off afterward." He flicked his knife open and pressed the stiletto's tip into Jesse's back.

Jesse's legs were wobbly. He shook his head, trying to clear the confusion. Blade tugged him toward JJ on the sofa and pushed him down next to his son. Jesse could see a small knot on the back of JJ's head. Melanie came in from the kitchen with a bag of ice and sat down next to JJ. Pastor Sonny paced a fervent path in front of the fireplace, as if he were preparing to preach a Sunday morning sermon on the proper fear of the Lord.

"Melanie, I warned you this would happen," Sonny said. "I begged you to listen, and now you see what you reaped."

"JJ needs a doctor." Melanie put the ice bag on JJ's knot, oblivious to her father's sermons. "You might have cracked his skull."

"That'll be Sully's problem in a few minutes. They'll get him evaluated, after they book him for kidnapping, plus whatever else the sheriff uncovers in his search. I told you to let this boy go."

"And I told you what your friend—the one who died in the motorcycle crash—told me in my dream," Melanie said.

"Hush with that sacrilegious nonsense. Stop repeating dribble you've heard from gossip-mongers…and your mother," Sonny commanded his daughter like a Pharisee issuing an edict. "I've warned you."

"He wanted me to warn you." Melanie mocked her father's imposing tone. "He knows what you've sown, and he knows what you'll reap."

Jesse listened as their argument grew more venomous with each exchange.

"You're talking yourself right into a psychiatric hospital." The pastor stopped pacing, as if he'd been struck from above by an idea. "That might be the best place for you anyway. We can tell them you're suffering from Stockholm syndrome. That boy just encouraged your blasphemy. You put his Georgia charges on top of these new charges, something serious is gonna stick."

"How can he kidnap his new bride?" Melanie asked, holding up her wedding ring to her father.

Sonny's eyes narrowed.

"For the love of God," the pastor screamed. He picked up the rocking chair and hurled it across the room.

Melanie took two steps toward the sofa and JJ, but then turned away and ran upstairs crying. A few seconds later, Jesse heard a door slam. The pastor's jaw was clenched so tight it was pulsating. Sonny's only intention was to squash the source of his paternal pain—JJ. Pulling at the cuffs, Jesse needed something akin to an El Paso left hook.

"I hope that chair wasn't an antique," Jesse said, trying to trump Melanie's sarcasm. "I guess you and me sorta equally suck at the whole fatherhood thing."

"What did you just say?" Sonny stepped closer to Jesse.

"I'm curious about something else we've got in common. Does Becky still do the trick with her hand when she's on top? I taught her that in just one night. No need to thank me."

"How dare you," Sonny barked, inches from Jesse's face.

"How dare either one of us? But we do. Because we're special. We're successful. We wear tailored suits," Jesse said with authority, finally on the other end of a sermon. "Does Becky know you used her cell phone to text JJ one night? Doesn't matter what she knows. What does your family know? My wife knew, and I'm sure the lovely Mrs. Suggs knows. The real heart of this evening's question is what's it worth to you to keep your façade rolling? Make sure those five thousand suckers show up every Sunday morning to hit the hip when the shiny brass plate is passed down the pew? You want to keep your platinum-player pastor status or you want me to blow it all up with one phone call?"

"I'm going to shut your filthy heathen mouth."

"Before you hear my deal?"

"Where's the Taser gun and some duct tape?" Sonny bellowed to an absent Blade.

"Okay, no deal. Maybe nobody'll be surprised by another hypocrite preacher preferring poontang over the gospel. It's probably not the biggest lie you've ever told. It wasn't mine."

The pastor backhanded Jesse across the face, knocking him off the sofa. Rolling away from the pastor, Jesse met up with the incoming biker, slowing his retreat. Jesse balled up, dodging Blade's kick, but the biker pressed the knife to his groin.

"Now, Reverend," said a slow, thick drawl entering from the foyer. "You're not benefiting too awful much by beating and stabbing a man in cuffs, and we really don't want to explain any bruises or cuts. You best allow professional law enforcement to control the suspects."

RECOVERING FROM THE HAZE, JESSE SAW A TITAN WITH
a brown Stetson and a khaki sheriff's uniform stride into the
living room.

"What took so long?" asked the pastor, attempting to regain
his control. He motioned for Blade to back away.

"Dad-blasted, didn't I tell you to cease and desist going through
town flashing your fake blue lights?" the sheriff asked, looming
over Jesse. His boxy face was deeply tanned and his chin jutted
out like the point of a shovel. Beneath the brim of his cowboy
hat, his forest-green eyes smoldered with a roguish savvy. "Phone
rings off the receiver every time you do that. People think Elvis
has landed leading a zombie rebellion."

"Tell them I own most of this county." Sonny reached down
to pull Jesse off the floor, and the stubby biker clumsily stepped
around the sheriff to help before lumbering out of the room. "And
this was a serious emergency."

"We'll get to the owning the county part later. What's your
side of the circumstances?"

"My teenage daughter was kidnapped this morning when she

was on her way to school by this whacked-out drug dealer," Sonny said. "He jumped bail, and I suppose his father is some accomplice to this whole mess. Their van is stashed in the garage."

"Accomplice? Father-son kidnapping, drug-dealing mob?"

"It appears so, but that's your end of the stick."

"You're 100 percent accurate in that assertion," the sheriff said. "Gratefully, I'm fully confident in our investigative abilities. We concocted sufficient probable cause to do a search on the van. Based on your man's phone call, my deputies are completing that about now."

"Just handle it," Sonny said. "I'm going upstairs to check on Melanie. She's quite upset, and we need to call her mother."

The sheriff walked around the room, kicked at the shattered chair, and shook his head. A young, lanky deputy, nearly as tall as the sheriff, walked into the living room carrying a white cardboard box and showed it to the sheriff.

"What you got?" the sheriff asked.

"We discovered this box here in the back of the van parked in the garage. There's a good half ounce of a white, powdery substance that tested positive for meth. Based on the way it's wrapped, the additional baggies, and the scale—possession and intent to distribute."

"Are you claiming that came from my son's van?" Jesse screeched. "It's not even—"

"That's total bullshit," JJ screamed over his father, rocking back, trying to propel himself off the sofa.

"I'd suggest you two best cease and desist," the sheriff said, holding up his hand and pointing his colossal palm at Jesse and JJ.

"Also, the white Escalade we seen earlier pulled up in the driveway," the lanky deputy said. "Some man claiming to be an uncle and a young girl that says her brother and father are in here."

"What're you doing with them?"

"Paul and Bryant are questioning them. The girl won't say nothing, but the older man," the young deputy said, "he rattles off too much nonsense to understand. But he might've said he was a lawyer or something about F. Lee Bailey, whoever that is."

"You keep them out there, for now." The sheriff rubbed his gray stubble. "Leave the evidence, and let me converse with these two suspects on my own."

"Yes, sir." The young deputy prepared to leave. "Oh, Grandma called and told me to remind you not to forget what she said about staying out too late tonight. She's worried about your night vision."

"I appreciate the reminder, Deputy, but tell your precious grandma not to fret...or nag." The sheriff gave a half-grimace of a man who comprehended too well the rewards and the burdens of running a family business.

The sheriff peered in the box for a moment and then aimed his green eyes at Jesse and JJ. Yanking JJ up by the cuffs, he quickly frisked him, and then studied JJ's pupils before easing him back on the sofa. He pulled a knife off his belt and cut JJ's cuffs loose.

"Gentlemen, good evening. I'm Sheriff Salvatore Sullivan," the sheriff said, pulling Jesse up by the cuffs and patting him down. "My drill sergeant called me Sally Sully in my Marine Corps days, but now, here in Rudolph County, I'm just Sheriff Sully." He pulled Jesse in close, considering his face intently. The sheriff set Jesse down next to his son and popped his wrists free. "But enough about me. What's your story? What song are you singing from the hymnal?"

Again, JJ rushed to speak, but Jesse put his hand on his son's chest. He reached across the sofa and picked up the ice bag Melanie left behind.

"Here, put this on your head. Melanie's dad gave you a good-sized knot," Jesse said, giving the ice to JJ.

Recalling what Pastor Sonny had told him the first time they met, Jesse now realized that Sheriff Sully, as the initial police officer on the scene, was the first line of justice, which in Rudolph County, made him the ultimate arbitrator—the supreme purchasing agent. Now was the moment for Jesse to sell his ass off.

"I appreciate you cutting us out of those cuffs, Sheriff. I'm Jesse Few, and this is my young son, JJ. I've got ID if you like," Jesse said, forcing his voice to be calm and his words slow as he worked to warm up the sheriff. "Tonight was the first time I've ever been zapped by a Taser gun."

"The reverend has a long reputation of using a sledgehammer when a flyswatter would be sufficient."

"Still, I'm sorry we caused a problem for you this evening." Jesse was searching for a way to build a bridge. "I'm sure you and your men have got more important matters to attend to than a family squabble from Georgia."

"Heckuva family squabble," the sheriff said.

"You're right there. Truthfully, my son is out on bail for a couple of charges, which are partly my fault," Jesse said. "My wife and I are split up, trying to reconcile, and I've spent a lot of time here recently, focusing on my own mother's health problems."

"How old is your momma?" The sheriff sat down on the arm of the love seat next to the sofa.

"She's eighty-two and has a touch of the dementia, among other things. I left my job to take care of her. She's living with me now." Jesse shook his head, knowing something more than the truth was needed to set them free tonight. He squeezed his eyes shut. It was all in the presentation. "In fact, when you'll allow us, I need to check on her. See that she's settled down for the night."

"We'll see." Sheriff Sully nodded.

"Now the main thing JJ is guilty of is being in love with the pastor's daughter. There was no kidnapping. They eloped and were married by a judge this morning. You know young lovers?"

"Indeed. My wife and I practically eloped before I volunteered for Vietnam." The sheriff took off his Stetson and ran his fingers through his thick, white hair.

"If you don't mind me saying, Sheriff," Jesse said, deciding now was the time to push, "I don't know what's in that box. My son has never seen that box before. This is a disagreement between two families that we should've settled over coffee and pie back home in Georgia, out of your hair. Here's what we'd like to do. Go home and regroup with family, our people, so we don't have a problem with the bondsman."

Sheriff Sully put his Stetson back on and stood up.

"So far as bail, as long as he makes it for court, the bondsman don't care. But we'll get to that. The box is problematic. It's odd," the sheriff said cautiously, like a judge weighing the evidence out aloud. "Not many drug dealers use banker storage boxes to run their illicit business or own brand-new scales. After nearly forty years in law enforcement, I know there's two sides to each coin. I heard your side of the coin. You're in sales, aren't you, Mr. Few?"

"Uh, yes, sir," Jesse mumbled.

"I trust there was a bit of wheat mixed in with the chaff." The sheriff gave Jesse a wink. "From my vantage, one could allege this discovery warrants some serious criminal charges. The district attorney and the grand jury have zero tolerance for drugs—absolute zero in Rudolph County."

The sheriff made a big zero sign with his thumb and fingers before continuing.

"I've dealt with the reverend for about ten or twelve years now," Sheriff Sully said, wrinkling his nose as if he'd smelled sour milk. "You see, some residents suggest we need outsiders like Pastor Sonny to keep our young people here. Maybe he'll develop a bluegrass gospel theme park or start a four-square gospel Bible College, like he promised. Others—the more inflexible kind like my kinfolk—believe there'll be enough refugees from the cities hazarding up this way when the End Times comes anyway. Either way, Sonny and I are always latched up like Jacob wrestling with the Angel of the Lord. So there's my side of the coin."

The sheriff had now given Jesse the opening to use his favorite sales trick.

"Sheriff Sully, I just want to help you. How can we help each other?"

"That's good. How is it you started asking the questions?" the sheriff said with a laugh. "I'd wager that you could sell cow patty pies at the church bake sale and probably slip your hand up the church ladies' choir robes."

"I love my son, Sheriff," Jesse said, the raw emotion suddenly choking up. "He's not perfect—far from it—but he's not a whacked-out, drug-dealing kidnapper. You see that."

"You might be right, probably are. But I'm dealing with a complaint registered by a respected supporter of the community and evidence collected by duly sworn officers of the court," Sheriff Sully said, leaning in to Jesse. "But if you had home-grown counsel, there could possibly, just maybe, be an effortless route to ascertain the facts and expedite a resolution. I know a good lawyer. You interested in retaining him tonight?"

"Of course, yeah, sure." Jesse smiled, and the tension in his muscles eased.

"Smart choice, Mr. Few. It happens that Billy Joe, my grand-daughter's husband, recently passed the bar exam and established the best criminal law firm in this part of Alabama." The sheriff paused. "He's green and expensive, too."

"I'm in. How much?" Jesse asked, unpleasantly familiar with the process.

"I'd say, around fifty thousand dollars—cash, no wires—and definitely no checks," Sheriff Sully said casually like a used car salesman explaining payment terms.

"That's a stout retainer."

"High-priced but worth the value received. I don't reckon you've got fifty grand in your wallet. So I plan to hold your boy overnight or until you get back." The sheriff hesitated, his eyebrows and forehead rumpled together. "And for my extra well-being, I'll keep the other two outside—the mouthy uncle and your daughter. Call it additional collateral."

Jesse had never encountered a lethal compound like Sheriff Sully—one part homey lawman and two parts cutthroat pirate. Looking over at JJ, Jesse was thankful his son didn't have the pistol when Sonny or, worse, the sheriff arrived. This could've easily become a parent's worst nightmare. Oddly, his gut told him he could trust the crooked sheriff to a degree, but he didn't want to leave without his family. Denise would lose it if he did. JJ might've been smart pawning the pistol for what he wanted the most. Now that the law and order line had been breached, Jesse saw a similar gambit without considering the consequences.

"I've got an idea," Jesse said. "We could barter for the legal fees like the old days. I've got a cache in my truck worth far more than fifty grand, maybe closer to one hundred thousand dollars."

"Go on. What do you propose? What you got?"

"I'd rather not say." Jesse decided he couldn't afford for the sheriff to see the guns without him being there to at least attempt to control the situation, leaving a bit of ballsy hardball as his best move. "You want to take a look?"

Sheriff Sully made a faint clacking sound with his tongue.

"Why not? Absolutely. I'm willing to engage in a late-night bargaining session."

They walked out to the driveway, now crammed with SUVs and police cruisers, flickering blue lights reflecting off the house and trees. Sully's deputies held Haymaker and Amie in a corner of the yard. Jesse led the sheriff around to the back of his Escalade, parked behind the pastor's black Suburban, raised the tailgate, and pulled the cover off the wheel well. The dim interior light revealed Jesse's hidden collection of arms.

"I'm a bit of a gun nut—licensed, of course," Jesse said, stepping aside, allowing the sheriff to get closer. "These are all registered in my name and legal, even insured."

Sheriff Sully shined his flashlight on the stockpile of weapons.

"The pistols are all in the original boxes, a couple of Glocks and some machine gun pistols, all valuable, but some more than others." Jesse treaded softly, trying to let the product sell itself. "And there's a few rifles, nothing more American, more

Constitutional. These might be vital if your folks are right about the End Times coming soon."

"Dad-blasted," the sheriff said, reaching in to pick up the AK-47. "The last time I seen one of these, the NVA was shooting at me across a rice paddy on my final day in the country." Sully inspected the rifle from barrel to butt, rubbing his hands along the wooden stock. "Is this the genuine article? Not a cheap Chinese clone?"

"I've had it examined by an arms expert," Jesse said, thinking there was no end in how to describe Haymaker, "and he assured me that it is; the threaded barrel, the smooth—not the ribbed—dust cover, and all the markings are stamped in Cyrillic. But the best way of telling is the sound."

"Your expert is 100 percent accurate on that claim. I'll never forget it." Sully leaned into the back of the Escalade and pulled out the loaded clip for the AK-47.

"Here comes the preacher," the young deputy shouted, "and he's beelining your way."

Pastor Sonny appeared at the back of the Cadillac.

"Sully, what's going on?" the pastor asked, less of a question and more of an accusation. "Let's wrap this thing up so I can get my daughter home." The pastor noticed the AK-47 Sully was holding. "Holy Moses, forget accomplice. Looks like we can nail the dad on gun-dealing charges. This will be a nice bust for you, Sully."

Jesse realized he was running a risky ploy, and he wasn't a cowboy gunslinger. He was a salesman who relied on persistence, determination, and the ability to read people. Success depended on him trusting his instincts that Sheriff Salvatore Sullivan was, at heart, a more honorable marauder than Pastor Sonny Suggs.

"Is it all clear in front of the Suburban?" Sully yelled.

"Yes, sir," replied the young deputy.

"Everybody, back up, or duck, or both, and cover your ears." The sheriff jammed the magazine into the rifle, flipped the safety with his thumb, and squeezed the trigger.

Takka takka...takka takka...takka takka.

A round of shots exploded into the rear of the pastor's SUV, shattering the back glass.

"What in the world?" Pastor Sonny screeched.

"Just like I remember—100 percent the genuine article." Sheriff Sully released the magazine and rounded the next bullet out of the chamber, disarming the rifle. "Tell you what, Mr. Few. We prefer cash-on-the-barrelhead, but I think we can trade. We've got a deal."

"You and I had a deal, Sully," the pastor said. "There won't be another one, no how, no way."

"Reverend, 'had' is the critical element in that statement," the sheriff said, stepping toward the pastor and poking his chin toward Sonny's nose. "Perhaps you're gathering now that I'm fully aware of you trying to sell our land, Rudolph County, to the video poker developers."

"Now...now...now, Sully," the pastor stammered. "I can explain what it is you think you know. It's bigger and better for the county, and more important, it's better for you."

"Rudolph County ain't having no casino. We'll never need jobs that bad."

"Hold on a cotton-picking second." Sonny pushed back from the sheriff. "Our deal is separate from this whacked-out, drug-dealing kidnapper and his gun-smuggling father."

"It was, until you brought your private Tar-Baby fiasco over here and tried to pawn it over to me and my family. We'll be deciding on our new arrangement shortly. You better hope I can save your chubby fanny from the Feds. I suggest you take it back inside the house."

Sheriff Sully turned to address Jesse.

"You throw in the Escalade as boot, and I'll hold the reverend and his henchman in jail for a couple of days, pending an investigation on charges of impersonating a law enforcement officer and falsifying evidence. I might even let the Feebees interrogate him a bit."

"Oh, okay. I suppose we can drive the van home," Jesse said, trying not to gasp, grateful even if it meant returning home in Jack's commie van. "Will I need to mail you the title or something?"

"Nope," the sheriff said, grinning. "My salvage operation is close by—no title, no problem."

"So, we're free to go?" Jesse asked, extending a handshake to the sheriff.

"Here's what I need you to do." The lawman grabbed Jesse's hand, squeezing it tightly. "You take the reverend's daughter directly home to her mother. I've met Mrs. Suggs, and she don't deserve this wolf in a shepherd's costume. I'd offer an outsider's suggestion that the young newlyweds live separately with their folks, at least until this mess is settled. That's what my wife and I did, until after I returned home from the war."

"All right. That might be best."

"And as far you and your son," Sully said, clamping down harder on Jesse's hand. "You both deserve a second chance, but I don't expect you'll be receiving one in Rudolph County. Don't come back for bluegrass gospel, Bible College, or the End Times.

Tonight and this place has taught you all it can. Life is mean, but it's tougher when you're shortsighted. You comprehend?"

"Yes, sir, 100 percent," Jesse said.

"Good. Now you best saddle up your folks in that van," the sheriff said, releasing his grip and patting Jesse on the back. "I wouldn't stop until you reach the interstate or, better yet, the Georgia welcome center. The best of luck with your boy's charges back home and your momma."

34

AFTER RETURNING HOME FROM RUDOLPH COUNTY, Jesse was astonished at the seamless shift from bizarre back to mundane, easily ignoring the flimsy beaded curtain between the two extremes. As long as he enjoyed a humdrum weekend, sleeping fairly soundly in his own bed at night, he could accept newlyweds living separately and vengeful preachers lurking in the shadows or rotting in a redneck jail. According to Haymaker, a triumvirate of assholes—Bin Laden, the Lehman Brothers, and Sarah Palin—conspired to make fucked-up the new normal in the neighborhood. Forget fresh air and front lawns; suburbia preferred to breathe in crisp denials and enjoy the smell of finely manicured contradictions. The next time reality would intrude was for JJ's Monday morning court appearance.

JJ and, especially, Denise, appeared surprised when Jesse showed up in his gray pinstripe suit and tie to meet them in front of the courthouse the morning of the hearing.

"Good morning. Everybody feeling good?" Jesse asked, balancing between a cheery drive-time deejay and a somber evening newscaster.

"Yeah, sure," JJ replied, tugging at his shirt collar and barely pulling away from his cell phone. "I'm just praying for this to be over."

Denise stood next to JJ, clenching her coffee cup. She gave Jesse her tight-lipped, half-smile half-frown, the look of the ever-accepting mom.

"You're especially dapper this morning," she said.

"Thank you. You know what they say—every girl's crazy for a sharp-dressed man." Jesse didn't want to confess that this was the third suit he'd put on that morning, aiming for the over-forty male model look of *GQ* magazine.

"Good, here comes Blaire," Denise said, checking her watch and looking past Jesse toward the front door.

Blaire McMahon—the lawyer Jesse helped pay for—showed up in his seersucker suit and white oxfords and hastily told them in his high-pitched voice what they could expect to happen. He had a plea arraignment worked out with the DA. Provided everything went according to their agreement, the drug possession charges would be dropped and JJ wouldn't face any jail time. He'd just pay a three-hundred-dollar fine plus court costs, serve forty hours of community service, and have his license suspended for six months, but the judge probably would give him a permit to drive to school and work.

Now sitting next to JJ and Denise in the front row of the oak-paneled courtroom, Jesse was reminded of the only time he went to one of his son's school plays. He couldn't remember the name of the play, but he recalled that JJ had the role of Mozart and how cute he looked in his costume and faux powdered wig. JJ was playing a new part today, dressed in a dark-blue suit and tie with his fresh haircut and clean shave. He was starring in a one-act production, but this time, instead of teachers directing the performers and whispering the lines, it would be the defense attorney and the district attorney, guiding the drama for an audience of one: the Honorable Judge Willis McCone.

According to Blaire McMahon, it wouldn't be complicated. All they had to do was stand by in the courtroom until their case was called. Fidgeting on the hard wooden bench seats, Jesse debated if this is where he'd come to file his bankruptcy papers, or if shitting your financial bed was a federal court matter. Now that his most valuable guns were gone and his aunt's lawsuit dragged on, he'd probably find out soon enough. Either way, he'd make the same deal with Sheriff Sully every time, gladly trading the self-loathing of insolvency for the honor of safely returning JJ to Denise.

Jesse peeked at his ex-wife's tan calves, allowing himself to reminisce about the fading tattoo that she'd gotten on their last trip to New Orleans. He could close his eyes, anytime and anywhere, and picture the black stem leading up to the pink blossom on the outside of her right ankle. It had taken Jesse years to realize that she'd let him tease her into enduring the pain and the leering Cajun tattoo artist, not simply to prove that she could still be naughty, but as one of her last attempts to save their marriage, a bolder move than he'd ever made. When the bailiff finally called JJ's case, Jesse shifted in his seat and focused on the front of the courtroom.

JJ and Blaire McMahon took their places at the defense table across from the DA while Denise anxiously eyed Jesse. According to McMahon, the charges would be read aloud, the judge would ask the lawyers if they were ready to proceed, and before JJ pled guilty and accepted the sentencing, the judge would recite a couple of paragraphs of legalese, making sure that JJ understood what he was consenting to. It was four quick and easy steps.

They had sailed smoothly through the first two steps when Judge McCone stopped the proceedings and put on his glasses; he rocked back in his chair and began reading JJ's case file. Both lawyers and JJ stood still, looking straight ahead at the judge. McCone's bald head shone in the bright courtroom light like he had waxed it that morning. His jaw was set firm as he perused the details in JJ's case. McCone put down his reading glasses and rocked his chair forward so that he squarely faced the three players before him, ready to adjudicate.

"Mr. Taylor," Judge McCone said, addressing the district attorney in the regal tone of a man who enjoyed the weight of his own words. "It's come to my attention that there was another individual involved in this incident, the traffic stop."

"Yes, sir, I believe so, Your Honor," the DA said nasally, giving a perplexed shrug to JJ's seersucker advocate. "A young woman."

"An underage young lady." Judge McCone turned to JJ. "Is that correct, Mr. Few?"

The question hung in the courtroom.

JJ turned around to his dad. Denise and Jesse glanced at each other. McMahon gave JJ a gentle pat on the shoulder and whispered to him.

"Uh...yeah," JJ said, his voice barely audible. "I mean, yes, Your Honor, sir."

"Speak up, Mr. Few," the judge commanded.

"Uh, I'm sorry," JJ replied, now loud enough for even the spectators in the back row to hear.

"Mr. Taylor, what were the blood-alcohol concentrations of the defendant and his passenger?"

The DA flipped through his files before responding.

"Your Honor, according to my copy of the police report, the defendant's BAC was 0.04 and the passenger's was 0.09."

"Where did you get the alcohol, Mr. Few?

"My dad." Fear for his son's future made Jesse mad enough to Taser Haymaker straight in the ball-sack.

Judge McCone scrutinized the case file again and then turned to the district attorney. "What about the drug possession charges, Mr. Taylor? Didn't the arresting officer find evidence of Schedule II drugs in the defendant's automobile?"

While DA Taylor rifled through his file once more, Blaire McMahon reached back and dug into the seat of his seersucker pants. Great, Jesse thought, for five thousand bucks we hired a clueless courtroom butt-picker.

"The State didn't have sufficient evidence to pursue the charges, Your Honor," Taylor said.

"Mr. Few, regardless of the legal issues, I presume you have an idea of the potential danger involved in allowing a teenage girl to consume alcohol and narcotics together?"

"Yes, sir, I do," JJ said.

"I'd like to go back to my earlier question. How exactly were you able to obtain two bottles of liquor to share with a high school girl? Your father gave you liquor?"

"No, not really. We—I sorta took 'em." JJ's voice shifted from dull to shaky.

"I see. You stole the alcohol and the drugs and then proceeded to share them with an underage girl, all while driving around Lewallen County. Does that about summarize it?"

"Yes, sir, it does," JJ said, lowering his head and staring at his feet.

Jesse could see that Denise's face had gone pale, and that JJ's case was on the edge of escalating way out of their control. He wanted to stand up and explain it all to the judge—to let him know that he was to blame for having a party animal as a roommate, for keeping booze and pills around the house so he could self-medicate, and most of all, that he was guilty of being a shitty father, worse than the ones who let their kids run around in a busy parking lot or get tattoos on their necks after they dropped out of high school. Evidently, the judge and he were on the same wavelength.

"Young man, is your father here today?"

"Yes, sir, right here." JJ and McMahon turned to face Jesse.

"Please have him stand and come forward to the bench."

Jesse's knees quaked and his throat went dry as he walked up to face Judge McCone; he could only imagine how JJ must be feeling.

"Sir, are you aware that I could charge you with contributing to the delinquency of a minor?" Judge McCone asked, covering the microphone with his hand.

"No, sir, I wasn't." Jesse was trying his best not to look at the judge when he noticed the lapel pin on the collar of his robe. It was the American flag with the praying hands over top and the diamond accent—the same as Pastor Sonny's. Jesse had ignored the pastor's advice regarding the importance of the docket. He and his butt-picking attorney knew nothing about McCone or Sonny's ability to control the courtroom, even if he was still in Rudolph County.

"Those charges are punishable with up to twelve months in jail and a one-thousand-dollar fine."

"Yes, sir," Jesse said, preferring the day's earlier tedium. "But I'd like to explain—"

"I didn't bring you up here to debate," the judge said, cutting Jesse off. "So I suggest you be quiet and consider the consequences of your negligence. Take your seat, please."

Returning to his seat, Jesse turned his eyes away from JJ and Denise; his face was warm. The judge continued before he made it back.

"Now, young Mr. Few," McCone said. "I understand you wish to enter a plea in your case. Is that correct?"

JJ looked at his lawyer, who nodded his head.

"Yes, sir," JJ said.

"And how do you wish to plead?"

"Guilty."

Hearing his son say "guilty" burned Jesse hotter, but at least the case was back on script.

"Sir, before I impose the court's sentence, I need to make sure that your plea is voluntary, and it isn't the result of any force, threats, or promises?"

"No, sir."

"You also understand that you're waiving your right to a trial and to file an appeal?"

"Yes, sir."

"Therefore, your plea is accepted, and the court sentences the defendant," Judge McCone said, scowling at Jesse, "to twelve months in jail."

Jesse heard "twelve months in jail," and he nearly convulsed before McCone continued.

"To be suspended with time served, twelve months of probation, a one-thousand-dollar fine plus all court costs, one hundred hours of community service, revocation of your driver's license for six months, and mandatory attendance at thirty Alcoholics Anonymous meetings, the defendant to be accompanied by his father as well."

JJ spoke softly to his lawyer after Judge McCone finished.

"Your Honor," Blaire McMahon said, his treble squeal heard in open court on JJ's behalf for the first time. "The defendant would like the right to apply for a limited driving permit in order to attend work, school, and the AA meetings."

"I don't think so, Mr. McMahon," Judge McCone said, standing up from the bench. "The young man was a menace. I suggest he make his father drive him; it'll do them both good."

35

"THAT WASN'T A DAMN THING LIKE TELEVISION," JESSE said, standing in front of the courthouse with Denise afterward, while JJ and Blaire McMahon completed JJ's paperwork. "I hope like hell I never have to go through anything like that ever again."

"Oh, my God, my nerves are totally shot," Denise said, holding out her still trembling hand.

"Either our seersucker Perry Mason doesn't know his bailiwick very well, or that judge was trying to prove a point with JJ." Jesse knew that Pastor Sonny had laid his courtroom trap before the elopement. Evidently, McCone pushed the sentencing guidelines as far as he could without disturbing the system.

"I wouldn't know where to find an AA meeting. Do you?"

"I didn't know he could do that, but JJ and I have got plenty of time to figure it out," Jesse said, imagining the benefits of the court-ordered father-and-son time. Attending thirty AA meetings wasn't like taking camping trips, but fucked up was the new normal, and at least JJ and Jesse wouldn't have to brawl and bargain through each meeting. They might ride out with

Momma to visit Virgil and Roberta Lee. JJ and he could sit on the back porch with Virgil in his man cave and work on calming their crazy monkey minds, maybe learn the difference between white gravy and brown gravy. "My encore career as a self-storage tycoon, gopher, and Momma manager gives me some free time."

"How is she doing? How's she doing without Lizzy?"

"I've heard other people say it as long as I can remember, so it must be my turn, but it's like they say—she's got good days and bad days. Losing Lizzy was pretty hard on her, but we're adjusting to living downtown, so it might just all work out."

"I'm happy if you're happy," Denise said with a warm, wide smile that showed off her dimples. "Listen, for some weird reason, this is hard for me to tell you, and it may be harder for you to hear." Denise blew out her cheeks and released a rush of air, her dimples vanishing as if they never existed. "But I don't want it coming from someone else, so here it is—Jack and I are getting married this summer."

"Really? That's awesome. Congratulations to you both." Jesse's lungs and stomach seized up like an engine run without oil.

"Thank you. I was so nervous about telling you or having you hear it from Schaff," Denise said with a calm relief in her voice. "You don't know how stressed I was. I'm so relieved now that I've told you myself."

"I knew it would happen sooner or later." Hearing the lift in her tone, Jesse was satisfied with his obedient lies. "I bet you guys are planning a big soirée for that one."

"Actually, we're getting married in Bali."

"Bali? The island that's—I don't know—where?"

"To tell you the truth, I really don't know either," she said, her smile returning. "But Jack has a friend who owns some kind of retreat down there, and he says it's absolutely beautiful with black-sand beaches and rain forests."

Denise continued to talk about her wedding and the trip, but Jesse couldn't really hear her words. All he could do was wish there were a way off his carousel of resentment. As much as it hurt him to admit it, the bad puppy, even in a gray pinstripe suit, wasn't ever coming back into the house.

"You should have seen Mother's face when Jack told her we were going to have a chakra-clearing ceremony at sunrise on the beach. I thought she was going to faint on the spot."

"I'm not sure what a chakra is, but I bet your mother needs hers unclogged, too."

"Thank you, Jesse, for not going all ex-husband on me." Denise wiped her moist eyes with the back of her hand. "Go figure. After all that crazy stuff last week and now court, here come the waterworks. I hate crying, even when I'm happy; it really sucks."

"No problem. You let me know if I need to straighten Ms. Mary out on anything at this soirée. I'll always have a special place, somewhere, for my ex-mother-in-law." Seeing Denise's tears, Jesse felt a tiny sprig of joy in knowing that she was enjoying the bliss of love.

36

DRIVING TO DOREEN'S HOUSE, THE PINK SUNSET reminded Jesse of blush wine. He peered at the two bottles of Oregon pinot noir riding shotgun next to him in the passenger seat like a couple of snooty tourists. A modest chilled rosé or white zinfandel would've been simpler, more laid-back, but this far out in the country, he'd be lucky to find a gas station that sold anything besides cheap beer and night crawlers. He grabbed his earlobe, giving it a hard tug like his third-grade teacher did when she caught an unwary student chewing gum. He'd bought the two bottles, some flowers, a six-pack of his favorite German beer, and walked down the family planning aisle of the grocery store, hesitating in front of the condoms and personal lubricants, but he'd rushed on; his hands were full.

After winning the club championship, he'd celebrated with Haymaker and the gang for one or two beers longer than he'd intended, but he'd managed to slip away before he sabotaged his plans with Doreen. Now he just needed to find her house. He'd never been there before, but he knew it was in the southeast part of the county, far away from wine stores and sommeliers.

Locating a gravel road—a thin, silvery-white path materializing on the side of these backwoods highways—was tough at sunset, but after dark, it'd be worse. Momma's old Cadillac didn't have a GPS navigation system. Thankfully, he'd texted her that he was on his way before he left home because his cell phone showed a faint signal. He was untethered, off the grid.

Doreen had told him to look out for pecan trees. The gravel road to her house ran through the middle of the grove. During their last lunch date, she'd given him directions to her house. The directions deviated into a story about Doreen moving from California to Georgia, then to her buying her aunt and uncle's old farm from her second cousin, and finally settled on Doreen confessing that her aunt once operated a roadside produce and fortune-telling stand and she'd lived on the farm with Doreen's uncle and another man, her lover. The frisky way she told her meandering tale only increased Jesse's infatuation with her but made the directions difficult to recall. He remembered her aunt's and uncle's names were Molly and Cotton, but he couldn't call up the landmark Doreen told him to watch out for before the pecan grove.

A darkening wall of pine trees enclosed both sides of the highway. He'd gone over a set of railroad tracks a few minutes back, and Jesse thought that might be the landmark he needed—yet still no pecan grove. The road tightened as he crossed a narrow creek bridge. Coming up the hill from the creek bottom, the left side of the road expanded into open terrain, and in the dwindling light, Jesse detected the dusky, sprawling contours of enormous pecan trees stretching out in succession across the field. There was a dim sliver of light in the distance that began twirling as Jesse neared.

Spotting the gravel driveway, he flipped on his blinker, and the tiny beacon spun faster. He turned into the driveway and rolled down his window. The light went off, and a silhouette approached his car.

"Doreen?" Jesse called out.

"It's me, just watching the stars, actually Venus," Doreen said, her tender voice straining in the field. She leaned into the car window. She wasn't wearing the white dress of Jesse's beach dream, but her powder-blue pullover accented her tan skin and velvet-brown eyes. "The sky is so clear tonight."

"You wanna hop in?" Jesse grabbed his grocery bags and put them in the back seat.

Doreen jumped in the passenger seat, and as Jesse turned back around, she wrapped her arm around his neck, giving him a deep kiss. "Congratulations on your big victory. Sorry I had that regional meet today. I'm sure you were epic."

"Many thanks," Jesse said, tasting the freshness of Doreen's lips. "I gotta say, if you hadn't been out here playing human lighthouse, I'd probably still be driving around lost."

"I guess I spared us from becoming two ships passing on the roadside. So let's go see the house, champ, *tout droit*," Doreen said with a playful skip. She guided Jesse between the sprawling pecan trees. The rolling of the tires over the gravel road resonated across the farmland. The daytime heat had drained from the air, and the dewy current of the grass flowed through the front seat. Warning him to watch for ruts and raccoons, she relayed more of the farm's history, leading him past the shadowy ancestral home on the outskirts of the grove, over a shallow creek bed, and through a patch of hardwoods to a break in the thicket and a small pasture.

"And that's my teeny place over there," Doreen said, pointing to a cabin on the edge of the meadow with a spectrum of colored lanterns strung across the front. "They called the main house back there in the grove, where Uncle Cotton and Aunt Molly lived, Creekside, but I haven't come up with a name for my cottage. They say it's where my aunt's lover lived, the farm overseer, who was something like a runaway European blueblood or a bootlegger on the lam. But you know, I don't mind the slightly sordid reputation; it's got a wonderful energy. It vibrates this beautiful plum-colored aura. You'll see."

After the kirtan and their lunch dates, Jesse was learning not to judge her statements. She was freeing him to experience the unfamiliar, as if he could go back and sit at a different table in the high school cafeteria. He parked next to her silver Prius. Beyond the rustic cabin, the surrounding area was veiled in nightfall.

"I didn't come empty-handed." Jesse pulled out his six-pack, put it between his legs, and hoisted the wine from the bag. "I brought us a couple of nice bottles of Willamette Valley pinot noir to go with dinner, or before, if you'd like."

"How sweet; thank you so much," Doreen said, reaching over to give Jesse a quick peck and grabbing the beer from his lap. "But I'll take one of these for now."

"Please do. I brought them for you, but they're not super-cold," Jesse said with a gracious laugh, surprised at Doreen's choice, but pleased that she was feeling at ease.

"That's fine. Let's go inside. I'll give you the cook's tour." Doreen showed Jesse in, checked on dinner in the oven, and gave him a brief walk-through of the house. The purple pastel Buddha statue and art deco loveseat were as funky and friendly as she was. Jesse was curious to see her bedroom, but she walked past her closed door, describing it as her *boudoir*. Finally, they settled in two lounge chairs on the back porch overlooking a pond. Drinking warm German beer and listening to the croaking frogs, warbling birds, and an occasional howl from the woods, they started a conversation that floated along and turned like inner tubes drifting down the river. They glided through her account of her regional swim meet, "the longest meet ever, ever," Jesse's hole-by-hole replay of the golf tournament, and into her worries about burning dinner. Sprinkled throughout was her giggle, reminding him of why he rode out all this way.

"Okay, champ," Doreen said, springing up from the lounge chair and handing Jesse her empty beer. "I'm going to the powder room and then see if I burned dinner yet. You good?"

"I'm fine, but hurry back," Jesse replied. "I'm worried what's coming out of the woods."

"Don't be scared. Just make sure you've got another beer ready for when I get here." Doreen gave Jesse a lingering kiss and went into the house.

Other than the potential for having to choke down a few mouthfuls of gluey tofu lasagna, Jesse's evening was going splendidly. Doreen seemed to be having fun, and her natural whimsy gave Jesse a sense of calm. His attraction to her wasn't forced. It welled up, not just from the curve of her hips, but from the way the porch light illuminated her wavy, auburn hair draping her face, framing the sleek angle of her jaw and the elegant arch of her neck when she laughed. Mattie was staying with Momma tonight, and he was hopeful that he'd break his streak of accidental celibacy.

The screen door slammed, and Doreen came back out to the porch. "Okay, I've got a confession to make," she said, pulling up the back of her chair, trying to sit up straight. "I got home a smidgen late and practically forgot to put in the lasagna, so dinner's still about ten minutes away."

"No problem. Good things are worth waiting for." Jesse handed her a slightly warm import.

Doreen reached over and exchanged a kiss for the beer. "You know, tonight while I was out by the road watching the planets, I kept hearing this '80s song playing in my head, Bob Seger's 'We've Got Tonight.' And I loved what I thought the universe was telling me, but then I got scared when I remembered back to when I first heard that song—when I was living in LA with the wanna-be hanger-on crowd, all the stupid, stupid, selfish choices I made, way worse than big hair and shoulder pads."

Letting her words sail out across the pond, Jesse sat up on the edge of the chair, facing Doreen. "I've made more than my share of the stupidest choices possible. Never a mullet, but worse than MC Hammer pants. And I've never limited my mistakes to strictly fashion."

"Yeah, I wish mine were only neon-pink leg warmers." For a second, Doreen turned away from Jesse. "All right, so I've got another confession." She looked back toward him again. "I talked to my friend at the swim meet about you."

"Okay," Jesse said, worrying that she was going to insist on knowing his number of sex partners or that it would be difficult getting along with her friends. He'd never had any sales training on building genuine personal connections. All he knew was various formulas for overcoming buyer's objections, but he didn't want to treat her as another prospect to close.

"She told me about your hot tub parties and all these real estate agents. I guess you dated them all?" Doreen paused, waiting for a reaction, reluctant, as if she'd been forced by the master to whip a loved one.

"Dated? I mean, yeah. I had just gotten divorced." Jesse fought for a blank expression, imagining the black streaks in the granite that made up the gravel road, grateful that the porch light was shining more on Doreen than him.

"Then there was something about this thing, an affair, with some married younger woman who divorced her husband because of you."

"Wow, geez, your friend gave you the real lowdown. She work for the FBI?" Now he wanted to fall back on the chair and roll up in a ball. Kimberly would be pleased to know that she was still wreaking collateral damage.

Doreen pointed her beer bottle squarely at Jesse's chest. "I like you, a lot. You sorta remind me of Paul Newman, and I feel your generous old soul, even if you don't. But your reputation scares me." Her voice quaked as she delivered the last of her beating. "I'm not another amusement ride. I'm begging you, if that's what you want, please don't. I'm not a tilt-a-whirl."

Doreen was done with her lashes, but Jesse didn't know what salve to put on their wounds. Avoidance and denial wouldn't provide the cure. Keep playing with those long-standing buddies, and he'd be the lonely guy wearing the off-kilter toupee who eats dried-out pork chops and drinks coffee every meal at the same shitty diner, praying the waitress would ask him for a ride home. Doreen was a treasure he'd stumbled upon, a teacher. His heart drummed in his chest. The sensation of the woods encircled him. Out yonder here, as the rest of the county mindlessly gasped for air, you could feel each breath, one after the other in rhythm.

"Everything your friend said was probably, definitely true. I did what I thought I wanted to do, believing it was, I guess, bargain basement intimacy." Jesse glanced down at the gaps in the worn porch boards, not focusing on Doreen's face. "I've never met anyone like you. You're so foreign to me, like you're, I don't know, Austrian or Australian. I don't spend a lot of time thinking about things like what's at stake, but I don't have many more chances at getting this right." Now searching for her eyes, he presented his own pleading confession.

"So maybe I'm a tad like your unnamed cottage here. I've got a local history, a slightly sordid reputation, but I must have some good vibrations, that generous old soul you believe in who looks like Butch Cassidy. If your Uncle Cotton, Aunt Molly, and her lover could find a way to make a life together on this farm, I gotta believe we can somehow at least try and do the same."

Doreen grabbed Jesse's forearm, pulling him into her lounge chair. They linked in a kiss. She wrapped her leg around his waist, coiling him closer. Caressing her body, Jesse brushed the waistband of her blue jeans. Doreen's hips tilted up.

"Wait, wait, it's burning," she whispered.

"What? What's wrong?" Jesse snatched his hand back.

"Dinner. It's probably ruined," Doreen said, slipping out from under Jesse and standing up. She straightened her sweater and checked the button on her jeans. "I'm going to go inside and see."

"You want me to help?" Jesse hoped he didn't sound like a disappointed teenage boy.

"You can stay out here; too many cooks and the soup thing." Doreen took a step back. "I'm sorry. I just—" Her voice flattened out. "I just need to make sure that I'm doing the right thing, for me. We'll break bread and just talk about stuff. Okay?"

"Sounds marvelous," Jesse said, adding an upbeat emphasis.

"Maybe start by dissecting your infatuation with Marcia Brady," Doreen said, her soft lilt and giggle returning. She kissed him again, lingering before she went inside.

Sagging back into the lounge chair, Jesse surveyed the inky black night. The stars were easier to see out here, free from the light pollution of the city. But despite the improved clarity, he still couldn't pick out Venus. He'd never had the temperament to distinguish a planet from the thousands of stars or draw the invisible lines that created the constellations. This was the exact same sky that hung over his own backyard, yet he knew it was different. But perhaps that was like convincing Doreen that he wasn't the same womanizer who had cheated away his marriage or tried to build a future with another man's wife. It could be the only change in his life and the night sky was the circumstances, his position on the planet, and the impurities obstructing his view. Tired of trying to find a shooting star to wish on, Jesse closed his eyes. A reddish-purple light flooded his mind, and he decided tonight was the perfect night for cozy conversation and crispy tofu lasagna.

THE END

ACKNOWLEDGMENTS

Over the course of eight years, a significant number of people have generously helped me complete Jesse's story. First and foremost, there's my lovely wife, Donna, and the "kids," Heather, Stephanie, Alison, and Davis. I am grateful for all your love and support and for never questioning what I was doing locked away for all those hours. However, I did appreciate all the unsparing questions from my fellow students and the faculty at Queens University in Charlotte. David Payne, Ashley Warlick, Naeem Murr, and Myla Goldberg, your gracious guidance and insight were beneficial beyond belief. Thanks to ALL my Pod members: your critiques, comments, and eye rolling laughter kept me writing. I'd especially like to tip my cap to Jim Button, Andy Harp, Evan Williams, Ricky Finlan and Richard Patrick. I've also been teamed with three excellent editors along the way. Emily Carmain, Jason Frye, and Joyce Mochrie were each vital in the honing of my manuscript. Lastly, I'm indebted to Bethany Brown of the Cadence Group for steering me through the final steps in my journey to publication.